BLINK OF AN EYE

Cath Staincliffe

Constable & Robinson Ltd
55–56 Russell Square
London WC1B 4HP
www.constablerobinson.com

First published in the UK by C&R Crime,
an imprint of Constable & Robinson Ltd, 2013

A copy of the British Library Cataloguing in
Publication data is available from the British Library

ISBN 978-1-78033-567-4 (hardback)

Typeset by TW Typesetting, Plymouth, Devon

Printed and bound by CPI Group (UK) Ltd, Croydon, CR0 4YY

1 3 5 7 9 10 8 6 4 2

BLINK OF AN EYE

ACKNOWLEDGEMENTS

For help with research thanks to crime writers Martin Baggoley and Roger Forsdyke, Peter Grogan from JMW Solicitors LLP and Martin Walsh from Stephensons Solicitors LLP. Thanks to Maggie Wood for advice on the world of social work. All mistakes or departures from normal procedures are mine.

For all my social worker friends:
Anne, Jacqui, Lynda, Maggie and Margaret

CHAPTER ONE

Carmel

Before and after. Two different lives. Before – did we really know how lucky we were? How wonderful everything was? How fragile?

A warm May day, the sun golden, the air soft with a hint of humidity, the silver birch offering dappled shade in the corner of the garden. I'd spent most of the afternoon on the swing seat there, doting grandma, three-week-old Ollie dozing in my arms. Phil, as besotted as I was, taking photographs, dozens of photographs. I had not believed people when they eulogized about the emotional impact of having grandchildren, but meeting Ollie had been like a punch to my gut, the sensation close to that I'd felt when our girls were born. A mix of overwhelming love and rabid fear – the urge to cherish and the fearsome drive to protect. Part of me was bemused, though, thinking, how did I get here? Like the Talking Heads track. When did I get to be a middle-aged woman? Fifty-two and still feeling like a seventeen-year-old inside.

The place was brimming with guests, mainly friends of Suzanne and Jonty, a sprinkling of kids, a couple of their neighbours, Julia and Fraser from the end cottage.

Jonty was living it large at the barbecue, florid with heat, his ginger curls damp, sporting a butcher's apron, garish Bermuda shorts and flip-flops. A bear of a man next to our daughter, who is petite, neat, who can get away with buying children's clothes.

Phil, at my side, traced a finger down Ollie's nose; the baby's eyelids flickered in response.

'He takes after Suzanne,' I murmured. 'The fair hair.'

'And the build, thank God,' he replied. 'Maybe they'll have a girl next, big as Jonty; she can take up rugby.'

'Don't,' I shushed him.

We had speculated plenty of times what an odd couple they made. Suzanne so crisp and competent, always in control, bossy even; and Jonty, who had something of the overgrown schoolboy about him. Exuberant, expansive, generous to a fault. Phil reckoned Jonty was a work in progress for Suzanne. Whatever – it seemed to work.

I loved to see her happy, in her element, socializing, serving drinks, prompting people to take another kebab or choose a dessert. She and Jonty were foodies, an interest verging on obsession in my opinion; you couldn't eat a thing they'd made without a spiel about its provenance and preparation. But it did make for a stunning barbecue: filo parcels of cheese and spinach, sizzling lamb patties, spatchcocked chicken seasoned with lemon and cardamom, peppered beef and tuna steaks, seafood or veg kebabs, puffy golden garlic-mushroom rolls. There were huge bowls of glossy purple-black olives, Colcannon mash, a table of salads: watercress, pepper and avocado, wild rice and chilli, Moroccan couscous. A cheeseboard and puddings: tropical fruit salad, cranberry pinwheels, chocolate mousse, lemon cheesecake, lavender sorbet. The colours a feast in themselves.

Jonty and Suzanne shared an energy, a drive which had underpinned their life together so far. They were both on good salaries – Suzanne as a buyer for Debenham's and Jonty as a television producer – which enabled them to get a mortgage and buy the house. It was on the outskirts of the city, an old weaver's cottage with thick stone walls and tiny windows. One of three original cottages on the cul-de-sac. The only other houses were two new-build detacheds opposite.

The previous owners had modernized it inside. Suzanne and Jonty had redecorated and remodelled the garden, replacing the lawn and cottage borders with a patio and barbecue pit, gravel paths and specimen plants: mimosa, ailanthus, bamboo, birch. Now that they had a baby, Suzanne would take three months off work, then return part time until Ollie started school. Jonty was in the process of producing a series of historical documentaries that would keep him in work for the next two years. They were on a roll.

Things had been tougher for Naomi, our younger daughter. She was still out of work, though she helped out in Phil's music shop whenever his assistant was on holiday or off sick. She was one of thousands of graduates who had found that their hard-won qualifications – hers was a degree in tourism and leisure – didn't translate into better job opportunities. Not yet, anyway. Though she had got an interview at long last, for a job as a teaching assistant. We tried to keep positive with her; the recession wouldn't last for ever. Naomi's boyfriend Alex was struggling too, eager to put his law qualification to some use. The pair divided their time between our house and his mother's. We rubbed along okay, but of course they wanted their independence.

Ollie began to fuss, nose creased, head turning. Suzanne heard, set down the plates she'd been clearing and came over to feed him.

'Tea?' I offered, and she nodded.

'Thirsty work.' I smiled. 'He's gorgeous.'

'Of course he is,' she said.

'And you're amazing,' I said.

'What? Why?'

3

I gestured to Ollie, then at the guests. 'All this. I don't think I made it out of bed for the first month. Certainly didn't get dressed properly for a year, never left the house before midday.' Whereas she looked cool and composed in a white linen skirt and a white blouse with pale gold trim.

She raised an eyebrow as she settled the baby at her breast. 'It's just a question of routine.'

I bit my tongue, swallowed a smile. She was serious. Phil and I swapped a look. She noticed. 'Well, you and Dad, you were all hippy-trippy.'

'Punk!' Phil protested. 'Totally different scene.'

'Man,' Suzanne said, putting the word in inverted commas, teasing Phil. She snorted. Ollie paused for a moment; she stroked his head and he continued suckling.

Naomi

The sun is shining and I'm ravenous and there's bound to be a really good buffet: Suzanne's a great cook – well, they both are.

I want to show Alex off, shout his news from the rooftops. It finally feels like everything is falling into place. I haven't felt this good for ages; it's not been a brilliant few months really. I want to dance, they might have dancing later – in fact I'll make sure of it. I've sorted out a playlist.

Alex pulls me back just before we go in the side gate. Kisses me, and I get that hollow, sexy feeling inside. I kiss him back harder, and he groans a little and then pulls free, laughing. He's excited. 'Better stop now,' he says.

'You started it,' I say.

'Yeah?' His eyes dance, green eyes, teasing me. 'Well I'll finish it later.'

This is so corny, I crack up laughing and he does too. And I hold the champagne with both hands, making sure I don't drop the bottle.

He grabs my waist and turns me to face down the path, leans his chin on my shoulder and says quietly in my ear, 'Come on then, into the dragon's den, eh?'

'Maybe motherhood has mellowed her,' I say. 'Hope so.'

He kisses my ear and smacks me on the bum and we head on in.

Carmel

When I came back out with Suzanne's tea, there were calls and greetings at the side gate. Naomi and Alex were arriving. Naomi made a beeline for Suzanne. She was swinging a bottle of champagne. 'Hello.' She bent down and stroked Ollie's leg, cupped his foot in her hand. 'Oh, Suze, he's so sweet. He looks bigger already. Can I hold him after?'

'Of course,' said Suzanne.

Naomi is dark-haired, like Phil and me. She's a taller, darker version of Suzanne. Apart from that, the girls have the same dark blue eyes, pointed chin, Phil's long slim nose. Naomi was wearing a short-sleeved blue dress in a waffle cotton, the dye faded and the hem a raw fringe, part of the design.

She straightened up. 'Glasses?' she said, hoisting the bottle up.

'Kitchen,' said Suzanne. 'Ask Jonty.'

'Splashing out?' Phil remarked. 'The real McCoy.' It wasn't cava.

'Celebrating.' Merriment danced in Naomi's eyes. 'Alex has got a job!'

We all jumped in with congratulations.

Alex grinned. He's a lovely-looking boy: pale skin, dark hair and green eyes.

'Training contract with a legal firm in town,' he said.

Even better. I knew he had looked far and wide, but the pair of them wanted to stay in Manchester if possible, dreading a move somewhere out in the sticks or to some soulless small town where there was nothing going on.

'So you'll be getting a place together at last?' Phil teased. 'Shall I book a van?'

'Give us a chance, Dad,' Naomi said, punching her father on the shoulder.

Alex took the bottle from Naomi, raised it and caught Jonty's attention. Jonty disappeared inside and came back moments later with a tray of glasses. Alex popped the champagne and filled the glasses and Naomi handed them round. I caught Phil's eye and winked. He winked back.

'New job!' Naomi led the toast.

The champagne was fresh and lemony, tingly on my tongue.

We sat and chatted. Suzanne wanted to know about our travel plans. We'd been saving up. I was about to book leave, some of it unpaid. It wasn't a good time to be doing it really, as there were cuts on the way (I'm a social worker on the emergency duty team). But we had finally paid off our mortgage after twenty-five years, and that made it financially doable. I felt that if we didn't get away and do some travelling soon, we never would, and I didn't want to live with that regret.

We had fantasized for ages about seeing more of the world; we'd never been beyond Europe. The idea was that we would take off for two months. If the worst came to the worst and I was made redundant or Phil's shop went under, then we could always sell the house and rent somewhere. While Phil explained which cities he wanted

6

to visit in the States (New Orleans, Chicago, Memphis, Detroit, San Francisco – music Meccas every one), I watched a toddler diligently placing pieces of gravel in a plastic cup. Someone was blowing bubbles, the light catching the oily rainbow colours as they drifted about the garden.

We stayed another half-hour or so and then left them to it. Phil had a gig that evening at a pub. He played lead guitar. A dream that had turned into a hobby somewhere along the way. They do a mix of rock and blues. He looks the part, an ageing rocker, greying hair down to his shoulders, jeans and T-shirt his uniform. No need for the ubiquitous leather jacket on that warm day. He was growing thicker round the waist but I still fancied the pants off him. And thought there might be a chance to prove it if we got home before too long.

I kissed Ollie goodbye, hugged Suzanne, found Naomi and Alex and congratulated them again. He was beaming and she clapped her hands. 'I can't believe it! Now I need some of his luck for my interview.'

'Fingers crossed.'

At the car, Phil kissed me, long and slow. Just the way I like it.

Naomi

Everyone's congratulating Alex. Suzanne's waiting for Jonty to bring glasses, and she flashes this look my way. A spark of irritation in her eyes, her lips tight. My stomach sinks for a moment. Maybe I'm overreacting? Is she pissed off with Jonty for not being quicker with the glasses? I wait to see if she'll roll her eyes or pull a face to let me in on the joke. But she doesn't. She turns away and says something to Mum.

7

Perhaps it's not me she's irritated with. She could just be tired with having Ollie, or she's got a headache or something and the look wasn't directed at me. But if it was, what have I done wrong now? Is it because we brought champagne? Or made a thing out of Alex's job offer? Doesn't that just make the barbecue even more of an event? It's not like we're taking anything away from it.

The glasses arrive, and Alex unscrews the wire cap and pops the champagne. It froths out of the bottle and we fill the glasses and I hand them round then make a toast. I drink most of my glass; it's so fizzy that it's hard to swallow fast and my throat burns.

I could just ignore her. But I don't want to be stuck with this horrible sour feeling inside. So I walk around and sit next to her.

'He really is gorgeous,' I say, looking at Ollie. I mean it. He's so perfect and other-worldly. His eyes are very, very dark, and his head is pointed at the back. He's delicate and really pretty. 'How are you?' I say.

'Fine,' she says, though it sounds brittle. But then she says, 'It's good news about Alex.'

So maybe I am wrong? 'Can't believe it,' I say, 'and I've got an interview for a teaching assistant job.'

'Right.' Ollie's gone to sleep and she starts to look around as though she needs to get away. The dutiful hostess.

'Probably be a lot of competition,' I add.

'God, yes,' she says. 'Anyone can apply, can't they? For that sort of thing?'

It's a put-down. A typical Suzanne snub. It's hard to tell if she's even aware she's doing it.

'Thanks for the support,' I say, fed up now.

She raises her eyebrows. 'You've got to face facts, Naomi. It's tough out there.'

8

'I know,' I snap at her. 'I'm the one sending off twenty application forms a week.' Why do I let her wind me up like this?

'Top-up?' Alex is there holding the champagne out to Suzanne.

'I can't.' She nods at Ollie. 'Feeding. We've got some in the chiller, actually. We were saving it for a bit later on when everyone's here.'

Now I get it. We've stolen her thunder. But I make myself sound bright. 'Great! This is nearly finished anyway. I bet yours is a good vintage, isn't it?' I say, though I'm not sure if champagne has vintages in the same way wine does. 'Save the best for later, eh?'

More guests arrive and she goes to greet them. Alex can tell things have been a bit tense. 'You okay?' He rubs my back between my shoulder blades, where I can feel the stiffness.

'Families,' I smile.

Why can't I just ignore her? What pisses me off is that I let it get to me. I wish there was a magic formula, something I could just switch on so I'd be immune to her sarky comments or her needling at me. Why do I care what she thinks? It's not like I want to be her or anything. I don't want her life; I'm not bothered about status and having loads of money. She never puts a foot wrong, but is she happy? She spends all her time watching eagle-eyed for other people (especially me) to make mistakes. I'm twenty-five and in a steady relation-ship and I've got a degree, and still she pushes all my buttons and I've not found a way yet to brush it off. Distance, absence helps. If I don't see her much. But put us together, and like some species of animal – rabbits or hamsters or something – if we have to share a cage, one of us gets savaged.

Any time I try talking to her directly, being really open

about it, saying, 'Why are you so bitchy to me?' or 'Why do you always have to be so negative?' she either denies it or says she's simply being honest.

Alex has a job, I tell myself, I've got an interview for a post I actually like the sound of, even if the money's not great, and we will soon have a place of our own. No way is my snotty sister going to spoil it. Fuck her, I am going to celebrate.

I raise my glass and wink at Alex, and he smiles back. 'To everything,' I say, and he echoes me and we toast the future.

Carmel

Before.

When the sun burnished everything and bubbles floated over the laughter and the future brimmed bright, ripe with adventure.

Before.

Were we smug? I don't believe so. But I dared to be happy, thinking that the girls were grown and building lives of their own, that Phil's business was ticking over in the teeth of the downturn, and a new generation had joined the family.

There wasn't any sense of entitlement, but relief rather. Like any family we've had our share of bad luck and misfortune. From the terror of Suzanne's bout of meningitis and the shocks of my dad's sudden death, Naomi's teenage high-jinks and my father-in-law's cancer, to the more mundane upsets of burglaries and credit-card debts. And I didn't for one minute think this phase of contentment would last – life's not like that.

It wasn't perfect. Naomi had been finding it increasingly hard to motivate herself after so many rejections.

And Phil, one of the most laid-back people I know, was on medication for high blood pressure. His latest tests had been disappointing, and the GP was keen to try and get it down to an acceptable level. Then there was my mother in a nursing home, lost to dementia. But that hazy afternoon it seemed like things were pretty damn good – and I was thankful. I was counting my blessings.

We left Suzanne's at about five. Phil set off for his gig at seven. It's nearby, a place they play two or three times a year, and they don't need long to set up. I could have gone along, but it wasn't like I hadn't seen them a million times, and I was more interested in catching up on some television.

I watered the garden first. We have a small square patch at the back of the house laid with flagstones, so everything is grown in containers. It's handy: no grass to mow, little weeding to do. Our home is one of four flat-roofed, split-level modern houses, three bedrooms, picture windows, open stairs. When I say modern, they were built in the sixties to replace the end of a terrace that had been demolished. They still look like a glaring anomaly in an area of identical terraced rows. The flagstoned garden is the back yard of the original property. I'd never imagined Phil and me living in what he describes as a little box, without the features and character of the older houses all around. But when we bought it, it was a bargain we couldn't ignore, on the market at a knock-down price due to problems with the flat roof. It was handy for schools and shops and a great place to raise the kids (apart from the windows, which were smeared with finger marks and kisses, traces of jam and Marmite for months on end).

As I filled the watering can from the butt and drenched

the pots, the day was ending, the sky a lavender blue draped with shreds of coral-pink clouds over in the west.

It was five to nine when I sat down and began flicking through the channels, a glass of wine at my side.

It was five past nine when the phone rang. And everything changed.

CHAPTER TWO

Naomi

Run! Run! Freaking out, fear squirting inside. Run! Can't move. Something squats on my chest, heavy, cold. Choking. Shout, warn them! Shout for help. Mouth stuck, tongue too. Can't even open my lips. Scream trapped in my throat, loud and red raw. Got to get away. Get away!

No light. Pitch dark and cold. Buried alive. Suffocating. Can't smell. Dark, still, silent. No – thumping, hammering. Something, someone, hammering. Thud, thud, thud, thud. Digging to reach me? Nailing me in? Each thud rocks me. Am I the nail? Salt in my mouth, brine.

Help! The scream echoes round inside my head. *Alex! Mum! Dad!*

There! Going up the escalator. I'm running. Legs like rubber bands, heart exploding, yelling and yelling. They never turn. They don't see me. No one sees, no one hears.

The ground trembles, hammering louder. Everything shudders and cracks. The pillars shatter and collapse, great clouds of dust billow, huge discs of stone fall and tumble, rocking the ground.

Running, dodging, everything thick with gritty dust. The ground splits, like cloth tearing, a massive wrenching noise and the world erupts. Tongues of fire and a blizzard of ash. I can't stop.

Falling.

Falling.

Like a puppet bumping off the walls of the canyon. Thump, smack, thump. To the bottom.

Crouching in a ball, arms over my head, coughing. I hear the beast coming, a river of molten lava, stone and gravel and debris. Thundering.

Battering me.

Burying me. Deep in pain.

No one will ever find me here.

Carmel

It was Alex's mum, Monica, on the phone. We had met briefly a couple of times. I was a little taken aback, then I assumed she was calling about Alex's new job and began to talk. 'Alex told us this afternoon, it's wonderful for them—'

She cut me short. 'Carmel, listen, I'm sorry, I've got some bad news.'

I laughed, I think I laughed, awkward, wrong-footed, trying to deny the danger in her voice. It seemed preposterous that there could be bad news. Was she ill, perhaps? Why was she sorry? My mother? Did she know her? Had Mum had another stroke, or an aneurism? That might be a blessing – something that allowed her to escape from the bizarre and frightening world she now inhabited.

'What is it?' I said. 'What?'

I heard her sniff or swallow, felt my skin chill and my stomach tighten.

'I'm sorry, there's been an accident. Alex and Naomi . . . in the car, there was a collision.'

My heart imploded; that was how it felt, a collapse in my chest, pain and my vision blurring. All that was left was the voice on the phone, the words that I was trying to decipher, the gaps between the words where the truth hung.

'Are they all right?' I could still speak, though I sounded odd, fractured, jerky. 'Monica?'

'I've talked to Alex,' she said. 'I'm waiting to see him. He's got broken bones, bruising.'

'Naomi?' I was trembling and shuddering. I thought about hanging up. I didn't want to know. It must be bad; she was breaking it slowly, gently. Couldn't come straight out with *Oh, she's great, not a scratch* or *Just a bump or two, miraculous escape.*

'I don't know,' she said quietly. 'Alex said they were working on her.'

Working on her. I swallowed. 'Which hospital?'

'Wythenshawe.'

In the taxi, I texted Phil, my fingers slipping, missing the keys, then I realized he would have his phone off while they played. Directory enquiries put me through to the pub. I could hear the band in the background, 'Stagger Lee'. We once learnt to jive to that, rockabilly style. Broken chicken walk, they called the step, almost like a limp, and the moves included lots of spinning round and away from each other, then back together. Me getting the giggles and losing the rhythm and setting Phil off. I repeated to the barman that he must interrupt the set at the end of this number and tell the lead guitarist, Phil, to ring his wife urgently. A family emergency. He promised.

Phil would be tapping his foot as he played, exchanging banter with Hugh on bass and lead vocals, supplying the odd backing harmony when the fancy took him, jamming with his mates at the end of a perfect day, no idea what was about to hit him.

A collision, Monica had said. So what about the other

vehicle? Another car? A bus? A lorry? Where had they crashed? It was about a twenty-minute drive from Suzanne's to ours. Were they coming back to ours? I couldn't remember. It's not like there were any fixed arrangements; they had their own keys, made their own meals. Or were they going to Monica's? Her house was even closer.

A new moon, a sliver of white, cut the inky sky. The roads were quiet: Sunday evening, people facing work the following morning. *Working on her.*

As we approached the hospital, the lights glared out from the corridors and entrance bays, the car park.

At A&E I paid the driver and got out. An ambulance was approaching, still out of sight, but its siren, insistent keening, filled the night.

Outside the entrance there was a couple standing with two policemen. The man had an arm round the woman, hugging her close, and she was weeping into his chest. He was smoking, his own eyes bright with pain. I quickly averted my gaze, not wanting to intrude, hating the sudden surge of empathy that quickened my pulse and stung my eyes. Why were the police there with them? Had they done something wrong?

My phone rang and I slid it open. *Phil.*

'Carmel?'

'Oh Phil, it's Naomi, there's been a car accident. I don't know . . . I've just got here, Wythenshawe. Come now, you must come now.'

'Oh God.'

There was a chant in my head, *pleasepleaseplease*, a frantic mantra. Not to any particular higher entity. To the world, to the world and everything in it, *pleasepleaseplease*.

Naomi.

* * *

The enquiries desk was quiet. Half a dozen people waited on chairs nearby, subdued. One man had a dressing pressed to his ear. An older woman opposite him was bent double. I rang the bell for attention, my eyes skating over notices about abuse of staff and no-smoking policies.

A woman came through and sat down behind the counter. She asked how she could help and I gave her Naomi's name and said she'd been in a car accident.

'Date of birth?'

I reeled it off. A September baby. An Indian summer. The nights had been sultry, the days baking. I'd moved in a daze, barely sleeping, trying to look after her and Suzanne, who was two and a half going on middle-aged and patently jealous of the baby. We had laid blankets on the flagstones and filled a paddling pool with water, kept it topped up. Sometimes I'd pull up a chair and rest my feet in it, feeding Naomi while Suzanne water-boarded her dolls: 'Naughty baby, you so dirty.' Phil took a couple of weeks off, got a mate to staff the shop, so he could cover the washing and shopping and feed us. We lived on salad, bread and cheese.

'Are you next of kin?'

'Her mother.'

The nurse checked a clipboard, then the computer. 'Yes, she's here. I'll ask someone to come and have a word. If you'd like to take a seat in the other waiting room, along the corridor on the left.'

There was no one in the waiting room, just two rows of plastic chairs and a low table between them with magazines on. Garish colours and chirpy headlines exhorting the reader to *Eat for Health this Summer* and *Exercise for Energy!*. Posters on the wall advised about bowel cancer and stroke, chlamydia and smoking cessation.

It was impossible to sit still and there wasn't enough room to pace. I checked my phone. Where was Phil?

Naomi. My heart felt unsteady, beating more quickly than usual, and with each thump I felt an ache inside, as though the shock had bruised it.

In the end I settled for sitting down, elbows braced on my knees, head in my hands, rhythmically drumming my feet in an effort to release some tension.

I hadn't let Suzanne know yet. Would they still be partying? We'd found it easy to maintain a social life when Suzanne was very small; she'd sleep anywhere and accompanied us to parties, concerts and festivals. But she probably already had a set bedtime for Ollie. She'd be feeding at four-hourly intervals through the night rather than on demand, and getting him to sleep through like a dream as soon as he'd gained enough weight. Suzanne didn't do failure. She might be asleep herself, it was after ten. Or she might still be clearing up; she'd never leave a mess overnight.

I was selecting her phone number when there was a knock at the door. A man in a doctor's coat. 'Mrs Baxter?'

I dropped my phone as I sprang to my feet, then winced and scrabbled to pick it up.

'Yes, how is she? Is she . . .' My throat closed up, suddenly dry. I could feel the drum of a pulse under my jaw, hear a humming from the strip lights. *Pleasepleaseplease.*

'She's being prepared for theatre,' he said.

'Oh, thank God.' The pictures I had been holding at bay – Naomi decapitated, Naomi crushed, Naomi on a slab – flooded in. I began to cry.

That was when Phil arrived. He said later that when he heard me crying, he thought we'd lost her.

The doctor sat us both down and explained that

Naomi's heart had stopped and she had been resuscitated at the scene. She had sustained a fractured skull, broken ribs, a broken collarbone and a broken ankle, and she also had extensive internal injuries. Their first priority was to isolate and stop any internal bleeding and repair damage to vital organs.

Phil kept asking questions: would she be okay, exactly what organs were damaged, how long would the surgery take, would she make a full recovery?

The doctor stressed that it was impossible to say at this stage how she would respond, or what they would find once they had her in theatre. He said it could be several hours. He had questions too about whether she'd had any previous surgery, any allergies or pre-existing medical conditions.

'Nothing,' I said. 'She's always been really healthy.'

'And Alex?' asked Phil. 'Her boyfriend?'

'I believe he's in X-ray.'

'Monica said he was okay, broken bones and bruises,' I said.

'Monica?' said Phil.

'That's how I knew,' I explained. 'She rang me.'

'The accident,' I turned to the doctor. 'Do you know what happened? Was it another car?' Or an HGV, I thought, pinning Alex's Honda Civic beneath the chassis. Had the fire brigade needed to cut her free?

'I don't know, I'm sorry. But the police are here and they'll be able to tell you more.'

The couple at the entrance doors, the man smoking, the woman weeping: were they in the other car? In the absence of hard facts, my mind was hyperactive, swooping on anything to fill in the blanks.

'She will be all right?' I said, as he took his leave. A plea as much as a question.

'We'll do our very best,' he said, confirming my fears.

Once he'd gone, Phil turned to hug me and we sat like that, twisted in the chairs, until I broke away, my arm deadened and my neck cricked.

He kissed my head.

'We'd better ring Suzanne,' I said.

He sighed. 'She can't do anything at this time of night.'

'I know, but we can't not tell her.'

He rubbed his face, sighed again, cleared his throat as he stood and keyed his mobile.

I listened to his side of the conversation as he spoke first with Jonty and then Suzanne. I closed my eyes and leant my head back against the wall. She was alive – now she had to stay alive. That was all that mattered. *Pleasepleaseplease*.

Phil had finished talking, promising to update Suzanne the moment there was any news, whatever time it was. Insisting there was absolutely no point in her coming to the hospital yet, while Naomi was on the operating table. Now he sat on one of the chairs opposite me, frowning, deep grooves between his bushy eyebrows, his mouth set. He looked over at me, shaking his head, his eyes raw. I walked across to him and put my arms around his head, pulled him close, felt the heat of his head against my belly, noticing how the hair on his scalp was thinning. Daft the things you see at times like that.

'What on earth happened?' When he finally spoke, his words were muffled.

I shook my head and exhaled, a long breath. There was nothing I could tell him.

Time passed. My eyes were closed, not because I was trying to sleep but because the harsh lights were unbearable, when a sound startled me, a door banging somewhere in the bowels of the building. My mouth was tacky. I signalled to Phil for the water: he had found a vending machine earlier and got drinks. He handed me the bottle; his eyes were bloodshot, his jaw darkened with stubble.

The next thing I remember, some time later, was the door opening. 'Mr and Mrs Baxter?' There were two police officers, a woman with freckled skin and glossy red hair pulled back in a French plait, and a stocky man with his hair cut very short. It made him look like a soldier. I wondered if they still had rules about hairstyles. Was he allowed to have a skinhead? I met plenty of police in the course of my work, but hadn't come across anyone with such short hair. Maybe he'd had chemo or shaved his head for charity?

He introduced himself and his colleague. I forgot the names as soon as I heard them, but he gave us his card. He was John Leland and he added her name in biro, Phoebe Jones.

'What happened?' Phil said straight out, but the man put off answering, saying they would tell us what they could but they needed to ask some questions first.

Outrage flared through me. Were they bargaining with us? Naomi was seriously hurt, her skull cracked, her insides torn, on the operating table; no one would or could tell us if she'd be okay, and now the facts of the accident were being withheld.

'We want to know what happened.' My voice was loud and shaky as I got to my feet. 'Why on earth can't you tell us that?'

'Carmel . . .' Phil tried to calm me down.

'The investigation into the accident has only just got under way.' The woman had a high, breathy voice which sounded at odds with the authority she held.

'The bare facts, then,' I insisted. 'We don't even know where it was or how they crashed.'

'Mottram Lane,' Leland said, 'just after the junction with Lees Hall Road, near the school.'

Only five minutes from home. I pictured it in my mind's eye. There were traffic lights on Lees Hall Road and it was a right turn into Mottram Lane coming back from Suzanne's. The river ran along the left-hand side of the road for a couple of hundred yards until the end of an S-bend where houses began. Opposite, on the right, were houses then a school. The start of the bend was sharp; you couldn't see round the corner and there had been a successful campaign to get a green-man crossing instead of relying just on a lollipop lady to help people negotiate the traffic.

They were nearly home.

'What about the other vehicle?' I said.

Leland stilled and blinked a couple of times; his colleague shook her head almost imperceptibly but I caught it.

'What?' I asked. 'There was another vehicle, wasn't there?' I looked at Phil. 'They said a collision. Monica . . . or the doctor.' Suddenly my memory was unreliable. Had someone said that? It was Monica, wasn't it? Or had I dreamt it up to plug the vacuum of knowledge?

'A cyclist was involved,' Leland said. 'It appears that there was a collision between the car and a cyclist.'

'Oh God, no.' I sat down. Cyclists were at real risk of accident. Drivers didn't see them, didn't give them enough room; our whole car-first culture and the lack of separate cycleways always made them vulnerable. Phil cycled to work most days unless he had anything bulky to carry. The girls had both used bikes to get around as teenagers, but we wouldn't let them ride into town, the route was too dangerous.

I imagined a bloke, a mountain biker on his Sunday ride out to the Peaks and back, tired and mud-splattered, lurid Spandex and a fancy water bottle. Or a woman, someone like me, with a butcher's bike, sit-up-and-beg, a wicker basket in front, cycling home from a picnic with friends. Alex seeing them, a fraction too late.

'How are they?' Phil said, his voice gruff.

Phoebe Jones was picking at her nails, her knees and shoes close together.

'Didn't survive the accident,' said Leland.

I gasped, and Phil reached and took my hand, gripped it hard.

'That's terrible,' I said. I saw Naomi holding up the champagne and Alex's dazzling smile and the patchy shade beneath the birch tree. And some poor person lying like a rag doll on the road, their bike a tangle of metal.

Phil shuddered.

But there was worse to come.

'It was a little girl,' Phoebe Jones said, in her breathy voice. 'Nine years old.'

I struggled to take it in. 'No.' Then, 'You're sure?' Desperate. Stupid. As if there was some chance they had it wrong, might backtrack, find a get-out clause. As if they would tell us something like that if there was the faintest margin of doubt.

Leland coughed. 'I'm sorry.'

'And you don't know why, how?' I asked. 'Was she crossing the road? Where was it? Was it a blind spot? Could Alex not stop in time?'

Silence. The fizz of the lighting, Phil's breath unsteady, a swift intake of air from Leland, who shifted on his buttocks and said, 'Apparently Naomi was driving.'

'Sorry?' I was numb, something clotting my senses, my comprehension.

'Naomi was driving the car; Alex was in the passenger seat.'

Naomi was driving. The enormity of what he was saying tore into me. I could not speak. With my hand clamped to my mouth, I shook my head over and over, my eyes burning. *No no no no. Please no.* A child was dead. Naomi was driving. Naomi. *They were working on her.* She was in theatre. *Naomi was driving.*

After. When everything changed.

CHAPTER THREE

Carmel

Sometime the following morning, a nurse came to take us to intensive care. She led us along the warren of corridors, the walls covered with artwork, and introduced us to the surgeon. Mr Hakim was a tall, thin man with piercing eyes and a thick, throaty accent, Greek or Turkish I guessed. He explained that they had repaired damage to Naomi's small intestine and bowel, and removed her spleen. Broken ribs had perforated her left lung, but they would be carrying out a further procedure to drain and reinflate the lung in due course. After such invasive surgery her recovery would be gradual, and they could not rule out the need for further intervention. We could expect her to be in hospital for several weeks. They were monitoring the skull fracture, but it was a linear one and all being well would not cause any complications.

There were two parallel reactions vying within me: a wash of relief, of gratitude that Naomi was alive, that she'd come through so far; and alongside that a stupefied horror at the litany of injuries she'd sustained.

I glanced at Phil, saw my own apprehension reflected back at me. 'Can we see her?' I said.

The doctor nodded. 'Yes, but don't expect a response. She's sedated at the moment, and even when that is withdrawn, she will probably sleep a great deal over the next few days.'

He handed us over to a nurse from the unit. She

indicated the hand-gel machines dotted along the ward and told us to use them before and after every contact with the patient. She asked us to put on aprons and gloves from a dispenser outside the room before we went in. All part of the drive to minimize the spread of infection that continued to plague hospitals. And of course, people in intensive care were most at risk.

My first sight of her, head bandaged and hooked up to tubes and wires, brought with it a lurch of pity and grief. I sniffed hard and grasped Phil's hand. Heard him breathe, bracing himself too. Her eyes were closed, her face and hair visible beneath the dressing. There were brown streaks in her hair, sticking it together in uneven clumps. Dried blood. Her lips were cracked and dry, her eyes stamped with bruises, and through the oxygen mask I could see traces of blood rimming her nostrils. There was a patch of raw skin on her cheekbone. A frown marred her forehead. I wondered if she was in pain.

Phil pinched the bridge of his nose and turned away for a minute. Then he brought a chair from the corner of the room and set it beside the bed for me. 'I'll find another,' he said.

I sat down. Naomi's hand was cool and limp. I held it for a while.

It was like being underwater, in a submarine, submerged in the murky light, enveloped by the cacophony of noises, the beeps and soughs and gasps of the machines, the clicks and whirrs. An echo chamber. For a moment I was six again, on the carpet in front of the television, heart racing as the admiral in *Voyage to the Bottom of the Sea* gave the command to *dive, dive, dive* and the hooter sounded. There was always a happy ending for the *Seaview* and her crew after their adventures fighting aliens and monsters and thwarting spies. But for Naomi?

'Hello, darling,' I said in a whisper.

Phil called her name, told her she was in hospital.

We waited some more, quiet, each lost in our own thoughts. Finally Phil suggested we come back later on.

A nurse checked our details so they could contact us if needed. In case she gets worse, I thought, in case she dies. What was Naomi's status? Poorly, serious, critical, stable, seriously ill, gravely ill? All the code words you heard on news reports. I asked the nurse. 'She's doing very well, a long time in theatre,' she said.

'Please?' I wasn't looking for reassurance; I needed to know where we stood. 'How would you describe her status?'

'Critical,' she said, 'but half of them are – we have an excellent record.'

I didn't dare ask for percentages or success rates; it was enough to know she was on the danger list.

'What about Alex?' I said to Phil. 'We should see him.'

'I need to lie down,' Phil said, 'before I fall.'

'We can just ask how he is, then,' I suggested. 'Visit later.'

He nodded.

The staff were obviously used to this sort of situation, and one of them spoke to her counterpart on one of the acute medical wards. Alex was comfortable and visiting was between two and five, and six and eight. We could visit Naomi any time. Another pointer to how ill she was.

Naomi

The sun is in my eyes. Dazzling. Too close. And a humming noise. The noise is in my head. A great ball of it, pulsing like a phone stuck on vibrate. I try to wake up, to drag myself away from the glare and the drone, but there is too much weight. Like someone has altered the strength of gravity, or like I'm underwater where the pressure is heavy on all sides. Snorkelling? Scuba-diving? I did it once, a trip to Tenerife, all four of us in flippers and wetsuits. Suzanne being anal about how long we'd be down there and the straps on her tank.

I can feel the ripples around me like the ocean, but the light is white, not blue or green. So I'm not sure.

When I try to move, to kick, or wake or float up, nothing happens.

I picture my hands and knees and feet away in the distance, like one of those rubber toy animals that stretch and stretch and stretch. Like looking into the wrong end of a telescope. I try to connect with them. If I can just twist my ankle or close my hand, it should do the trick.

But everything is sleeping, lazy.

The pressure is growing and the hum in my skull is getting louder. Am I drowning? If I were, wouldn't I be coughing and spluttering, like when I learnt to swim? Dad standing in the water with his arms wide open, calling to me. Or did I already do that, the choking? And this is the next stage, my lungs full of seawater. I can't find my breath. When I search for it, for my lungs in my chest, I can't find them. They're hidden in the blaze of light and the din in my head. The ripples tilt me again, to and fro. I like that. There is someone singing, a simple tune, a children's nursery rhyme, but I can't put a name to it.

Spinning round and round makes me dizzy. I love that feeling, like being full of bubbles. Out of it. Am I tripping? Are we living it large at some club or a party? But it must be pretty heavy-duty stuff, because I can't see anyone or hear the music, not even the singing any more. I think there was a party. Now the sun's gone and there is just a hissing sound. A waterfall of noise. I like the dark. Floating in slow circles, round and round and far, far away.

Carmel

We got lost on our way out, had to ask directions twice. Then Phil couldn't remember where he had parked. We wandered up and down the bays like zombies until we found the car. It was almost funny.

Before we set off, I called Suzanne.

'How is she?'

'She's in intensive care,' I said, and repeated the list of procedures the surgeon had relayed to us, glancing at Phil in case I had missed anything, but he just nodded. 'They say she's critical.'

'Oh, Mum.'

'I know, darling. They've got her sedated, so she's sleeping. We're going home for a bit now, but you can visit her any time. I'll ring you later.'

'Right.' There was a catch in her voice. 'Do they know what happened?'

I didn't want to say it out loud. I wanted to keep it smothered, safe, secret.

'Mum?'

'All they've told us is that Naomi hit a little girl, on a bicycle . . . She was killed.'

'Bloody hell!'

'I know, it's so awful.'

'What the hell was she thinking?' She sounded angry. 'Suzanne?'

'She shouldn't have been driving.' Tears in her voice, and a tight rage. 'She was drinking all afternoon!'

The shock of what she said hit me like a thump in the

29

guts. *Oh God!* I could barely speak. I finished the call and told Phil what Suzanne said, and saw him blanch.

'She's never driven when she's been drinking,' I said.

'Not that we know of,' said Phil.

'No, she doesn't. When they go out, she and Alex, her mates, they always decide who's going to drive. You've heard them.'

'Yes,' he admitted. 'I don't know, maybe she lost count, meant to have one or two and then stop like I did.'

'And why did Alex get in the car if she was drunk? He's not an idiot.'

'I don't know.'

'Perhaps Suzanne was wrong,' I said. 'You know how giddy Naomi can get if she's having fun.'

'We saw her with the champagne,' Phil said.

'Just a glass, and that was hours beforehand.'

I heard him sigh. 'Suzanne wouldn't say it if it wasn't true,' he said eventually.

'She exaggerates when she wants to make a point. They must have checked, the police or the hospital. They couldn't breathalyse her, but they'd take blood, and that would show how much was in her system.'

'So until we know that,' Phil said, 'we don't know if she was drink-driving.'

'Anyone can take a bend too fast, anyone can swerve.' I could hear the desperation in what I was saying, a plea for things to be not as bad as I feared. 'Alex will be able to tell us, won't he? He'll know.'

Phil gave a nod, then stretched and rubbed at the back of his neck. He started the engine.

They'd been so happy, I thought: the new job, the way Naomi's eyes danced as she raised the bottle of bubbly. Alex would have heard his news when he picked up the post from his mum's. Came round to ours to tell Naomi and collect her for the barbecue. A red-letter day. Why had she had taken such a risk? Had she, or was Suzanne mistaken?

'I want to see where it was,' I said.

'Now?'

'Now. Please.'

'There might not be anything there.'

But there was. We approached it from our end, as though we were heading for Suzanne's. The road was cordoned off, *Road Ahead Closed*, and diversion signs were the first indication before we reached the stretch leading to the S-bend. Blue and white police tape was strung between barriers, shivering though there was no breeze to speak of.

Up ahead we could see several vehicles – police cars and vans – and a prefab, a mobile investigation unit. On the steps that led up to it, a young police officer was smoking a cigarette, a large polystyrene coffee cup in her other hand. Beyond that were people in protective suits, their heads covered, working. And a white structure in the middle of the road. A square tent. I knew it must be where the girl had died.

Phil parked and we got out. Only as we crossed to the river side did I see the car. A blackened, mottled heap, resting on its roof, the front end partly on the narrow grass verge, the rear crushed, mangled with the railings that edged the riverbank. The trees immediately above were stripped of foliage, their branches burnt and black, blasted like something in a war zone.

'Jesus,' Phil said under his breath.

From where we stood, the stink of molten plastic, the charry smell of burning caught in the back of my throat. Crumbs of glass, fragments of metal and a layer of white powder covered the ground, and curls of grey ash riffled in the breeze, echoing the shivers of the police tape. Larger pieces of debris were scattered all over the road and beside them bright yellow markers, like mini sandwich boards, each numbered.

There were birds singing too, oblivious, a song thrush in the canopy of the trees further along, its sweet, trilling melody clear in the relative quiet of the day.

'She wasn't burnt,' said Phil.

'No, they must have got out before.'

I turned and looked across at the school and the pedestrian crossing beyond. The playground was deserted. Were they in lessons; would they be kept in, as though it were raining, because of the tragedy? It struck me that perhaps the girl went to the school. That her friends and teachers would be in mourning for her today. Maybe school was cancelled.

'Oh, Phil.' He put his hand on my shoulder, squeezed it. I thought of the parents, of the dark place they must be trapped in. Of their anguish. Imagining what it would be like if one of my girls was dead, if one of mine had been killed as a child. Never grown up.

'See the gatepost?' He nodded to the school gates, where one of the stone posts listed to the side. There were lots of markers close to it, and labels on the post itself as well as the railings further down next to the yellow sign: *Show You Care – Park Elsewhere.*

'They must have hit the post,' he said.

Or the child did? I didn't say it aloud.

A plane flew low overhead, the roar something to be endured. I watched its shadow ripple over the school roof and then the road, darkening the little white tent before moving on over the trees that fringed the river. In its wake a quiet fell before the song thrush resumed its serenade, one of the CSI people called to another at the far end of the stretch and a hornet whined close to my ear, perhaps mistaking my earring for a flower.

Looking again at the car, I noticed the dark pools on

the ground around it. Blood? There had been blood in Naomi's nose; had she spilled more on the road? Or had Alex? Monica never mentioned that he had any wounds like that. When I pointed it out to Phil, he thought it was probably something else, molten plastic or burning fuel. 'It's melted the road surface, see? You can see the difference.'

The heat. My stomach swooped as I imagined that heat, what might have happened if they hadn't got out.

'She wouldn't have stood a chance,' Phil said, his voice old with sorrow. Momentarily I thought he was imagining the fire, and then realized he was looking at the white tent. The glow of guilt licked my cheeks.

One of the CSI people picked something up and placed it in a bag, then wrote on it.

'She might not have used the crossing. Thought she'd risk it,' I said.

'You think she was crossing the road?' When I didn't reply, he touched me. 'Carmel?'

'Because that makes more sense.' I tried not to sound defensive, but all my muscles were stiff, there was a tension across the back of my skull and down my neck, and I had to force the words out. 'There wouldn't have been time to stop, to swerve. Naomi's not a bad driver.'

'You heard Suzanne, she'd been drinking.'

'It was an accident,' I said, as if that was some sort of excuse. I was unwilling to face the facts head on, even though they were laid out for me in the charred metal chassis by the trees, in the markers that littered the tarmac, and the bright white canopy concealing the site where the girl had lain. It was all too new, too raw, and I wanted to twist it into a different pattern, to bend it and weld it until it was something less dangerous, more palatable.

Phil had no such compunction. 'If she'd been drinking and then drove that car and that child is dead . . .' There was steel in his voice, and disgust, disgust for his own daughter. So unlike Phil. My vision blurred and I blinked to clear it.

That child. My mind veered away whenever it came close, like a wild animal smelling smoke, instinctive, protective. It hurt to think of her, of her and her nine years and her family.

Above the trees a flock of starlings came wheeling and turning in formation, then settled in the branches. Their high piping cries overlapped, fast and insistent, like a mob running rumours, trading gossip. The sun was hot on my scalp and my shoulders but I was chilled to the core.

'We might lose her, Phil.' I turned to him, my back to the police tape and everything beyond it.

His mouth tightened and his brow creased and he gave a fierce nod.

'We have to just ...' I broke off, uncertain what I meant to say. I tested the notion: Naomi dead, her injuries too great. Please, no. *Pleasepleaseplease.*

Had she cheated fate? Had she been marked to die in the crash but escaped? Was fate now stalking her, drawing inexorably closer? You can run but you can't hide. I knew I was trying to articulate that we had to stand by her and believe that she would come through, support her.

'Whatever it takes, you know that,' Phil said. Pain harrowed his features, and he pushed his hands either side of his temples and raised his face to the sky above and groaned.

The hornet returned, droning by my face, and I waved it away.

The woman who had been on the steps of the Portakabin was walking our way. She smiled as she reached us. 'Hello, can I help?'

I shook my head, tried to smile but failed.

'No,' said Phil.

'You live locally? Did you see anything yesterday evening?'

'No, sorry,' said Phil. 'Just passing.'

We didn't want to say it; neither of us could bring ourselves to own up. *It was my daughter. See the car. Her fault.* Let Suzanne be wrong, please, I thought. If Naomi *had* been drunk, then whatever the child had done, even if she had been in the middle of the road doing handstands on her handlebars, the fact that Naomi had got into what amounted to a lethal weapon with a bottle of wine sloshing through her bloodstream meant she was the guilty one. So we did not introduce ourselves to the police officer, but turned and slunk away. I could feel the shame rippling through me, wide as a river, deep as the sea.

It was surreal, travelling home along the tree-lined roads, past the shopfronts with their pavement displays. And it was peculiar finding the house as we had left it. Almost as if I expected the very bricks and mortar, furniture and fittings to be loosened or altered by the accident. Sleep eluded me, I went through the motions – a quick shower – then lay in bed with the curtains closed. Tried to empty my mind, listened to Phil snoring, imagining the noises he made were really waves breaking on a vast tropical shore, that I was lying on the hot sand, my muscles softening in the heat. But however much I tried to relax, the images of Naomi still and silent in a hospital bed, the blackened car and the stark white tent swam to the fore. And questions, persistent as the starlings' chatter had been: why had Alex let her drive? Why didn't they get a taxi or stay at Suzanne's? Where had the child been? Could Naomi have avoided her if she had been sober? *Was* she sober? I prayed that Naomi would be conscious when we went back, out of danger and able to explain it all to us.

CHAPTER FOUR

Naomi

Everything hurts. An awful dragging pain in my belly and deep in my bowels. Tearing me apart.

If my pain was musical, that would be the bass, and the percussion is all the things beating in my head, but there are these tight, sharp, cutting pains too, like glass daggers in my side. They'd be the strings maybe, high and off key. Like when I learnt violin for a term in Year 5.

There's a sound like traffic, shushing on and on, and lots of computer beeps and clicks. And something like the wind, a moaning noise.

That's me! I get it, me moaning. I'm the vocalist. I don't know where I am or what's going on. I could open my eyes; I consider it, but it would be very hard to do. And it might hurt, too. Then something tears inside me. Savage. Hot molten metal floods through me, and a pool of black, black oil rises, taking me down.

Carmel

The phone rang. The hospital. Naomi had deteriorated; she was in theatre again. Internal haemorrhaging. They were doing all they could.

We hurried, but there was nothing for us to do when we got there. The nurse on intensive care promised to let us know when Naomi was back. She said it like she meant it, pragmatic and positive, and it was a hope to cling to. Neither of us wanted to leave the hospital.

Phil rang Suzanne and arranged to pass on any news as soon as we heard, so she could visit again.

'We really shouldn't expect her to be doing this when she's a tiny baby to cope with,' I said.

Phil shrugged at me. 'Wild horses, you know Suzanne. Besides,' he exhaled loudly, 'it's . . . well, it's serious, isn't it?'

She might die, he meant, she might not recover. And her sister would need to know that she had done all she could to be with Naomi.

The girls had fought like cats in a sack when they were growing up. An endless bout of sniping and name-calling, one-upmanship and out-and-out rivalry. Any honest mistake or calamity that befell Naomi, Suzanne imbued with malicious intent – *she broke the shower, she ruined my DVD, she took my plate, she knew it was mine* – while Naomi complained that Suzanne was always trying to get her into trouble and boss her about. At eleven, Naomi spent several months referring to her sister as Mrs Hitler. The verbal clashes sometimes turned to physical brawls, in which Naomi, who was bigger and tougher, had the upper hand.

But when it really mattered, the animosity dissolved like salt in water. Naomi insisted on seeing Suzanne when she had meningitis, and was distraught when she had to wait until the antibiotics we had all been given kicked in and safeguarded her against contracting the infection herself. When she finally got there, she sat stroking Suzanne's cheek with a sticky hand and making little cooing sounds, promising to give her all her worldly goods when she got better and came home. Phil and I didn't know whether to laugh or cry.

When Naomi broke up with her first serious boyfriend and become very low, it was Suzanne who took the time to provide some treats and distractions: a makeover by one of the stylists at work, some casual shifts helping towards a charity fund-raiser that Suzanne was planning. And further back, when Suzanne was just starting school, I'd opened the door to an upset neighbour brandishing a note and holding a weeping child by the hand. The note, in Suzanne's purple felt tip, on Barbie notepaper, read: *dont be so mean or I will killl you, from Suzanne.* I think the extra 'l' added feeling.

I'd called Suzanne in from the back garden.

'What is this all about?'

'He was mean,' she said disdainfully, 'lots of times.'

'Glenn is smaller than you,' I scolded her. 'He doesn't understand yet.'

'Not mean to me,' she said scornfully. 'He's horrible to Naomi and she's more smaller.'

We had a talk there and then about death threats and bullying and how to ask for help, then I made Suzanne apologize and got her to tear the note up in front of the boy.

'It's not nice when anyone is mean,' I said, hoping his mother would get the message and maybe pull him up on his treatment of Naomi, but she just looked at me with a humourless smile and said goodbye. Maybe she did it later, behind closed doors. Secretly I was pleased that Suzanne had tried to protect her sister, even if her methods were a bit full-on. It reassured me that she cared for Naomi when so much of the time they acted like sworn enemies.

I was getting a stream of calls from friends and colleagues who knew only that Naomi had been in a car crash and was seriously injured. I hadn't the energy or inclination to reply to them yet. Though I did call my closest friend Evie, who also works in my department. She'd pass on any stuff for public consumption and keep quiet about anything I wanted to remain confidential. She listened while I gave a summary of what had happened.

'Oh God,' she said, then, 'Okay, what needs doing?' Her practical, social-worker side kicking in. 'Shopping, cleaning, dog-walking?'

'Idiot.' We don't have a dog. 'We're fine at home, but the office . . .'

'Yep.' I could see her, poised to write, snazzy glasses on, blonde curls wild. Often as not she'd scrawl notes on her arm if there wasn't paper to hand. It drove her partner Lucy mad. 'The last thing I want when things are getting romantic is to read about a court date or a custody hearing,' Lucy once complained.

'Get somebody to cover my shifts. I'm on tomorrow and Wednesday. And can you check the diary? I think there's something pencilled in during the next couple of weeks.'

'Call me when she's out of theatre,' Evie said.

'Promise.'

'She'll be all right,' Evie said. How could she say that? She should know better. It was there in all our training. Don't make promises you can't keep. Only offer what you can realistically deliver. I prayed for Naomi's deliverance, but to speak the thought aloud would be reckless, dangerous, tempting fate. I felt a prick of anger, hot beneath my breastbone. 'I'd better go,' I said.

'Take care,' she said, and hung up.

It was another two hours before we had news. Naomi had come through surgery; further repairs had been made to her lower bowel. She would be moved back to the ward once she had come round from the anaesthetic.

We waited outside intensive care and were there when the porter appeared pushing the trolley with her on. She was awake but barely with it, groggy. She had a cut on her lip which was bleeding. I asked the nurse about it as they settled Naomi back on the ward, attaching a saline drip and the pulse monitor to her finger. 'It'll be from the anaesthetic; it's not unusual for there to be minor damage to the mouth, broken teeth even.'

'What do they use?' Phil muttered. 'A hammer?'

The nurse laughed. 'We are a bit more advanced than that. Now, she's still nil-by-mouth, but if she gets thirsty we can bring some mouth swabs for her to suck.'

Naomi's eyes were closed; she hadn't even acknowledged us yet. Did she know who we were? Was there any brain damage? The thought hit me like a cold shower. They'd have said, surely? Warned us?

'Naomi?' I said quietly.

She opened her eyes a little, scowling as though the light was too harsh for her. She looked at me, then her eyes moved to Phil at the other side of the bed. She gave a small sigh but still didn't speak. In her gaze I saw the same blunt indifference that I found in my mother's. My stomach tightened.

'You're in hospital,' Phil said. 'You've been in an accident, love.'

'What?' she whispered.

'A crash,' he said.

She looked numb, still woozy. 'I don't remember,' she said, and closed her eyes. I tried to read her face and failed. Was she thinking, processing the information? The nurse came back then, depositing a pot of pale blue foam lollipops on the bedside table.

'I think she's gone to sleep,' I said.

'Best medicine,' the nurse replied. 'If she does all right, she'll be transferred to another ward in a few days' time. She's doing really great,' she added, 'but she's not going to be up to much for a while.'

'Is she in any pain?' I asked.

'We'll be keeping an eye on that. There's always some discomfort after surgery. Especially given the amount she's had.'

My hands in the latex gloves felt hot and sticky; the apron was full of static and the skirt section stuck to my arms.

Naomi

It's a labyrinth; the tunnels run through the earth, the smell of mud is strong. The roots of trees, knotted and gnarled, poke from the soil like fingers or bones. I have to crawl, the roof is so low, and when I come to the end of the passage, it is blocked off. A dead end. There is no space to turn, so I have to shuffle back the way I came, my hands and knees raw, stinging from the pieces of grit, the grains of dirt.

I don't sense the chasm, don't notice any change in the air until I'm in it, falling, falling upwards and . . .

Awake. Dim light. Mum, her face all funny and . . . I can't see all of him properly, but enough to know Dad's there too. There is something I should tell them. Is there? Then a whooshing comes and the ink races through the tunnels, leaping up the walls, rising to take me back, lapping at me.

Carmel

A little later, Suzanne and Jonty arrived, calling to us from the doorway to the room. There were only meant to be two visitors to a bed, so we said we'd come out and see them. We took off our protective clothing and put it

41

in the bin, and left the room to meet them in the corridor. The sight of Suzanne made me feel wobbly again. I held her close, then Phil did the same.

'How is she?' Suzanne asked.

We told them. Jonty looked embarrassed, awkward. I wondered if he had a thing about hospitals. He kept rocking on his feet, up on his toes and down, his eyes wandering over the posters and notices.

'We can't stay long,' Suzanne said apologetically. 'Left Ollie with Julia down the road.'

'She's sleeping anyway.'

'You both look shocking,' Suzanne said with her customary honesty. 'You should get some sleep your-selves. There's stuff in your fridge,' she added. 'We'd loads left over.'

'Oh, Suzanne, that's so—'

'Well, you won't feel like cooking,' she said, cutting me off.

'We'll just say goodbye to Naomi,' I told her. Hand gel. Another pair of gloves, another apron. I bent close over Naomi and kissed her cheek. 'We're going home for a bit, darling. See you later. I love you,' I added. It wasn't something we habitually said aloud, but now it seemed important.

Back in the corridor, I hugged Suzanne again. As we stepped apart, she caught my elbows in her hands. 'Mum, you need to know. It's in the paper. The accident, the little girl.'

'On the local news, too,' Jonty said.

I nodded quickly, avoiding her eyes. I didn't want to know, I didn't want to hear.

We made our way to Alex's ward and found Monica in the waiting area just outside the ward itself. 'Oh,' she said, 'Carmel, Phil – how's Naomi?'

'She's had more surgery,' I said. 'Internal bleeding. She's back now. She came round for a minute but she couldn't remember anything about the accident – didn't seem to know what we were talking about. What about Alex? We've not managed to see him yet.'

'He's just gone down to have his casts done. The fractures are pretty straightforward, so he shouldn't need any operations. He'll need to use a crutch for a while.'

'Is it his leg?'

'Ankle and wrist. He was lucky.'

'Yes,' I said. It was relative, wasn't it?

'It's still such a shock,' she said. 'Alex said she took the bend too fast. If only . . . I passed them,' she shook her head, 'driving back from the gym. Tooted and waved, like you do . . .'

I nodded.

'Her driving was fine then, honestly, she wasn't speeding. If only I'd . . . Oh, I don't know.' She blinked fast.

What could she have done? Flagged them over? She'd had no reason to.

'I do hope she's all right,' Monica said. 'You'll let me know – and Alex wants to see her as soon as . . .'

'Yes. Thanks.' The words about Naomi maybe drinking before they drove home were in my mouth, lodged there. I should mention it, I knew I should, but I said nothing. I prayed Suzanne was wrong, that Naomi had switched from wine to soft drinks not long after we left the barbecue and her greatest sin was not watching her speed.

Phil stayed quiet, saying nothing either.

'There'll be an investigation,' Monica said. 'The police are going to talk to Alex tomorrow.'

'Yes.' My mouth was dry.

'I'll give you my mobile number,' Monica said.

I took her number and we said our goodbyes, and still I kept silent. I didn't want to be the one to tell her; I couldn't face her reaction.

And it was only Suzanne's word after all, wasn't it?

Evie and I spoke before I went to bed. I shared everything with her. And she listened. She didn't make excuses for Naomi, or dodge the sheer ugliness of what I was telling her, and this time, thank God, she didn't tell me it was all going to be all right. I think I'd have hung up if she had come out with any stupid platitudes like that. Because whatever happened, there was no gain saying that this was a tragedy, maybe plain and simple, maybe complicated, but an awful, awful tragedy. At the heart of it a nine-year-old, mown down on a Sunday evening as she cycled along the side of the road. Mown down by my daughter

I am used to other people's crises. It's what I do, how I earn my living. Social worker – emergency duty team. When someone's life is turned upside down and it's an emergency and out of hours (evenings, nights, weekends, bank holidays), the phone rings in my office. I do a rotating pattern of night shifts and back shifts (afternoon till midnight), and get one weekend off in four. I am the person who sorts things out: the admission to a mental health unit, the emergency accommodation, the removal to a place of safety. I act as an appropriate adult when a teenager is arrested in town, and am there for all the victims of fire or flood or explosion who find themselves suddenly homeless. I'm the person who can bridge the gap, hold your hand and list the steps that need to be taken the following morning or at the start of the week when normal service is resumed. I don't panic or freeze or lose my temper. My training has equipped me with all

I need to support you through the calamity in a calm and professional manner. I am objective, detached. If something about your particular case upsets or enrages me, you won't have a clue. I will save it for my report and assessment, for my recommendations, which feed into a cycle of monitoring and improvements.

The bulk of my work, the real routine, is child protection. An unending catalogue of cruelty, neglect and misery. From the child with the mark of a hot iron branded into his back to the six-year-old turning up at school on a weekend in an attempt to escape her stepfather's sexual abuse.

Of course there are some situations that stick with me, stark memories most of them of the cruel and desperate straits that people find themselves in. Like the little boy who survived the wholesale slaughter of his family by his father, or the elderly woman found wandering on the main London to Manchester railway line, abandoned by her son and his wife, or the young Somali woman who one evening escaped from the shed where her owners kept her as a domestic slave, running barefoot in a city thick with snow. But other memorable encounters are funny or heart-warming, because of the people, their tenacity and courage, and the kindness of strangers. Humanity in all its messy, mucky, glorious, beautiful colours. Like the young mother of a foundling baby boy who was traced and who went on, with support from her stepdad, to make a loving home for herself and her son. Or the retired head teacher who opened his house to a recovering drug addict and ended up adopting her. Or the lad poised to jump from his gran's roof because his medication sent him loopy. He teaches boxing now, mentors others.

Some events are overwhelming – we're on call for major incidents as well, and I was there in the aftermath of the Manchester bomb. That's with you for ever, too.

So, no foreigner to emergencies, the tears that appear without warning in the fabric of life, the cracks in the road, and the way we act to try and cope with sudden trauma. But it is a completely different thing to be on the receiving end. No doubt some of my experience and expertise kicked in, but I was powerless to act, powerless to influence. I had no role. Naomi's health was in the hands of doctors and nurses. They were the experts. There was nothing for me to arrange or fix up, no calls to make, no referrals to agree upon. I was a bystander; I was 'the family'.

That night I dreamt vividly. We were running, Phil and me and the kids. Naomi and Suzanne were still children. We were running and the wave of water was behind us, enormous, slate blue and foaming, howling at our heels. We had to reach higher ground; none of us could swim. I was yelling, screaming at the girls to run faster, tugging their hands. The wave rose above us, high as a house, a wall of water suspended for a moment before it came crashing down, wrenching our hands apart. I was tumbling over and over under the weight of it. When I surfaced, the water was littered with debris: metal and wood, tree branches. I couldn't see the others. Phil called my name. He was up on the bank. On the turf, above the raw clay that had been eroded by the sea. The girls beside him. I waded to the edge, cold and breathless, hauled myself up and on to dry land. Suzanne, now an adult, stared at me, horrified. 'Mum,' she said, 'where's Ollie? You've left Ollie!'

And the fear flooded through me like acid.

CHAPTER FIVE

Carmel

Thank God Phil was there, going through it all with me. I don't know how I would have borne it without him. We'd been together thirty-one years by then. God – thirty-one years! Phil was playing support at the PSV Club in Hulme when I first saw him with his band, the Blaggards. They were punk pirates, all black leather and zips and red stripes. A skull and crossbones on the drum kit.

I was revising for finals at the time and trying to get my dissertation written: 'Unmarried Mothers – Slatterns and Scapegoats'. Renting a room in a shared house in Fallowfield that was permanently damp and cold.

My housemates Karen and Gillian and I had hooked up with other friends and gone en masse to the gig.

The club was called the PSV because it was owned by a load of bus drivers and a PSV was the type of licence required to drive a bus. It was south of the city centre and meant we could walk home, unless someone felt flush enough to pay for a taxi. The door prices were reasonable, the toilets were a disgrace. Hold-your-breath-and-straddle-the-bowl kind of thing.

It wasn't a massive club, small enough to spot people you knew in the crowd. The stage was raised; the dance floor was ringed with a scattering of tables and chairs at the fringes, some of them dropping to bits.

I remember dancing as soon as they started playing, pogo-ing up and down to keep warm more than anything. They were loud and strident; I couldn't make out any of the lyrics that Ged, the front man, was snarling. I was single at the time. Gasping for breath in between numbers, I'd already scanned the crowd and worked out that the only good-looking blokes were already taken. So I turned my attention to the band. The bassist was a woman, Lorraine. Ged didn't do anything for me. The drummer was a possible: nice face, but the Mohican hair dyed lurid orange and spikes pushed through his ears suggested he might be too outgoing for me. I wasn't after a clown. Phil I thought was shy; he spent most of the set looking down, not connecting with the audience. He was skinny, bony, his shoulders sharply defined under a torn black T-shirt, tight black pants with zips, black Doc Marten boots on his feet. He had been at the hair gel, or sugar and water or beer or something, to stiffen his choppy black hair into a spiky fringe.

I watched him play, moved to the left through the crowd so he might notice me when he looked up. But he never did. He didn't seem interested. Maybe he was gay? I went home unattached and drunk.

It must have been a month or so later, at another club-cum-boozer called the Cyprus Tavern, on Princess Street, not far from the BBC buildings, when I saw him again, drinking with Ged and a couple of other lads. The shyness was gone. We must have spent an hour doing the glance dance, matching gazes then looking away, over and away.

'Go and ask him out,' Karen told me. 'Put him out of his misery.'

'No!' I objected. If I was going to risk making a fool of myself, risk rejection, I wasn't going to do it in front of an audience.

Time went on, Karen started talking about going for

the bus, but I didn't want to leave while he was still there. While there was still a chance.

Then his group got up, all of them, and pulled on jackets and coats. His was an ancient black leather bomber jacket. I swore, lit a cigarette, nervous, knowing they would pass us on their way to the door.

He was last in line. Karen nudged me with her knee as they got closer. I nudged her back, hissed, 'Leave it!'

I decided to play it cool, pretend indifference in some last-ditch attempt at flirting. But I could sense him getting closer with every hair on my body, with each beat of my pulse. As he reached our table, I swung my eyes up, took a drag of my cigarette. Aiming no doubt for some vamp-like appeal. I was wearing a tight-fitting green leopard-print dress, black tights, black Docs, half a wand of mascara, a slash of red lipstick, most of which was now on my fag end. My hair was dyed black with fuchsia-pink tips. All topped off with an acid-green beret. I thought I was drop-dead gorgeous.

He had blue eyes, dark blue with a black rim. Merriment in them as he slid on to the stool opposite us. 'Got a spare smoke?' His romantic first words. I pushed the packet over.

'Thank you.' He smiled. I laughed. He made me laugh. This popping feeling inside, mirth, excitement. He wasn't shy at all. I found out later that the reason he appeared like that at the gig was because he was only just learning the chords, was petrified of playing a bum note. Though whether anyone could have told the difference . . .

'I'm Phil,' he said as he lit a cigarette. He had a Zippo.

'Carmel, and this is Karen.'

'Want to go on somewhere?' He addressed us both.

My throat grew tight. Karen winked at me. 'Thing is, Karen needs to get the bus. Said I'd walk her.'

'I'll come too,' he suggested.

49

We ambled along Princess Street and through to Oxford Road, talking about his band and seeing them at the PSV and where they were playing next. I was coherent and outwardly calm, but inside there was a little kid, arms raised in triumph, jumping up and down on a bed yelling, *I got him! I got him! I got him!*

We didn't touch.

We saw Karen on to the bus. Phil had already suggested we get a late drink, and we walked down to Rusholme, to a little place hidden away off Moss Lane East. A shebeen, I guess. People knew him, let us in. It was smoky, crowded; most of them were West Indian, just a sprinkling of white faces. He nodded greetings and we squeezed through the couples who were dancing up close to rocksteady songs. There were huge towers of speakers with the bass set high, thudding through the floor; the dancers pulsed almost as if the beat itself was physically shifting them.

Phil led me to a table where shots of rum and cans of Red Stripe lager were all that was on offer. I had no money left but he had enough for a lager, which we shared, taking turns sipping from the can.

Someone passed a joint to Phil, who toked on it three times before offering me some. It was pure grass, seeds in it spitting as I took a long draw. I held the smoke in deep and passed the reefer on, resisting the reflex to cough. The buzz overlaid the loose, fuzzy feeling from the drinks and soon we were dancing. Not touching, but dancing. Maybe an hour later, we left. Outside it was dark, not cold. My ears were hissing from the music.

'I'm not far, just down the road,' Phil said. 'Or I could walk you home.'

I didn't usually go back with men I met on a first encounter. But I trusted Phil. He felt safe.

'Whereabouts?' I asked him.

'Just on Platt Lane.'

We meandered along. I was still walking when he called, 'Hey, Carmel.'

I swung back; he had halted outside a building.

'You live in a shop?'

'Upstairs.'

I read the sign *Rock Records*, saw the display of record sleeves (several I owned: Elvis Costello, the Clash, the Slits, X-Ray Spex) and the top twenty record charts through the grille over the window. There were other notices there: *Musical accessories sold here* and *Blank tapes best prices.*

'Who has downstairs?'

'Me.' He smiled; he had a dimple, just one on the left, and a chipped front tooth.

'No, really?'

'True.'

I stared at him. It seemed so grown-up.

'What?' he asked.

'Brilliant!' I said.

We had to go through the shop to reach the flat. He was careful about locking up; there were bolts and padlocks all over the place. 'Got robbed three times last year,' he said, flipping the lights on.

'How long have you been here?'

'Four years, started when I left school.'

'Do you make enough to live on?'

'Long as I can bum cigs off someone like you,' he joked.

He did all sorts to get by: sold records and cassette tapes, as well as accessories for guitars and drums and percussion. He had a PA to hire out for small events. And decks, too. Then there were the gigs the Blaggards played, though they probably spent more on drugs and alcohol at those than they ever got paid.

'This way.' He took me up the stairs at the back, rickety wooden steps, no carpet. Posters on the walls covering up the mottled paint: Iggy Pop, Bob Marley and the Wailers, Che Guevara, *Butch Cassidy and the Sundance Kid*.

At the top of the stairs there was a bathroom and the narrow hallway doubled back leading to two rooms: a kitchen/diner at the back and a bedroom-cum-living-room at the front. There were records everywhere, music papers and piles of books. The place was messy but not dirty. Not damp like mine.

I felt suddenly shy seeing his bed, a mattress on the floor covered in a brightly patterned blanket. And wondered where to sit, what to say.

'Tea?' he offered.

I agreed, and he put a tape on and left me. The music was lovers' rock, similar to the stuff on the sound system at the shebeen. The sofa looked like an antique, an enormous squashy pile of red velvet that I fell back into.

He brought mugs and a plate of biscuits, then bummed another cigarette off me and skinned up. We smoked it, finished the tea. We still hadn't touched. Was I reading the situation wrong? Only one way to find out.

'You want to dance?' I said.

He stood up, reached out a hand and pulled me up. Long, bony fingers, nicotine stains. His hand was cool and dry. He pulled me close so my breasts and belly were pressed against him, angled his hips so there was pressure there. Bump and grind. I closed my eyes, the music swirling through me, passion growing.

As the track faded out, he stopped moving and I opened my eyes. He had a warm, sleepy look on his face and nudged closer to me. We were kissing, slow-kissing, tasting of tea and tobacco and dope. He gave a little groan and broke it off. But I pulled him back, kissed him hard and started to take his clothes off.

He woke me at one-thirty the following afternoon with tea and fried-egg sandwiches, and the Sunday papers. We ate and swapped sections of the newspaper. He started the cryptic crossword, something I never even attempted.

He talked to me about my course and what I was going to do next. 'Apply for jobs, go wherever I can get something.' A pang as I said it, thinking that this might just last a few weeks then.

We watched a black-and-white western on television. His reception was rubbish; the picture kept fizzing over. We got high again using my last cigarette and made love.

I had to go. I'd still more to do on my dissertation and I hadn't been to the launderette yet, either. One of the few places open on a Sunday in Manchester.

Would I see him again? Would he say anything? Did he like me as much as I liked him?

'You busy Friday?' he said as I laced up my shoes.

'No.' A spurt of pleasure, warm inside.

'There's a do on, the West Indian centre. Go for a curry first?'

'What time?' Feeling giddy.

''Bout eight.' He named one of the curry houses. He offered to walk me home then, but I said there was no need.

We kissed outside the shop.

It was sunny, sunny and warm. The streets were busy with people going to the park opposite. I grinned all the way home. It could have been hailing stones and hurling lightning. I wouldn't have minded.

By summer, I'd moved in.

* * *

Wandering into the kitchen, I saw the little girl's photograph on the front of the paper, dark hair in plaits, a plump face, chubby arms. Dumpy. Overweight. Sucked in the accompanying headline – *TRAGIC GIRL ROAD DEATH* – before I had a chance to censor myself. Felt a rush of heat, of nausea as I understood what I was looking at. 'What on earth did you buy that for?' I rounded on Phil.

'Don't you want to know what they're saying about it?' he said, sounding puzzled, a little irate.

I gave a laugh. 'No, obviously not.' *Perhaps she was wobbling on that bike, lost her balance, veered too close.* My mind whispering things I'd not dare to voice aloud. Sneaky things. She was wearing a polo shirt; a school photo, perhaps. An uncertainty in the smile.

I moved to go and he caught my wrist. 'Carmel, we don't deal with this by pretending it's not happening. By sticking our heads in the sand.'

'So we rub our noses in it?' My voice broke. 'I can't . . .'

'We can't help Naomi if we're ignorant, blinkered.'

I looked at him, his frank blue eyes, his beard already growing in. I closed my eyes, wanting to be blinkered; more than that, wanting to be blind and deaf and dumb to all of it.

He hugged me and we stood like that, the heat of him warming through me, his hand moving to stroke my head.

He was right, I knew it intellectually, but my heart was lagging behind, my instincts were off kilter. At work, with any other family, I'd have been saying something similar: face the facts, accept the truth, only then can you act on the situation. Gather all the relevant information, analyse, understand, develop a strategy, a plan.

'I'll read it,' I said quietly. 'I'd rather not have an audience, though.'

'Hey,' he said softly, 'you sure about that?'

Why was he so fucking understanding? Tears burned at the back of my eyes. I nodded miserably.

When he left the room, I made a cup of tea and sat down at the table. Pulled the newspaper close. Stared at the photo again. Was it recent? Must be. Had she turned nine by then? The smile was small, slightly false, no teeth showing.

I steeled myself to read the article, aware of all the questions crowding in my head, insistent and intrusive: *was she the eldest, the youngest, what was her family like, what was her name, where had she been going on her bike, who broke the news to her mother?*

My eyes slid over the type, the two short columns, reading it like some foreign language, trying not to translate it into meaning and empathy and understanding. A barrier around me like a concrete wall, unyielding.

The nine-year-old girl tragically killed in a road accident in Sale yesterday has been named as Lily Vasey. Lily was riding her bike on Mottram Lane near the family home when she was hit by a car. Her parents Simon (37) and Tina (35) and brothers Nicholas (16) and Robin (14) are reported to be devastated. Police are currently investigating the circumstances of the accident. The two occupants of the Honda Civic, a twenty-six-year-old man and a twenty-five-year-old woman, were both injured in the collision and are undergoing treatment at Wythenshawe Hospital. Sgt John Leland of Greater Manchester Police said, 'This is a tragic incident that has resulted in the death of a young girl and our sympathies are with her family. We would ask anybody who may have witnessed the collision to contact the police.'

I let out my breath. *A twenty-five-year-old woman.* That was Naomi.

She was the baby, Lily. Two big brothers. An afterthought? A miracle? A mistake?

Nine years old.

At nine, Naomi had been a determined tomboy, refusing to wear girlie clothes, best pals with Anthony at school and Usman down the road. She had a BMX bike and we'd rigged up a basketball hoop on the drive. She liked to show off break-dancing moves and play Tomb Raider on the computer. I'd wondered then if she'd turn out to be a lesbian.

Now I was scared about her waking up, as she came through the pain and physical healing of the operation and the injuries, and remembering it all: the barbecue, the drive home, the split second before impact when it was too late to act. She'd have seen the child, the bicycle, knowing in her bones that it was too late to stop, too late to avoid hitting her. The slow-motion last moments as the car flew closer.

Until she woke, there was this weird limbo, a breathing space. The sudden silence before the storm breaks, before the earth shakes. Though in fact the damage was already done. When Naomi sat up and remembered it all, it would be an aftershock. The rest of us were already experiencing them, on waking, and in between, all those little tremors when the mind and body forgets for a moment and then stumbles over the memory.

The girl's family – they'd be doing it too, like being at sea among waves the size of houses, each one cresting, slapping the truth at them. And all their nine years' worth of memories rising up on hind legs like shadows, like ghosts hungry for grief.

CHAPTER SIX

Carmel

I kept thinking about them, the Vaseys. I said to Phil, before we left to visit Naomi again, 'They're waiting for a post-mortem or whatever. Having to bury their little girl.'

'Yes,' he said.

'Out of nowhere,' I said, 'out of the blue, bang, and a whole life, a whole life . . .' There was no other way to say it: Lily and all she encompassed, all she might have become. Destroyed. Gone. 'I just feel so sorry for them. I can't imagine . . .'

'I know,' he said, his voice close to a whisper.

After we'd been there about half an hour, Naomi opened her eyes and groaned a little, then scowled. 'Mum?' My heart swelled up and almost robbed me of speech, but I managed 'Hello, love.'

Her eyes moved to Phil at the other side of the bed. He set down his paper, half the clues already filled in in the crossword, and reached for her hand. I moved my hand to cup her cheek, very tenderly, fearful of hurting her. 'Hello,' I said again. 'You're in hospital, there was an accident.'

Phil and I had agreed that we needed to give her the information gradually. She'd be weak and vulnerable. She didn't say anything; she was still frowning, her eyes creased up. Had she followed what I'd said? 'You've had some operations. They had to remove your spleen and repair damage to your bowel. You've broken your collarbone and your ankle. You've a punctured lung, too, broken ribs.'

'Alex?'

I told her how he was. Then she flinched and her eyelids fluttered. 'Are you in pain?' I asked her.

'Yes,' she said, her voice squeaky. I wanted to give her a drink, she sounded parched, but the nil-by-mouth sign was still there. I offered her a foam lollipop, explaining that she could suck it if she was thirsty, but she gave a slight shake of her head.

'Okay, I'll get the nurse,' I said.

The nurse came and took various readings. Naomi responded to her enquiries in monosyllables and the nurse gave her some pain relief.

I expected Naomi to have questions for us, or at least to share something of the trauma she had been through, but she didn't speak again. After a while she closed her eyes, and soon her face relaxed and we could see she was sleeping.

We weren't out of the woods, but I felt a lightness, a lifting of the dread that had shadowed us since first coming to the hospital. She knew us, she could talk. The spectre of brain damage, of finding her incapable, incompetent, receded.

Naomi

'An accident,' she says.

It makes sense. The weakness, the awful pain, the weird dreams.

She tells me how I am hurt, a list of stuff. It's like a present, this explanation, a gift. I had no clue what was going on, where I was, how messed up I was, but now I've got an answer. *An accident. Operations. In hospital.*

'Alex?'

'He's okay. Some broken bones, bruises, he's on the mend,' Mum says. 'Concentrate on getting better,' she adds. How? Maybe I just have to imagine myself all healed, nothing hurting. Back to normal.

I'd like to smile to show her I'm okay, but the simple things are so hard.

Still. I will get better, and go home, and everything will be all right again. I feel weepy for a moment, then sort of calm. Like I'm a little kid and they're both there so I know everything's going to be okay.

An accident?

Mum's talking again, but my head has gone all swimmy and I can't stay with her. She squeezes my hand and it hurts, but not much compared to everything else.

Carmel

'We should eat,' Phil suggested.

We went to the café and bought lunch, salad and quiche for me, chilli and baked potato for him. I found it hard to swallow even though I was hungry, my stomach still tense.

The canteen was busy with people, most of them older than us, many with sticks or wheelchairs. Ailing but still active, still out in the world. Unlike my mum, whose life existed in the confines of her nursing home and the wilderness of her imagination.

After we'd finished eating, I suggested we get some air. We were waiting for visiting time to start so we could see Alex. We had to walk a bit to escape the smokers dotted around the building's exits. There are no grounds to enjoy in the complex; it's carved out of brownfield sites and has grown and sprawled over the years. We sat on a bench with an unlovely view of the car park. The sunlight twinkled and glimmered on the windscreens and the chrome trims.

I watched a car arrive, drive slowly around the parking bay, find it full and make for the next one along.

'I've been thinking about Petey,' Phil said.

So had I, somewhere in the back of my mind. Petey, our friend who'd been run over and killed. A drunk driver. Though it turned out to be more complicated than that. There were bound to be echoes for us. 'Yes,' I said. 'I know.'

Phil's phone went – Archie, his assistant, with a problem he couldn't answer on his own. 'Tell them we can try and get the parts but it could be costly. They might be better buying a replacement.' Archie said something, then Phil answered. 'Better than she was. She's been awake for a few minutes.' He sounded exhausted. We both were. Living on adrenalin and air.

A bus trundled past, over the speed bumps, pulled into the stop and disgorged its passengers, who streamed up to the main entrance.

I rang Suzanne.

'Mum?'

'She woke up; your dad and I were there. She recognized us, she talked, only a word or two, but it's really good news.'

'Oh good,' she said, but there was a shade of something in her tone that didn't fit.

'What?' Was something wrong with Ollie? Or was the whole thing just too much for Suzanne?

'The police are here.'

'Oh God!'

'I'd better go,' she said.

I told Phil. 'They'll want to talk to all of us, I imagine,' he said, 'and Naomi of course.'

'Not yet,' I said. 'She's not fit.'

'No,' he agreed. 'I'm sure the staff won't allow it until she is.'

I nodded, barely reassured.

The sky was unbroken blue, the sun warm again, but I shivered, cold to my bones.

Alex was in a four-bed room, asleep in a semi-upright position when we reached him. He looked terribly pale, his skin blue-white like skimmed milk. He had a cast on his left arm and one on his right leg. There were bruises like plums on his forehead and his jaw, and cuts peppered his face and hands.

'Alex?'

He opened his eyes a little bit and there was a bleary, drugged look to them. He was probably on strong painkillers.

'Hi, you feel up to visitors?' I said.

He swallowed, nodded. 'You thirsty?' I offered him some water. He nodded again and I passed him the cup. He sipped, coughed, sipped some more.

'How's Naomi?' His voice was hoarse when he spoke.

'She's hanging in there.' I discerned the tremor in Phil's voice, and his careful choice of words. I understood we should be gentle with the boy, gentle with the truth. But I needed to hear his account.

'She's very groggy. No one can tell us exactly what happened,' I said.

He stilled. I saw him press his lips together, make a strange movement, balking as if he would retch.

'We're so sorry, Alex,' Phil said.

'Yeah,' he said huskily.

'If you're not up to talking . . .' Phil said.

I will rip your head off, I thought in my desperation.

Alex dismissed Phil's offer with a shake of his head.

'You thought Naomi was safe to drive?' I said.

He frowned. 'What?'

'Suzanne said she'd been drinking.'

'No!' He shook his head again, frowning. 'Early on maybe, but she'd offered to drive. I was celebrating.' He almost lost it then, the muscles around his jaw spasming with the emotion.

'Celebrating the job,' Phil said.

'She was fine with it, the driving.'

So they'd discussed it at the party. 'She wasn't drunk?' I said.

'No.' He looked from me to Phil and back. 'I'd never have let her . . . She wouldn't do that, she wouldn't.' *Oh, thank God.* He sounded absolutely certain, and it reflected what I'd thought when Suzanne first said Naomi had been drinking. The pressure in my chest eased as though someone had taken their hand away. I knew this didn't change everything – it was still a tragedy – but at least if Naomi had been sober, then she was less to blame.

'So – the accident?' I prompted him.

'We were on Mottram Lane,' he said.

I nodded, my fingers laced together tightly. 'Where it bends round?'

'Yes,' said Alex. 'Naomi, she took the bend too quickly . . .' He stopped, his Adam's apple moving in his throat. 'This . . . there was a girl on a bike.' He closed his eyes.

'Was she crossing the road?' I said.

He opened his eyes, his brow creased as if to focus. 'No,' he said.

My heart sank.

'No, she was at the side, my side.'

'Waiting to cross?' I couldn't let it go, so keen was I to comprehend, to find mitigating circumstances.

There was a kerfuffle in the room as visitors arrived and called out to the patient in the bed in the corner.

'Riding along,' said Alex.

'At the side of the road?' Phil said.

'Yes. Going the same way as us. Naomi had gone too far over on the bend; she must have tried to compensate. We swung to the left. I don't know whether she saw . . . We hit the bike,' he said dully, 'then . . .' He took a breath in, shaky.

Phil put his hand on mine. I unclenched my fingers, held his hand.

'. . . she was thrown into the air.'

He was so young, I thought, as I watched him sitting in that bed, young and vulnerable, wounded.

'Naomi braked really hard and we spun round. The road was dry, but . . .' He shook his head.

'I brought you some decent food,' one of the visitors was saying in ringing tones so we could all hear. 'Not the rubbish they give you in this place.'

I wanted to slap her. Couldn't she tell from our tense little tableau that there were hard things being discussed? That we had no need of entertainment?

'We hit the gatepost – there's a school there – and the airbags went off and we flipped right over.' His mouth trembled and I feared that he'd cry. I wanted to tell him it was okay, that there was no need to pretend a stoicism he didn't have, but at the same time I wanted him to keep talking.

'We went right across the road on the roof, towards the river. The railings stopped us, they ripped through the back. I was shouting, I remember shouting, but Naomi, she was . . .' He blinked, put his good hand to his forehead, a fist next to the swelling. 'She was . . . she didn't answer, she couldn't. I undid the seat belts, got my door open and went round and tried to get hers open. There was this really, really strong smell of petrol.'

Phil squeezed my hand. I put my other hand on his arm, needing more contact, more connection.

'I got her out, pulled her away from the car. She, erm . . .' Now his eyes glistened and he opened his mouth, a silent cry. After a few moments he spoke again. 'She wasn't doing anything, not breathing. Her eyes . . . I thought she was dead.' He dipped his head and sniffed. 'There was no heartbeat. Her face was bleeding. The bike was on the railings like it had fallen from the sky and the little girl, she . . .' He covered his eyes. I looked at Phil, tears welling in my throat. 'The petrol tank, it blew. And I rang the ambulance.'

There it was. The facts.

Unbearable.

'You saved her,' I told him, reaching out to touch his arm. 'You got her out.'

'Alex,' said Phil, 'you've no idea how much that means to us.'

'I thought she was dead,' he said again, and he began to cry, silently, his shoulders shaking, tears spilling down his pale cheeks.

I was delighted when Naomi met Alex. The boyfriend before had been very full of himself from what I'd heard, and unreliable. He'd let her down on several occasions. She'd get all excited about some arrangement, a concert or whatever, and at the last minute he'd rearrange or bring extra friends or be horribly late. If she complained, he accused her of being a whiner. He made her unhappy.

I tried telling her to talk to him calmly about it in between any actual crises, but she dismissed me. 'He won't listen, he hates that sort of thing.' *Being told his behaviour is unacceptable?* 'He just doesn't think.' *Doesn't care, more like.*

You can't tell them how to live their lives, much as I sometimes yearn to.

Alex was a ray of hope. He's exactly a year older than Naomi; they share the same birthday. 'How cool is that!' Naomi crowed when she told us. His parents are divorced and his dad, who's American, lives in the States. Alex is quiet, quieter than Phil, say, or Jonty, but not shy. He's clever, too, intelligent. I guess he'd have to be to study law.

He's a bit geeky, up with all the social networking stuff, Facebook and Twitter and so on, but perhaps that's my age showing. Nowadays that's normal, isn't it, not geeky?

Alex has travelled a lot more than any of us. His mother's an air hostess and they get reductions on flights. I was green with envy at that. It was something we talked about a lot, Alex and I, with me picking up tips for my world tour with Phil. Alex raved about Vietnam and Japan. Told us we must look up his dad if we ever got to San Francisco.

Neither Suzanne nor Naomi took a gap year to see the world, which was all the rage at the time. Suzanne was too intent on getting a degree and finding a job; she had her next ten years mapped out, and bumming round the planet wasn't on the itinerary. Naomi never really got the chance. She had to repeat the first year of sixth form when everything went pear-shaped, and just getting her back on track was the priority.

She was skint, anyway. The way things stood, if she had found a way to travel, I'd have been really worried that she wouldn't cope with the pressures and temptations. Or that she'd end up in danger, getting mugged or raped, or suffer some terrible accident and we'd have to fly out and bring her home. My faith in her was at a low point then.

But by the time she and Alex got together, some four years later, she was back to her old self. Even stronger. Still scatty at times, still prone to impulses (or from another viewpoint, open to fresh experiences and opportunities). But not reckless, destructive. She'd grown up. At least we all thought that. *I* thought that. I trusted her again, I thought she'd come through.

Was I wrong? Not according to Alex. He had faith in her too.

Back in 1981, my parents weren't best pleased to learn I was shacked up in Rusholme with a boy they'd never heard of. They weren't particularly religious, but even so, the swinging sixties hadn't really percolated through to the suburbs of Huddersfield.

'I only hope you know what you're doing,' my mum said when I went home for the weekend and broke the news over Friday night's fish supper.

'What's he do then, this Phil?' asked my dad. He looked terribly serious and I had a moment's anxiety that telling them had been the wrong thing to do.

'He has a shop, a record shop, and he plays in a band.'

Dad gave a weary sigh.

'We can't all be accountants,' I sniped. I had expected him to be more impressed that Phil had his own business.

'What's his turnover?' he said.

'I don't know.'

'So you're living with him and you don't know—'

'Bruce,' Mum chipped in.

'We've got separate bank accounts,' I said. 'He doesn't know what I earn either.'

'Rum do,' my dad muttered.

My mum was lively and outgoing; she liked nothing more than getting together with a group of friends. Didn't matter what for, it was the company she relished, the chatter and friendship. She worked at C&A, the department store in town, and had firm friends there. She liked work, liked going there. Hated being idle. They were always organizing social events, nights out at the Talk of the Town in Batley, cheese and wine parties, trips to the cinema or the Alhambra in Bradford for a play, even the seaside, when they'd book a coach and bring the kids to Scarborough or Filey or Bridlington.

My dad had gone along with it – enjoyed it too. There was more to him than just being an accountant. He had been a dancer, amateur ballroom, which was where he met my mum. And he'd played piano too, as a teenager, in a little jazz combo. We had a piano at home, and occasionally he'd sit down and spin out a tune. Back then, I suppose most people did play an instrument, made their own entertainment.

I'd got my first job by the time I moved in with Phil, in a residential children's home in Trafford. I worked funny shifts, doing some sleepovers, then having several days off, but it worked fine for Phil and me. In my free time I could go and see his band play, or we'd go and watch other people. Sometimes I helped out in the shop if it was busy. Saturdays were crazy: kids with their spending money eager to choose a record, people whose dole cheques went on music, the lucky ones in work with cash to flash. Phil had a Saturday girl, Amanda, who was into disco and kept up a running argument with him about how it was a superior musical form to punk rock.

The other members of the Blaggards used the flat like a second home, especially Petey, the drummer, who had troubles at home. He was from a big, brawling Irish family who seemed to get evicted every other week. Petey would turn up and stay with us for a couple of nights every so often. He never spoke to me directly about what happened, though Phil told me his father used to hit him.

Nights when I needed to go to bed because I was starting work early next morning, I'd have to turf Phil and Petey and Ged out into the kitchen so I could get to sleep. Later I'd hear Phil coming in, and sometimes Petey if he was crashing on the sofa. The pair of them stumbling about in the dark, whispering loudly or getting the giggles. 'Be quiet!' I'd hiss, but I couldn't be mad for long and I always fell back to sleep without any trouble.

Stealing out quietly with my clothes in the morning to get dressed in the bathroom. Eating Weetabix with hot milk. Painting my eyes with rings of black and peacock blue. There was no dress code in that first job. My outlandish style was a useful talking point with some of the older kids. And I ignored the taunts and abuse I got from complete strangers. What else could I do?

The job was two bus rides away, but I'd got a Walkman for my graduation present and Phil made me mixed tapes, so I listened to those or read to pass the journey.

My dad was wary when he first met Phil that autumn at the start of the eighties, though Mum took to him straight away. Because he was a talker too, not shy or tongue-tied like some young men are.

My dad and Phil never really found much in common. The only exception was space travel. Anything about the space shuttle missions to the moon or exploring the stars and they went at it hammer and tongs. But if nothing much was happening in space there'd be chat about how the business was going, the latest changes to the rates or VAT and problems with distribution, and then things would peter out.

With my mum it was different. Phil and she would natter on about everything and nothing, which made it all the harder when she began to lose her faculties, when having a conversation became difficult and then impossible.

CHAPTER SEVEN

Carmel

We went round to Suzanne's later that afternoon. We drove along Mottram Lane. The road was clear, but the mobile incident van remained, and the blackened trees and charred verge, the dark melted stains on the road were all there. The railings at the school were a gaudy riot of cellophane-wrapped flowers and soft toys.

That poor child. And her parents. Mixed with my sorrow I felt the sting of shame. My head was full of the accident, the moments Alex had recounted.

Jonty's car was gone, and when Suzanne let us in I asked her where he was.

'Belfast,' she said. 'They start filming tomorrow.'

I'd forgotten. 'If you want us to stay, with Ollie and everything . . . You'll need help. Or come to us?'

'I'm fine,' she said briskly. 'Meals in the freezer and I've a laundry service booked.' She looked amazing, given how tired she must be. Her blonde hair gleamed; it looked as though she'd got highlights, but it was natural.

'Moral support, then.'

How had she turned out so strong, so resolutely independent? As a new parent of a three-week-old baby I'd felt completely at sea, even with the help of Phil and both our mothers on standby. The simplest task took hours; I was achy and leaky and weepy as well as experiencing bursts of profound happiness. Everything had felt so precious, so challenging.

'Stop fussing,' she said. 'Tea?'

We accepted, and Phil went and lifted the kettle.

'Let me, Dad,' she said. 'You sit down.'

The house was quiet, the patio doors open and the sun streaming in.

'Is Ollie asleep?' I'd hoped to have another cuddle, to soothe myself with the simple innocence of holding a newborn. She told us he'd just gone down.

'What did the police say?' I asked her.

'They wanted to know everything about Naomi and Alex. When they arrived, when they left, what they said, what they did. Who they spoke to. They want to talk to Jonty, too. I'm to give a statement. I might be called as a witness.'

Oh no!

'Why was she going so fast?' I said suddenly. *One moment's thoughtlessness and the railings plastered with toys.*

'Because she was drunk.'

'She wasn't!'

Suzanne glared at me.

'We've spoken to Alex. She was the designated driver. She had some champagne, yes, but she was fine by the time they left.'

'She wasn't,' Suzanne said, shaking her head. 'She might have promised to drive, but that didn't stop her drinking. She's a selfish idiot.'

'Suzanne!'

'It's true, Mum. The only person she cares about is herself.'

'No,' I protested. I turned to Phil, seeking his support.

'What about the fire?' Suzanne pressed on. 'What about the time the police brought her home. And what happened to Georgia?'

THE FIRE. I thought of it in capitals still: a headline

70

moment in our lives. 'Suzanne, that was seven, eight years ago.'

'She hasn't changed.'

'She has. She was impulsive then, she didn't always think.'

'Exactly,' Suzanne said.

'She needs us more than ever. We have to support her, we nearly lost . . .' I was going to cry.

'Mum.' Suzanne came and sat beside me, her hand on my shoulder. 'Of course we have to help her, I know that. We all love her, but that's not the same as condoning what she's done.'

'I'm not condoning it! I can't believe she did what you are accusing her of.' I put my head in my hands. Fought back the tears. 'Accidents happen . . .' I tried to speak, but Suzanne talked over me.

'Yes, but if she was drink-driving, that changes everything. It wasn't *just* an accident.'

'But we've only your word for that, and Alex says differently. And I believe him.'

In the strained silence that followed, I looked outside to the garden, where the bamboo and the grasses were still and the only movements were the insects busy flying hither and thither and seeds drifting through the air. And tried to still my thoughts.

THE FIRE, just like this was THE ACCIDENT.

We had left strict instructions before going away that the girls were not to have a party. Later Naomi claimed it wasn't a party, just a few friends who'd come round.

They had reached an age, at eighteen and sixteen, when they didn't want to holiday with us and so we hadn't been away for over a year. I was exhausted by all the work involved in moving my mother into a nursing home and sorting her house out, and Phil had talked me into a week staying in a cottage in the west of Ireland. I'd have loved some sunshine but we didn't dare venture any further afield in case Mum took a turn for the worse. She had had a small stroke a couple of months earlier and there was a chance she'd have another.

There was a music festival on in a town near to where we were staying, and Phil was looking forward to that and to some nights jamming in the local pub. We were taking cheap flights to Cork, and if he'd brought his guitar he'd have had to pay through the nose, so he made do with his harmonica instead.

Suzanne was in charge and we knew she would take the responsibility seriously. But she was going away herself on the Friday night; she had an interview for a university course at Bournemouth that afternoon and was staying over in a B&B near the station. When we realized this, I panicked and talked to Phil about changing our dates. But Naomi came up with a solution: she would stay at Georgia's that night. Perfect.

Except she was lying to us. Maybe not from the outset, but somewhere along the line the plan shifted to Georgia and a dozen other friends coming to our house. Unsupervised.

There wasn't a good signal for mobile phones in the area we were visiting, but we were able to ring home each evening from the landline at the pub. The cottage was tiny and cosy; we used peat on the open fire and banged our heads on the sloping ceiling above the stairs each time we went down without thinking about it. Saturday we walked along the rocky shoreline, spotting seals off the rocks and trying to identify birds, breathing in the ripe smell of the great hanks of seaweed that clotted the sands. We had lunch at a little café in the bay and bought an outrageously expensive bottle of wine to share with our evening meal of freshly caught mackerel.

We were relaxed and windswept and glowing with contentment by the time we went out to the pub. It was a five-minute walk from the cottage, no street lights and the stars glittering cold and fierce in the dark blue sky. The air smelling of brine and burning peat.

We could hear the musicians tuning up in the main room as we arrived. We tucked ourselves into the phone booth by the door and closed its wooden folding door. Suzanne answered the phone and began to cry. I went cold all over. 'What is it? What's the matter?' Images of my mum dead, or a burglary at the house. 'Suzanne?'

'Oh Mum,' she cried, 'the house, there's been a fire.'

Oh God. 'Are you all right? And Naomi?'

'Fine.'

What on earth had happened? An electrical fault? We'd never bothered rewiring, we just loaded the sockets with extension cables and adaptors so we could plug everything in. Was it that? Or had one of the girls accidentally set a tea towel alight or let a pan boil dry? 'Is anyone hurt?'

'Georgia's in hospital.'

'In hospital?' I said. Phil was pressing his ear to the other side of the receiver so he could hear too. 'From the fire? But they were at Georgia's.'

'No, they were here. I got back this afternoon. It's such a mess.'

'How is Georgia? Was she burnt?'

'No. She's okay, I think, but Naomi won't tell me any details.'

'Put her on.'

'She's not here, she's at the hospital.'

'Where was the fire?'

'The lounge mainly, and your bedroom. The fire brigade came.'

My stomach turned over. 'Look, we'll be home by

73

lunchtime.' We had an early-morning flight back the next day. 'Are you okay staying there? Do you want to go to one of your friends?'

'I'll stay. Mr Harrison got the windows boarded up.' I felt sick; that image brought it home. The fact that it had been savage enough to damage the windows. And that our neighbour was involved in helping secure the place.

We talked a bit more, trying to calm Suzanne down rather than finding out any more information. Mr Harrison had told her not to clean up until we'd taken photographs for the insurance claim. An eminently sensible suggestion, but I knew how impotent she'd feel. I did try again to persuade her to sleep elsewhere, or at least get someone round. 'Naomi will be back,' she said.

'Tell her to stay there,' I said. 'She's got some explaining to do.' Even if the fire was an electrical fault, she should not have been there.

'I'll kill her,' I said to Phil, as we sat with our pints of Guinness going over what we'd just heard. 'And Georgia, I can't work out if she's been hurt in the fire or what. It's more likely to be smoke inhalation, isn't it?'

'We could ring Georgia's parents,' said Phil.

'Except I don't have their number.'

All the benefits of the holiday were wiped out in one fell swoop. The warm glow replaced by cold tension.

I've managed the aftermath of house fires a number of times at work. Dealing with shocked and displaced families, or even worse, the bereaved. Firemen with tears in their eyes carrying small corpses. One time it was deliberate. Arson. Three generations killed while they slept. The grandfather coming back from his night shift to Armageddon. Me there getting him a place to sleep, clean clothes and toiletries, money for food and a visit from the doctor. Sitting with him while the police spoke to him. His daughter's ex-boyfriend was convicted of the offence. She had ended the relationship and begun seeing another man. Seven people died that night, four of them children.

Naomi wasn't there when the taxi dropped us back from the airport. I was glad, actually. I might have lost it, in the first full shock of seeing the damage; said things that couldn't be undone.

It was bad enough from the outside: the ugly boards over the big lounge windows, and our bedroom above. Black smears on the walls, the front garden full of shards of glass.

Oh God! Our house. I'd been pregnant when we moved in. I'd loved the flat above the shop, with its bohemian flavour, but wasn't sure about having a baby there. We'd no central heating, washing machine or even a shower, just a stained old bathtub. There was nowhere outside to put a pram or sit out.

We scoured estate agents' windows and local newspaper pages to get an idea of prices. The biggest problem was the deposit. If we bought somewhere at the cheapest end of the market, with my salary and Phil's average income, we could just about afford the monthly payments. But we had no savings.

In the event, Phil's dad offered to help as soon as he heard we were considering buying.

The house had been empty and on the market for over a year. It smelt musty and damp from where the flat roof let in water. The decor was revolting: Anaglypta on the walls, and polystyrene tiles, swirly brown carpets and fussy ceiling lights. I relinquished my dreams of somewhere with a hundred years of history and high ceilings and attic rooms and bay windows. We saw that it had the potential to be a family home, though. And it was the only property we'd seen that was in an area we liked, not too rough and not too stultifyingly suburban. It was years before we could afford to replace the carpets or do more than slap paint on the embossed wallpaper, but we made it our own as best we could.

And here it was, blackened, ruined. Suzanne was in the kitchen and ran to us as we went in. She hugged us both and told us Naomi was at the hospital again but would be back soon. The smell was horrible, burnt plastic or burning hair.

'The lounge is the worst,' Suzanne said. She passed Phil a torch. We went up the half-flight of stairs and stepped in. The carpet was spongy underfoot from the water they had sprayed. It was dark with the windows boarded up. The sofa was a charred wreck, the books along the wall blackened. The television had exploded, its screen punched open. Next to it were Phil's records. Unrecognisable. Irreplaceable. The curtains had melted and fused to the carpet.

I couldn't speak. Just shook my head and bit my cheek.

Upstairs, our room was mainly smoke-damaged, apart from the smashed window; flames licking up from outside had destroyed that. Everything was covered with an oily black residue and tiny fragments of soot, like black snow.

We drank cups of tea, then Phil began to make a list of what we needed for an insurance claim, though he wanted to talk to Naomi before he rang the company so he'd got the facts straight. He thought they might have to send an assessor out. It could cost us thousands.

Suzanne had a note of the contact details for the fire officer responsible for investigating the fire. He'd be coming back to see us.

Phil goes very quiet when he's angry. He doesn't raise his voice or wave his arms about like I do; he doesn't even swear. He goes quiet and it is scary.

That was what Naomi faced when she came back. She looked awful, hair lank, her clothes rumpled, a crop of spots on her face. Crying as she came in.

I went to hug her, relieved to see her there, aching for her as well as angry. She smelled of smoke and sweat.

'Oh Mum,' she sobbed. I got her to sit down. Offered her tea, but she shook her head.

'How's Georgia?'

'Okay.' She gave a little nod.

Phil said two words: 'What happened?'

'People came over and I was in the bathroom. Then there was this massive bang and the smoke alarms went off. Everyone just got out and someone rang the fire brigade. And I had to get Georgia.'

'Where was Georgia?' I said.

'In my room.'

'Was she hurt?' I said.

Naomi hesitated, licked her lips.

'Naomi,' said Phil. His face was set and his eyes hard.

'She's in hospital.' She swallowed.

I didn't understand. 'What's she in hospital for?'

'Alcohol poisoning.'

Phil groaned.

'And she's okay?'

'They said she can go home later.'

'How did it start?' Phil asked.

'I don't know.'

'You must have some idea,' he said steadily.

'We had candles in the lounge. I think maybe that . . .'

I could see it. Them all pissed and rowdy, easy enough to kick over a candle; if it touched the curtains or one of the cushions . . . 'You shouldn't even have been here,' I said, 'and you know we've told you before, no parties.'

'It wasn't a party, just . . .' she protested, then fell silent. Realizing perhaps that splitting hairs would get

77

her nowhere. 'I'm sorry,' she said, wiping her nose with the back of her hand. 'I'm really sorry.'

Phil closed his eyes.

'I'm so cross with you,' I said, shaking. 'You've ruined—'

'I'll help pay.'

'How exactly? Don't be stupid. But once we're allowed to clear up, you can bloody well muck in.'

'I will,' she said in a small voice.

'Someone could have died, Naomi,' Phil said. '*You* could have died.'

It was horrible. The whole situation was horrible. I'd thought the shock of what had happened might make her buck her ideas up, but Naomi's rebellion had a way to run yet.

'I suppose it's the same old story,' I said to Phil as we drove back from Suzanne's. 'Suzanne's doing everything by the book, being Superwoman, and then Naomi's in trouble and it's all eyes on her. Whatever happens, we must make time to see her and Ollie. She seems so lonely sometimes. She hasn't really got any close friends. Perhaps you could do something with them on Sundays when I'm at work, take them out or something? While Jonty's away. I think you're more neutral in her eyes. She's cross that I won't just take her word about Naomi drinking.'

'Sure,' he said.

Suzanne appeared to have it all – beautiful home, successful career, loving husband, now a baby – but we weren't the only ones to find her prickly. Her judgemental attitude, her rigorous standards alienated people and left her isolated. Despite the brave front she was putting on about having Ollie, I couldn't believe she wasn't finding it a challenge at some level. I'd do all I could to make time for her and be available to help out, but I'd do it as subtly as I could, because I knew she wouldn't want to admit to needing anyone's help.

We drove on home as the light softened and the evening star rose in the west. My favourite time of year, but now everything beautiful was tinged with sadness. Our world had changed.

CHAPTER EIGHT

Carmel

Naomi stayed awake longer the next time we visited. Her voice still had that awful rasp and she didn't say much. But she did ask us about the accident. I felt a shrivelling sensation, but I knew I had to tell her. 'It was after the barbecue,' I said.

She didn't show any glimmer of recognition.

'You and Alex, a car crash.'

A flicker of alarm. 'But . . .' she said, then, 'Alex?'

'He's fine,' Phil said, 'couple of broken bones but—'

'Oh God!' She made a retching movement. I reached to fetch the cardboard bowl from beside the bed in case she was sick, but she didn't repeat the motion.

'A crash,' she said slowly. It was as if she couldn't understand what we were saying.

'On Mottram Lane,' I said, thinking that pinpointing the location might help her.

She gave a little quick breath in and out, then said in a panicky voice, 'I can't remember. I don't remember,' louder, frightened.

'Don't worry,' I said. 'You banged your head, banged everything. It might take a bit of time.'

'You remember the barbecue?' Phil said.

Naomi's eyes flicked from side to side. A trapped animal.

'At Suzanne's,' he said.

She shook her head. 'Why can't I remember?'

I took her hand. 'You've had concussion.' I didn't

80

know how much to tell her: *you died at the scene, they revived you there*. 'It's amnesia because of the trauma.' I tried to sound calm.

'But it'll get better?' she said. 'It'll come back?'

'Probably,' I said. 'We'll ask.' I nodded towards the nurses' station. I wondered how much time she had lost: days, weeks, years? She knew us, knew Alex, so the amnesia couldn't be that extensive.

She began to whimper again in pain; the dose of medicine they gave her acted quickly, and she soon became drowsy then slept.

The staff were brilliant but refused to give any prognosis regarding memory loss. Patients varied widely, the nurse said. The majority regained memory; for some it was gradual and could take weeks, while others recalled everything in one flash of illumination. A minority never recovered from the amnesia precipitated by the trauma. There were theories that it was the brain's way of protecting them; the memories could be too harrowing to countenance. I didn't say anything to Phil, but I knew Naomi's memory might never return. A woman we were called out to, who'd survived a stabbing by her husband, was similarly unable to recall the attack itself or the immediate aftermath. The body is wise sometimes. After all, how grotesque would it be to have total recall of something like that haunting you day in and day out?

We argued about when to tell Naomi the full truth about the accident: that a little girl had died. 'If she can't remember, then maybe her brain's doing that on purpose, waiting until she's built up some resilience,' I said.

'Or maybe this is as good as it gets,' Phil said.

'She hasn't asked for any details,' I said. 'She's not stayed awake long enough, she's not ready yet.'

'But the longer we leave it, the bigger a shock it'll be. We've always been honest with the kids, Carmel.'

'I know, but she died, Phil, she . . . It's too soon. Look, let's ask the consultant, ask to see him and get his advice. If he thinks the timing's immaterial then we'll tell her everything.'

'Okay,' he agreed.

'I told her it'll be all right,' I said, feeling my eyes prickle, 'but it won't be, will it?' Even if she remembered everything, even if she healed completely, there was a little girl dead and the emotional burden that would lay on Naomi for the rest of her days.

He held me and comforted me. 'She's alive,' he said finally, sounding gruff.

'For now that's all that counts. Yeah?'

The consultant, Mr Hakim, in effect told us to make up our own minds. He had no guidance as to what would be medically preferable. He'd given the go-ahead for her to eat and drink again, and she would soon be moved to a general surgical ward and assessed by physio and rehab, who would help plan her discharge. If all went well we'd be looking at weeks not months.

I was still reluctant to bite the bullet. Hoping that tomorrow or the next day it would all come flooding back to her and then we would do our best to help her to come to terms with what had happened. I just wanted her to be more robust, physically stronger to bear the impact of it.

Suzanne agreed with her father, 'The sooner Naomi knows the truth, the better.' I wouldn't have expected her to say otherwise. Suzanne never puts anything off. There's a bravery in that perhaps, a willingness to act immediately, to put a decision into practice as soon as it is born, but in this case I also felt there was a twinge of self-righteousness, a desire to punish Naomi for what she had done. Then I felt dirty for apportioning such motives to Suzanne, for seeing perverse intent when possibly she simply thought nothing could be gained by prevaricating. In my efforts to protect Naomi, I was thinking badly of her sister. As though they were either side of a see-saw and the only way one could rise was at the expense of the other.

'A compromise,' I suggested to Phil, after we'd asked Suzanne to honour our wishes and not give Naomi any details before we did.

I was putting things in a bag for her: nightdress and dressing gown, knickers, toothbrush and paste, socks and shampoo and conditioner. She hadn't had a shower yet, but when she did, I thought she'd like some of her own things.

'Once she's out of intensive care, we'll tell her then.'

'And if she asks before?' he said.

'Yes.' I put her hairbrush in and zipped up the bag. The room was messy, left just as it had been when Alex and Naomi had set off for the barbecue. Outfits on the bed that she must have been trying on, plates and cups on the chest of drawers. Alex's jeans on the chair and discarded socks and trainers nearby.

My phone interrupted us. It was Evie. She was pleased to hear Naomi was awake and out of danger, sent her love, checked if there was anything she could help with, then spoke to me about work. 'The thing you wanted me to check. It's the Cottesloe hearing, Wednesday the sixth.'

'Oh shit! I can't miss that.'

'You'll be in bits.'

'What time is it?'

'Eleven.'

'I'll do it. It'll be a right mess if someone else has to cover. I can't not go.'

Ivy Cottesloe had been a pensioner, recovering from a stroke, supposedly looked after by her daughter and son-in-law, who had submitted her to terrible neglect and inhumane treatment. She was tied to her bed (the couple claimed this was to prevent her falling out) and starved. The couple withdrew her pension and savings and kept GPs, the pharmacist, neighbours and old friends at bay with a mishmash of lies and evasions: *Ivy's in hospital again; she's at her sister's; she's too ill to come to the phone but I'll tell her you called.*

Her sister did eventually visit in person, travelling from Jersey, and when she was turned away it only served to confirm her suspicions that something was amiss. She spoke to the local police, who made a referral to the social work out-of-hours team. It was a Saturday afternoon. When my colleague and I arrived at the house, Ivy's daughter told us she had moved. But she grew increasingly aggressive as we asked for more information, and it was obvious she was hiding something. When it became clear that we were not leaving until we had seen round the house – and that we were more than happy to involve the police if she prevented us – she began to backtrack: Ivy was demented, she had been refusing to eat, she wouldn't use the commode, she was violent, we had no idea what it was like.

We found Ivy in the back bedroom. The stench was formidable. The woman was covered in open sores and lying in her own faeces, severely dehydrated and malnourished. Her sight and hearing had gone. Vomit rose up my gullet, scalding my throat and the back of my nose. I forced myself to swallow it. Rang the ambulance and the police.

Ivy died an hour after reaching hospital. A court case found the couple guilty of manslaughter. The hearing was intended to assess what lessons if any might be learned from the event. Should there have been professionals asking questions when Ivy disappeared so comprehensively? The sister's enquiries had not been taken seriously for several months. And it appeared that there had been a breakdown of communication between the hospital and the community nursing service on Ivy's discharge after her stroke. Why had that happened? And how could it be avoided in future?

You never forget something like that and there was no way I could tolerate the thought of missing the hearing and not contributing what I could.

Naomi

They are moving me to a different ward. I'm no longer hooked up to all the tubes and stuff. I've not been out of bed yet, though; even turning over is agony still, because of my collarbone and ribs, and I've got a cough. I try so hard not to cough. Now I can eat and drink, they let me have tablets for the pain instead of a drip, but they ration them out.

I smell awful. This sickly, sweaty smell. And my teeth are literally furry. How can the nurses bear it? If only I could have a shower. They took one of the other women yesterday. She couldn't walk but they had her in a wheelchair and she was smiling when she came back. Said, 'That's done me the world of good.'

Along the corridor the light is blinding and we hit patches of cold fresh air. The porter wheels the bed along. I wonder where Alex's ward is. Mum and Dad said he was here still. I'm so glad he's all right. I want to see him. We're soulmates. We have the same birthday, like twins. We look a bit alike too, the same height, both with dark hair, but his eyes are green, this amazing electric green. I could almost see Alex as my brother, not in a pervy incest-type way or anything, but we squabble sometimes like I did with Suzanne growing up, though not so viciously. We play-fight and then one of us catches this look, like a glint in the other's eye, and then we're in stitches. I've never laughed as much as I do with Alex. We're friends as well as a couple. We like the same stuff.

He likes to argue. It's his legal side. He's really quick to spot things he sees as stupid or contradictions. Like how if it's wrong to kill someone, then capital punishment is wrong too.

And the job! At last one of us with a job. A real job. It was getting pretty bleak there for a while. Sending out a million applications and not getting any replies. Slobbing off to the Jobcentre to be patronized by some idiot who keeps suggesting you update your CV or widen your options. What options? In the last six months I have gone for jobs at call centres, a packaging warehouse and a care home. Some options.

Mum's face fell at the care job. 'Oh, Naomi, it's awful terms and conditions. They treat most of the staff like dirt.'

I told her not to worry. I wouldn't get it. I was right. But then I got the classroom assistant interview. I've missed that, but at least I did get one. It's not totally impossible.

Alex hates the whole circus, too. He did economics at A level as well as politics and law and Spanish. And the economics means he's always arguing with the Jobcentre people about unemployment and the deficit and that.

'They want to blame us,' he said to me, 'pretending that if we only had a bit more about us, nicer suit, brighter smile, we'd find work. Totally ignoring the numbers. Over a million out of work under twenty-four. Where's the jobs?'

Him getting a job is our salvation. Even if I don't find anything for a while, we'll still be able to get a place of our own. He always wanted to do law, from high school, he says. He got a first at uni – really keen. He was chair of the law society and the debating society. I still don't know what I want to do. It's not like I've got a particular thing that I'm brilliant at. Or a passion like Dad and his music. They all had a career in mind: Mum, Suze, Jonty. Me – zilch. That's why I did tourism and leisure. It wasn't too specific. I was so sick of it by the end, but by then I'd met Alex and didn't want to mess up and leave, and so I scraped by with a pass, a third class in my degree.

He went round firms in Newcastle trying to get an internship or a training place, unpaid if necessary. He was determined to get something, and when he didn't receive any offers it drove him mad. I'd do anything just to pay the bills, but for Alex he also wanted it to be a stepping stone to achieve his real ambition, to be a lawyer. Things got a bit scary with money; there was no way we could manage on jobseeker's and housing benefit. Didn't even cover our bills. Alex had a credit card and he maxed it out. His mum ended up clearing it. Lucky sod. We were both pretty stressed out and we had a few rows, mainly about money.

When the nurses have gone, after I've had my checks and used the bedpan and got over all that and the throbbing pain has settled a little, I close my eyes and think. How hard can it be to remember? If I just focus properly . . . I tiptoe back along the tunnels of my memories, like exploring underground. Here is the moment I woke up in hospital. I was in the ICU. But behind that, before that, it's a hole, like a bomb crater with ragged edges. I skirt around it. It's a dangerous place; the ground is crumbling at the rim and I might fall in. It is a bullet hole in my brain, the flesh torn, the matter missing, a smudge of blood. Edging round the gap, I try from different angles, but my teeth are on edge and there's a jittery feeling in my stomach. Any moment something could rear up and bite me, devour me. Am I too scared to remember the crash? Because it was frightening? I can't remember any of it, sights or sounds, what the accident felt like; it's like catching smoke.

And earlier, further down the dark corridor? Outside their house, Alex kissed me – yes. Were we coming or going? And food. Piles of food, lots of colours. So beautiful you'd think it had been airbrushed for a magazine. Was that the same day? It could have been some other time. Suzanne always goes all out for it; the way it looks is as important to her as how it tastes. I see the food and try and touch on something either side of that recollection, but there is only space, empty space, grey and swirling in mist. It's like blind man's buff, fumbling my way further back with my arms out-stretched, fingers stiff, holding my breath. All the other players have gone and left me there, blindfolded, flailing like an idiot. I give up.

I try a rational approach: if we were at the barbecue, then we must have got ready beforehand. This thought produces sweet FA. No glimpse of what I wore or when we left or whether we took a bottle to contribute.

I remember hearing about the job, though! There like solid ground, land ahoy. I remember Alex getting back to ours, his face all bright, and yelling at me with excitement. Punching the air and shaking his head. And me running at him, launching myself at him, wrapping my legs around his thighs and clinging on, kissing. Kissing him. That's it. Kissing him at home and then again at Suzanne's . . . then the ICU. No stepping stones in between. The film stops running and there aren't even any snapshots unless you count the food, and I don't count it, it tells me nothing. Some crappy product placement: here is Suzanne's feast! Cut and pasted on a blank page. So there is nothing until service resumes at the hospital.

I want to see Alex. I want to kiss him. Though the furry teeth need a deep clean first. I want to be better and go home and get on with everything. Looking for a flat or rooms in a shared house. And he'll need to get some clothes: shirts and suits. God, sounding a bit Suze-ish there (she hates being called Suze). She chooses Jonty's clothes, you know. Buys stuff for him.

Alex doesn't understand it when I talk about Suzanne. He thinks she's fine – maybe a bit scary, I got him to admit that much. He reckons I'm exaggerating the way she has to control everything and boss me about. He's never experienced anything like that because he's an only child. He only had his mum to quarrel with and they actually get on really well. She's so proud of him and she worked and brought him up pretty much on her own, though her mother looked after him when Monica was away.

Alex thinks Suzanne's funny, the way she criticizes people, and she can sometimes be very arch, dripping with sarcasm, though it's not such a laugh if you're the target.

It'll be so cool to be on our own again. I hope I get a job; I'll do anything really. I wouldn't want to be stuck at home while he's out in the world doing stuff.

I wonder who crashed into us?

CHAPTER NINE

Carmel

I walked up to the shops and bought some food. It was the first chore I'd done for days and it had that unreal quality to it, like the first hours home after a foreign holiday. Everything's familiar but you notice things with a keener eye, an edge of objectivity. The high street looked neglected, everything from the tatty awnings outside the shops to the litter on the pavement and the carcass of a bicycle, its wheels and saddle missing, chained to a metal pole.

After I'd got some fruit and vegetables and bread, I went into the butcher's for chicken. The butcher was making conversation with the customer ahead of me, talk of the summer weather forecast, complaining how they never got it right.

The door opened and Cynthia Stiller came in. Shit! Her daughter and Naomi had been friends at high school. I wanted to run. To sink from view. I wasn't ready to face people, brave the topic, accept expressions of sympathy or shock or anything else. But she couldn't help but see me, and we always stopped to swap the latest news about the girls.

I took a breath, tore my eyes away from the shopping list and turned to greet her. She looked away, studiously staring at the meat behind the glass, her face flushed pink.

Unnerved, I dropped my list, then bent to pick it up, straightened as the woman in front of me left and I ordered my fillets. While the butcher weighed and bagged them, fetched my change, I could feel Cynthia there: her censure, her refusal to acknowledge my presence like a miasma heavy in the air, making my chest tight and my ears whine.

Walking home, I felt hurt and indignant. She'd blanked me; that was the term the girls used when such situations were part of the currency of teenage feuds and alliances. *She blanked me, Mum.*

What would my mum's generation call it? Sent to Coventry? Would I have done the same if our positions had been reversed? And how did Cynthia know? Naomi's name hadn't been in the newspaper. Who could have told her? *It could have been you*, I cursed her in my mind. *It could happen to anyone.*

Of course neighbourhoods like ours are interconnected; people talk to each other, share the gossip and the news. One of Alex and Naomi's friends or someone Monica knows tells a friend, who tells her brother who mentions it to his wife, who tells the girls at work and soon the whole of south Manchester knows that the twenty-five-year-old driver in the Lily Vasey road death was actually Naomi Baxter.

I told Phil when I got in and he shook his head. 'Maybe she didn't know what to say,' he suggested. 'She was embarrassed.'

'*Sorry* would do,' I said. '*Sorry to hear what happened.*'

'Yeah, but you've done the training, love.' He tried to lighten my mood.

I swore at him in jest and began to cook, slicing garlic and ginger, spring onions, carrots and chicken for a stir fry.

'I'm thinking of going into work tomorrow,' Phil said. 'Archie needs some time off.'

'That'll be fine,' I said. 'I'll go in to visit in the afternoon and you can come with me in the evening.'

The last thing we wanted was for the business to go under on top of all our troubles. It had been a long haul – Phil's life's work really. In the mid nineties Rock Records was teetering on the brink of insolvency. When his dad, Ian, died after a miserable year fighting cancer, Phil inherited his estate. The house sold very quickly, and once the bills were paid there was just under forty thousand pounds left. A small fortune for us.

At the same time the shop next door to Phil's, called Dolly's, which sold wool and haberdashery supplies, ceased trading and the property went up for sale.

Phil was making more money from the musical instruments than from the records and CDs. It made sense to grow that side of the business. If he invested in buying Dolly's, at least he'd have some capital, and if the business didn't thrive, he could sell the property and rethink.

Phil closed Rock Records at the end of August, having spent weeks supervising the alterations and improvements for next door, including a sign: *Baxter's Music.*

I went with him to help with the move and for a last look around. The upstairs was no longer a flat but was used for storage. There were still things I remembered there, including the ancient red sofa, now only fit for a skip. And when we moved boxes away from the corner of the kitchen, I found one of Petey's cartoons stuck to the wall: me and Phil in caricature, arms and legs entwined, seeing stars.

Suddenly I was back in those days, giggling with Petey. He was never still. If he wasn't tapping out percussion rhythm on anything to hand, he was scribbling little cartoons and bits of graffiti. He was left-handed and did that crabby, sloped writing that lefties often have, unless he used print. So most of the time his little phrases or puns or bits of lyrics were in block capitals.

He wrote most of the words for the Blaggards, though they were pretty basic: punk rock songs delivered at breakneck speed with a ravaged vocal style, courtesy of Ged and his forty-a-day fag habit. Petey's cartoons were caricatures, really funny. At the flat we used the walls like blackboards or canvases. It was all part of the creative DIY ethos. Same as I made my own clothes, touring the second-hand shops for fabrics that I liked, chopping up dresses to make tunics and tops, adding zips or fun fur or strips of neon nylon to jazz up old cardigans and trousers.

Petey was such a sweet guy. If I hadn't been so in love with Phil, I'd have made a play for him. He took all those drummer jokes in good humour: *what do you call a drummer with half a brain? Gifted.* Petey had nothing to fear on the intellectual front. The doodles he did were peppered with quotes from poets and politicians, philosophers and novelists. Sometimes we'd play a game: Petey coming up with a quotation and the rest of us trying to guess the source. Is it one of the Brontë sisters? Martin Luther King? Is it Norman Mailer, John Cooper Clarke, Sylvia Plath?

He resembled a dandelion, his hair golden and curly when he let it grow out. I thought it looked better then than when he shaved the sides and spiked the top.

We became close in the youthful, lively way of our age. Because I was besotted with Phil, there wasn't any sexual tension between me and the rest of the band. I'd sprawl on Phil's lap, my feet across Petey as we huddled round the gas fire to watch *The Old Grey Whistle Test* or *Blackadder*, or I'd paint Ged's eyes before a gig.

Petey never talked about his family, I don't suppose any of us did really: families were something to escape from, to distinguish ourselves from; there were far more exciting topics of conversation. But we were always running into some cousin or nephew or sister of Petey's. I think he once said he had more than thirty cousins. They'd always be chatty and friendly and eager to talk and be introduced, and there was no indication at all that anything was less than peachy in the clan. Maybe they didn't know. I'd done enough social work by then to understand how violence and abuse thrive because of the taboo surrounding them. Not something you talked about. Pretend it's not happening and it'll go away. Laugh and joke loudly enough and you won't hear the cries.

I often wonder if Petey was sexually abused as well as beaten. That might account for the fact that he never seemed interested in dating, didn't have a lover for all the time we knew him. Plenty of girls tried, flirting and buying him drinks, asking him to give them a drumstick as a souvenir, or sign their arms. He'd do a little self-portrait, sticks akimbo, whirring above the drum kit, skull and crossbones and all, and scribble his initials.

Back then the extent of child sexual abuse was still unknown. Domestic life was sacrosanct. Rape in marriage didn't exist as a crime. This was before ChildLine started and journalists began writing about sexual abuse in families. At the sharp end, in social work, we were trying to comprehend that the greatest threat to children was not from strangers, as we'd all been led to believe, but from those in the family home who had charge of them.

The Blaggards put out two singles, 'In Your Face' and 'The Park in the Dark', which sold in miserable numbers. No one really expected anything else. Phil kept sending sample tapes in to John Peel, hoping the champion of eclectic new music would play something on the radio, but he never did.

Seeing Petey's cartoon after fifteen years brought tears

to my eyes. Suddenly it felt as if we were destroying a little bit of history.

'It's just a shop,' Phil said.

'But those times . . .' My emotions got the better of me.

'Hey,' he tapped his temple, 'it's all in here. Good times.'

But it wasn't all good. Some of it had been terrible.

'If Baxter's doesn't take off,' I said, 'and you have to sell the place, we'll put some towards travelling. Once the girls have left home.'

'Deal,' he said. 'Where to?'

'Cuba and India and Australia,' I said.

'What about the States?'

'There too, if they'll let us in.'

He laughed. There was something on US visas at the time about links to communists, and we had friends in the party. 'You might have to take your earring out,' I warned him. He still wore a silver sleeper.

But he hadn't had to sell up and cut his losses. Baxter's carries on. No two years are the same, but there are enough people in the city still playing music, learning music, to keep the place afloat. And Phil is still happy there.

Naomi

'I can't remember,' I tell them. 'You said we crashed, but I still can't remember it. What happened?'

Mum looks peculiar, like I've said something offensive, and when I turn to Dad, he's behaving strangely too. *What's the matter?* I don't say it out loud; maybe I've read the signals wrong. But the pause goes on too long and I feel sweat prickle my armpits and round my hairline.

Mum starts speaking very slowly, like I've got brain damage not just memory loss. 'You and Alex were travelling home from the barbecue, at Suzanne's. Do you still not remember the barbecue?'

The table, groaning with food. That's all. 'No,' I say.

'You left about eight o'clock,' she says. I see her lip tremble, like she's going to cry. I wish she'd just get to the point, but my chest hurts too, like something's trying to burst out.

'You turned into Mottram Lane – where the school is.'

I nod. We must have passed that school millions of times, but I've never paid much attention to it. It's on the right, I know that much.

'The road bends round there . . .' She clears her throat, glances at Dad. Shit. He looks like he's going to cry. I peer at my hands, rub at the sheet even though it's not creased or anything. '. . . There was a little girl riding her bike. The car swerved on the bend and . . . you hit her.'

Something gives way inside me, shattering, falling. *Is this for real?* Mum's eyes are wet. 'The car spun round and travelled across the road and hit the gatepost, then it rolled over on to its roof and went back across. The railings by the river stopped you.'

A little girl? We hit a little girl.

'Alex pulled you out. The car went up in flames.' She pauses, as if she expects me to agree with her. All of this is news to me.

'You were . . . they had to revive you at the scene,' Dad says quietly.

'The girl?' I say.

'She didn't survive,' Mum says.

Oh God, no! Please, no! 'Who was she?'

'She was called Lily, Lily Vasey, nine years old. They live in the estate off Mottram Lane. She had two older brothers.'

96

The shock makes me gasp. It's unbelievable. If this has really happened, how could I not know it, remember it in every cell, in every pore?

I'm crying and they are touching me and saying stuff to try and calm me down. My heart is going really fast, making it hard to breathe properly, and there is this dark, oily, sick feeling in the pit of my stomach.

I want her to take it back now. All of it. I want them to go. I want the whole world to go away.

'Was he speeding?' Everyone does it, now and again. Even if they don't all get caught. Neither of us has ever had a ticket.

'Alex wasn't driving,' Dad says in a really quiet voice. 'You were.'

What? Have I heard him wrong? But his face, Mum's face . . .

I can't describe what it's like. A tearing. A guillotine cutting off everything that has been, severing connections to all the good things in my life. Or like one of those traps, nets that scoop up animals in the jungle, hoist them into the trees.

They stay for ages, insist on sitting with me even though I don't want to talk. They say Suzanne will come later, but I don't want her to, I don't want to see anyone.

The awful thing about it is that I have done this terrible, terrible thing and I can't remember the tiniest bit about it. How weird is that? It's like I'm a fraud, a fake, all upset about something even though I've no recollection of it. Who am I crying for? My thoughts are churning round and round, probing what they've told me. Each time I light on the girl on her bike, or the car flipping, or Alex hurt, it scalds me and I shrink inside, but I can't stop doing it. I'm hypnotized by it.

Mum keeps saying it was an accident, as if that makes it all right. But if I hadn't lost control of the car, we

97

wouldn't have crashed, so it's pretty clear whose fault it was.

At long last they go.

I'm so sorry. So so so so sorry. And there is nothing I can do about it.

I wish I was dead. I wish I had died instead. Or that Alex had left me in the car.

It can't be true. How could I forget something that massive? That awful? It dawns on me that everyone knows. The nurses are bound to have heard how I ended up in here. No wonder poker face looked at me like she did, gave me my medicine with a tight little smile, more of a snarl than anything. I don't blame her. I don't blame her at all.

CHAPTER TEN

Carmel

Naomi looked desolate, haunted, her face drawn, a sheen of fear in her eyes. This was something she needed to confront, to wrestle with and absorb. But how much harder it must be when the facts come from other people. When they arrive in a vacuum, robbed of context or sense-memory or reference points. No way to knit it together with your own impressions and sensations. A truth that you learn but do not know.

She cried, not making much noise. I stroked her back, my own face wet, aching for her. Eventually I broke the rhythm. 'Come on, have a drink and blow your nose.'

She did as I said, numbly, her face muddy with misery. There was little more conversation.

Naomi was lost in her thoughts, trying to disentangle what we'd said.

'Suzanne's coming later,' I said eventually.

'I don't want her to.' Naomi's face crumpled. 'I don't want to see her today, Mum.'

'Okay, I'll tell her you're not feeling up to it.'

She cried again as we hugged goodbye. 'I can't believe it, it's unreal.'

'I'm so sorry,' I said. There was only one crumb of comfort I could offer her, a tiny thing to help her feel less terrible. 'It was an accident,' I said, 'an awful accident.'

'But it was my fault,' she said, distraught.

All I could say was, 'We don't know all the ins and outs yet.'

And she wiped her eyes and slowly shook her head in defeat.

As I waited at traffic lights on my way to work one day, two and a half weeks after the accident, a funeral party drove past; it wasn't far to Southern Cemetery. I saw the flowers in the hearse first, spelling out the name LILY, then took in the white coffin. My stomach fell. A long, slow procession of cars followed. When the lights changed, I stalled the car, broke into a sweat, cursing as the driver behind impatiently blared his horn at me.

My heart went out to them, her poor, poor parents. I pictured their devastation. The empty bedroom, the absence of Lily that must feel like the withdrawal of air or the loss of light. Aching arms where she should be, missing her laughter and her foibles and the sight of her entering a room. The loss that would last for ever. The wound in their hearts that would never heal over. A yoke of grief. Not to be overcome but simply to be borne. And I was bitterly ashamed that there was no word or deed I could gift to lighten the burden of sorrow. It was not fair. It was so very cruel.

LITTLE LILY LAID TO REST. The front page of the local free paper. I felt the slap of recognition when I saw the photograph. A picture of her grieving family in their black clothes. The parents were the couple I had noticed with the policeman outside the A&E department on the evening of the accident: he'd had his arm around her; her head was buried in his chest.

The article included a statement from the police: *The investigation into the accident is ongoing and our sympathy is with the family at this difficult time.* The piece concluded with a quote from her father, Simon Vasey:

Lily was the light of our lives, a friendly, cheeky, loving little girl who completed our family. It is beyond devastating to lose her like this, but we hope that one day we will see justice done.

I took a breath. Felt a wellspring of grief for them, sick and sorry.

Friendly, cheeky, loving. That could have been Naomi. Naomi as she was. I wasn't sure she was still that girl. This had changed her. There's often some depression after major surgery, but I didn't think she'd smiled since it happened. Only the occasional wry half-smile, an expression of resignation or deprecation, not humour, certainly not pleasure or joy.

Naomi

It's hard to take it in. The terrible thing I've done. I feel filthy. Disgusted at myself, and still incredulous. The ugly truth is lodged in my head like a dense, dark lump. A clot or a tumour, heavy as lead. I keep repeating it like a chant. *I crashed into a little girl and killed her. I crashed into a little girl and killed her.* It sets off a current of panic that swirls and surges through me. If only I could run away, run from it all, outpace it until I was on safe ground and free of the sin, free of the deed. How can I ever make this right? Why was I so stupid? Why was I driving too fast? Why?

I wish I could freeze everything and turn back time and change something so I'd never got in the car and put my foot on the pedal. Change the past so we'd missed the barbecue. Or even that Alex didn't get the job so we weren't feeling up to going. Or go further back so I'd never met Alex, never been to uni, never got my A levels. I'd give all that up to save the little girl. I know I'm howling for the moon. What can I do? What can I possibly do?

Carmel

'I think we should talk to a solicitor,' I said to Phil.

'What?' He set down his fork.

'Get some advice for Naomi. They're likely to charge her, the police,' I said. 'It'd be better to talk to someone now rather than wait. She could go to prison.' I'd lost my appetite, stared at the slivers of vegetables on my plate, the grains of rice stained by curry sauce. 'I could ask at work,' I said. Plenty of our clients needed legal representation. 'Evie might know someone.'

'What about Hugh's bloke?' he said. 'Don, he does criminal law.' Hugh was the saxophone player in Phil's band. We'd met Don a few times, but like me, he didn't go to their gigs very often any more.

'Try him,' I said, 'and if it's not his sort of thing, I'll call Evie.'

Phil got Don's number from Hugh and managed to get through to him on his first go. I found it hard to sit still as I listened to him sum up the situation, so I ended up pacing round the room, stopping each time Phil spoke to hear what he said.

'Still in hospital . . . Yes, for some time, they say. Next Monday? Yes . . . If they move her to another ward I can drop you a text . . . Thanks, that's great.'

'Well?'

'He wants to see her. He does deal with driving offences and he wants to find out what her instructions are. And he says if the police show up before then she's not to talk to them without him there.'

'Okay.'

Phil started clearing up and I turned on my laptop. There were dozens of emails in my inbox but I hadn't the will to open any. Instead I googled *death and driving*, the page of links loaded and I went to the criminal justice website.

My eyes flew over the definitions, and the table of sentencing guidelines. Death by dangerous driving, twelve months where there are no aggravating circumstances. Seven to fourteen years for the most serious culpability. Further down the page a list of aggravating factors, among them alcohol and excessive speed.

Phil came and looked over my shoulder. I heard him sigh as he saw what I was reading. 'Up to fourteen years,' I said.

He put his arm round my shoulders. 'Worst-case scenario,' he said, 'if she gets convicted. She might get off. We've no idea. Don't think the worst.'

'I know.' I closed the laptop. 'You're right. And if her driving was fine when Monica passed them, then perhaps there was a problem with the car, with the accelerator or the brakes.'

'Go down to the river?' he suggested. 'It's lovely out there.'

There's a short cut behind the school playing fields and then it's a fifteen-minute walk to the Swan, a little riverside pub that has a large beer garden facing the water. The place itself was surprisingly quiet, although there were joggers and dog-walkers and people strolling and cyclists passing in a steady stream.

We stopped for a drink, had two. Hoppy beers brewed on the premises. The midges were out and I felt a nip or two on my neck. Phil never suffered. The surface of the river looked serene, silky, a shining ribbon of brown rippling between the banks. But this whole stretch had been used as a dumping ground for years. Building waste, litter, chemicals and rubbish chucked into it. Even after three decades of sustained clean-up, there would be all sorts lurking down there: old mattresses and paint tins, slabs of concrete, car wheels, shopping trolleys and bread trays.

Phil stroked my arm and I smiled at him. My back was aching from the tension of the last few days and fatigue rinsed through me. The beer was making me feel sleepy. 'I love you,' I told him.

He gripped my hand, kissed my knuckles. I rubbed at my neck; another prick from one of the gnats.

We walked back in the twilight, holding hands all the way. I caught the scent of barbecued meat at one point, plunging me back to that Sunday and the sweet happiness of the party. And on one of the cul-de-sacs near our house, two kids played out on their bikes. Just the sight of them was like a cold shower, extinguishing the tiny glow of peace I'd had in the simple pleasure of the walk and the quiet waterside drinks in Phil's company.

Phil put some music on when we got home, an old blues compilation that seemed to suit our mood, Billie Holiday and Muddy Waters making magic out of misery. I concentrated on writing a list of all the things that needed sorting out while Naomi was in hospital: everything from notifying the Jobcentre that she was incapacitated to checking that her bank account wasn't going to go over her overdraft limit and land her with mounting debts. I'd check her appointments diary, in case there were arrangements to cancel, and work out what to do about her phone contract, given that the phone had been destroyed when the car caught fire.

I assumed Alex would be dealing with the car insurance and so on, as he was the registered owner, though Naomi was a named driver. Their premium was astronomical, as they were young drivers. It made some sort of sick sense now, though, Naomi one of the faces behind the statistics about risks and demographics.

I went up to her room and gathered together Alex's clothes so I could return them. Would he be fit enough to start his new job? If he was, would there be any problem with the job offer given that he had been in the accident? I drew the curtains, thinking about it. They couldn't penalize him for being a passenger, surely. I remembered reading about one case where a passenger had been prosecuted because he had known the driver was over the limit and failed to stop him.

But Alex was adamant that Naomi was sober; he'd never have got into the car if he'd thought she was pissed.

I woke at three in the morning, slathered in sweat, my pyjamas twisted into tourniquets round my legs, my heart pounding. The tatters of the dream fading like smoke. An ancient prison cell, underground, dank, dark, a stone slab. The walls wet with seepage, the smell of earth and decay. Naomi there, her pale fingers clenched round the bars at the front, her face contorted and wild. Screaming 'Let me out, let me out!' On the slab behind her a child, still and waxen, lips and eyelids deepest blue, limbs mottled. A doll child. Head turning, eyes opening, empty sockets, savage black holes staring at me, swallowing me.

Naomi

He's here! Alex. He's here. There are bruises on his face and a cut over his eye and he comes on a crutch, with one arm and one foot in plaster, and sick gathers at the back of my throat.

He says my name, like he still loves me, but all I can say is sorry, sorry, sorry. 'Sorry, I never meant for this to happen.'

'I know that,' he says. 'Don't be daft.'

'The little girl,' I say, because it seems important to be honest and say it out loud.

'I know.' He looks so sad, his mouth turning down at the corners. He manages to sit down, and the crutch crashes to the floor with a clatter and the woman in the far bed makes a huffing noise, complaining.

I wish the curtains were drawn round the bed and we could have some privacy, but I can't do it. I can't even stand up yet, and I can't ask Alex to hop about. He can barely walk.

'You pulled me clear.' My voice breaks on the last word and I rub at my eyes. There's no point in bawling. I need to talk to him, to apologize.

'You remember?' he says. He picks up my hand, traces the line of my thumb. There are flecks and marks on his hand, cuts healing.

'No, none of it really. I'm so glad you're okay . . . well . . .' Okay doesn't quite cover it. He's all bandaged and broken.

'Me too – you,' he says. 'They're discharging me, so I must be doing all right.'

'Thank you,' I say, 'for . . . you know – and I'm so sorry. I'd do anything . . .' I run out of words, my throat too tight, and I can't stop the tears. I reach for the tissues. Then I have a drink. 'Sorry,' I say again.

He nods, his eyes shining. I've never seen him cry and he doesn't now. This is probably as close as it gets. Some people are like that, not just men either. Suzanne doesn't cry, not really, not that big, messy sobbing and letting go and her nose going all red and snotty. Sometimes she'll get like maybe three tears and they sort of squirt out;

more like tears of fury when she's spitting mad, and that's your lot. Mum cries like a tap. But she must be able to turn it off for work. Lots of the situations she deals with are really sad and she'd be no use to anyone if she went to pieces all the time. Dad rarely cries, but when he does, his eyes go pink and he makes a strange noise in his throat.

'I can't remember anything,' I say. 'The last thing I remember was you telling me about the job.' I have a clutch of anxiety then. 'They'll still take you, won't they? Is there a physical or anything?'

'Should be okay,' he says, knitting his fingers through mine, 'though I might need to negotiate a later start date, put it back a couple of weeks.'

At least that was going to be okay, then.

'And you kissed me, I remember that – were we arriving or leaving? We were at the side of their house.'

'Yes,' he says, 'we'd just got there.'

'That's all there is,' I say. I take a breath, feel the stabbing pain in my side. 'Was I going too fast – speeding?' I wait for him to answer. He squeezes my hand.

'Maybe a bit, yeah.'

The guy with the tea trolley pitches up and I feel like asking him to come back later. But we accept a cup each, and once he moves away, it feels safe to talk again. 'I can't have seen her, can I? Did I say anything?'

He shakes his head, frowning. I can tell how hard it is for him to talk about it; it's not just me. 'No, it happened so quickly. One minute we were coming out of the bend and sort of skidding, and then this massive bang. The bike ended up on the railings by the school.'

And the girl? Oh my God. The image of her impaled, like a rag doll. I have to know. 'And her?'

'She landed in the middle of the road. I didn't really

see her after.' He swallows. 'We hit the gatepost and flipped over on to the roof. It was so fast.' He pauses.

'Who called the ambulance?'

'Me. There was no one else around. You weren't breathing,' he says.

It must have been so frightening for him.

I think about it after he has gone. The car on fire, roaring with flames, like a special-effects stunt, the little girl and me on the road. Alex all alone, no one driving up or walking past – like some apocalypse movie.

Carmel

Phil told Naomi we'd found a solicitor to come and talk to her.

'What have the police said?' she asked. 'What'll happen?'

'Nothing yet. We don't know exactly,' Phil said. 'That's why we've asked Don to come and see you. He's an expert, he deals with this sort of thing all the time; he'll have an idea of what to expect and what to do about it.'

She put her hand to her head, her fingers knotted in her hair. The bandage was gone, the bruising round her eyes faded to mustard yellow. The big bruise on the left of her neck by the collarbone sling was more vivid. The graze on her cheek a large rust-coloured scab. 'I keep thinking it can't be true,' she said. 'I'll wake up and it'll all go away. But it won't.'

I struggled for something to say, some comfort to give her. In the end I just agreed with her. 'I know, darling, we just have to get on with it.'

She seemed angry at that, a hard glint in her eyes as she retorted, '*You* didn't do it, *you* don't have to . . .' then broke off, too agitated to articulate.

Phil intervened. 'Have you remembered anything else?'

She gave a shake of her head. Although she was frightened and furious and feeling guilty, there was a marked improvement in her physical state. The procedure to drain her lung had gone smoothly, and being able to breathe easily again meant she had greater energy and less pain. Apparently the scars from the operation were healing nicely, too. The staff had given her a shower and she now wore her own nightdress instead of a hospital gown.

'I've bought you a phone,' I said. 'There's credit on it.'

'Thanks,' she said, a little shamefacedly after her outburst.

I gave her my own phone so she could copy in numbers, and then talked to her about some of the practical things that might need sorting out. She found it hard to concentrate, I noticed, but was eventually able to remember that she'd only recently paid a credit-card bill and that the Jobcentre stuff was in a folder in her room. It did seem as though the memory loss was simply around the trauma.

We were going to be lucky. I hardly dared believe it, but any time I considered our situation, I was aware of the Vaseys. The accident bound us together, reverberated through our lives. If I could have, I'd have gone round there and sat with Tina and Simon and shared their grief, supported them as best I could. But I'd have been an intruder, the do-gooding ghoul. My place was with Naomi. But again and again my thoughts returned to Tina Vasey and the pain and wretched grief she must be feeling.

CHAPTER ELEVEN

Carmel

I began to read up on amnesia, wondering if I could do anything to help Naomi regain the missing hours. Sometimes visiting the place where the precipitating event occurred could trigger recall or flashbacks, in the same way that music or smells might. I thought of how I would retrace my steps when I mislaid my car keys and then remember where I'd left them. I could hardly re-orchestrate the barbecue for her, but it couldn't do any harm to find out more about it: who she'd talked to, where she'd been. I could also see if anyone agreed with Suzanne that Naomi had been drunk. Of course I was hoping that they would contradict Suzanne's version and confirm Alex's, bolstering my belief that Naomi would not have driven the car in a state of inebriation.

There was plenty I could tell Naomi from the time we'd overlapped at Suzanne's, but I'd need to talk to other people too: colour in the picture of what happened later. It was the least I could do. I had to do something to try and find out about the missing hours, in order to help her get her memory back.

I talked to Suzanne and Jonty first. She looked a little sceptical. 'You think it'll be any help?'

'I can try. I can't do nothing. Anyway, other people can tell me what state Naomi was in.'

'I've told you, she was drunk.'

'That's not what Alex says. Maybe she was just being

giddy, having a laugh. Maybe you misread the situation,' I said.

'You don't believe me?' Her eyes were shining with intensity. She didn't give me the chance to answer. 'She kept topping up her glass, she was the life and soul.'

'Then why the fuck did you let her drive home if she was in such a state?' I spoke more harshly than I intended.

Suzanne's face shuttered closed. Then she glared at me. 'It never occurred to me that she was driving.'

'I'm sorry,' I said, and squeezed her arm. 'Of course you wouldn't have let her go, if you'd known. You didn't see them off?'

She looked at me like I was raving. I saw it was hardly the sort of small, intimate event where the hosts would escort each set of departing guests to the door.

'Suzanne, this is family. If she's convicted but there are no aggravating factors like alcohol, then she gets a lighter sentence.'

'You're on to a loser there, then.'

Was there a trace of jealousy buried in all this? Suzanne had wanted to show off her baby, so she'd organized a fabulous spread and even been graced with fine weather. But had she then found herself overlooked once Naomi arrived and started entertaining people?

I was determined not to get deflected from my cause. I took a breath and said, 'Tell me everything you can remember about Naomi that day.'

'She was in the garden most of the time,' Suzanne said.

'Can you remember what she was doing, and who she talked to?'

'Erm, Julia from down the road and then Gordy later, and she was helping with the Chinese lanterns.'

'It wasn't even dark,' I said.

'Well, we wanted to do it while there were still some people here,' Jonty said.

111

'And then she was dancing with Pip. She talked to Alice and her husband, too,' she said.

Jonty said, 'And I saw her inside with Martin, I remember that.'

'He's my trainee,' Suzanne reminded me.

I wrote down everything I could manage and they helped me put a very rough timing next to some things, like lighting the lanterns at seven and the dancing not long after.

What else might she have done? 'Did she eat anything else? I know she had a plateful not long after they got here.'

Jonty had tended the barbecue on and off for about three hours so that as new guests arrived there were always freshly grilled steaks and kebabs. 'Tuna – that's right,' he said so loudly I jumped in my seat and Ollie twitched.

'Jonty,' Suzanne scolded.

'She did come back for more because she said she'd try the fish this time.'

'Any idea when that was?'

'Five-ish?'

'We left at five,' I said.

'After that, then. I was nearly done,' he said. 'Oh, and she borrowed my camera.'

'Could you copy me the photos?' Along with the ones from Phil's camera, I could put together a visual record of the afternoon.

'Sure, I'll put them on a data stick. I think there's some with her in too.'

'You said she kept topping her glass up?' I spoke to Suzanne. 'Do you remember when you saw that?'

'Every time I noticed her she had a glass in her hand.'

'But you don't know what was in it.'

'No, I don't.' She held my gaze, unflinching.

I backed away from the topic; there was nothing to be gained from quarrelling about it any further.

As we'd been talking, I'd made a list of the people who had figured, and now we went through the photos and I linked names to faces and got people's contact numbers. I noticed, though I didn't point it out, that of all the photos that showed Naomi, there was only one where she was holding a glass – and that was when we had the champagne. So there was no damning pictorial evidence to support Suzanne's story.

Ollie woke then and she fed him.

'How's work going?' I asked Jonty.

'Good, yeah. They've seen the rushes for the first film, Shrewsbury, and everybody's happy. We've a great editor on board. So we're hopeful we'll get a second series.'

'Brilliant. Where's next?'

'When Belfast is done, we're in Aberdeen.' His phone rang then, and he glanced at the display. Picked it up. 'Natalie, my PA. She must have heard me talking about work.'

I wondered how Suzanne really felt about Jonty working away while Ollie was so small. I knew she was loyal and would never admit any dissatisfaction, and of course she knew how things worked in his business, but she must miss him, I thought. Just to have someone there to share the load, someone who could do the early-morning nappy change. Someone to supply cups of tea and take the baby out for a walk while she had a bath or a shower.

I began with Martin, Suzanne's trainee, and asked if we could meet up. Although taken aback – he didn't know me at all well and we had not spoken at the barbecue – he agreed. He could do coffee at Piccadilly station after work.

The station was thronging with commuters, travellers

and shoppers. I'd told Martin I'd find a seat in the coffee shop and would be wearing a black jacket. Poor choice: there were four women in similar attire. When a potential candidate wandered in, looking right and left, I waved and he came over.

He was all togged out in a posh suit – well, it looked posh to me – and a startling puce shirt. He was young and seemed wary. I'd no idea if Suzanne had spoken to him since the accident. I couldn't see why she would have – she was still on leave – but he might have needed to check something out with her. He asked after Suzanne and Ollie, and Naomi, made all the right noises.

I repeated what I'd told him on the phone, that Naomi had amnesia and we were trying to find out more about the events leading up to the accident in the hope that it would help her get her memory back. 'Did you see Naomi, talk to her?'

'Saw her; she came in the kitchen a couple of times for a top-up.' The drinks were in the kitchen: beer and soft drink cans in a barrel full of ice cubes, a parade of wines and spirits and fancy fruit juices on the counter.

'Did you notice what she was drinking?'

'No idea, sorry. Just said hello, that's all. That was it.'

'Do you remember anything else – see her talking to anyone else?'

He shook his head.

'You were in the kitchen with Alex?'

'That's right, we're both footie fans. We were rehashing the Premier League.'

'Man City?' They'd won the title for the first time in forty-four years, pipping their arch-rivals Man United to the post.

Martin nodded. 'What about Alex?' I said. 'Was he drinking much?' If Suzanne was right and Naomi was pissed, that would account for him not realizing. And it would explain the difference between his recollection and Suzanne's.

'Vodka and orange,' Martin said. 'We were drinking that Ukrainian one they had. Rocket fuel. He'd got a job, right?' *So he'd be celebrating.*

'Yes. Can you remember who else was there?'

'One of the neighbours, didn't get her name.'

'Black hair and glasses?' I said.

'That's right.'

'Julia,' I told him.

'And a couple, Australians,' he said. 'They knew Jonty from golf.' One of the peculiar pastimes my son-in-law pursues when he isn't filming ruins or sourcing organic cheese. 'There were other people coming and going too,' he added.

'Did you see Alex and Naomi leave?'

He thought. 'Alex went out to fetch her. That's all.'

I was disappointed. Nothing much there to add to the picture I was building for her. On the train home I looked through the list of other party guests. After the fruitless meeting with Martin, I'd decided to establish over the phone whether people had been in the garden with Naomi for any length of time, and only if that was the case would I arrange to meet them face to face.

For all my concern and good intentions about attending the Ivy Cottesloe hearing and saying my piece, when I was actually there I found it claustrophobic and couldn't wait for it to be over.

I didn't know anyone else, which was a relief, and if anyone linked me to the accident they didn't let on. There were jugs of coffee, and hot water for tea, before we convened. I got a tea bag, added water and a splash of milk. Took a biscuit. But when I came to drink it, there was a foul taste of stale coffee, bitter and oily.

The chairman was the sort of character who likes the sound of his own voice and never uses one word when a paragraph will do. His laboured introductions and summations at every micro stage of the process were excruciating and had me grinding my teeth. And of course everything took far longer than it should.

I'd submitted a written report months previously which had been circulated, along with other contributions, to those attending. When it came to my part there weren't any questions. Things became marginally more energized as we attempted to agree on where mistakes had been made – the failings in the system – and on the wording of our recommendations as a result. The general view was that human error had led to Ivy slipping through the net. Either someone in the hospital discharge team had failed to pass her case through to the community social workers, or the office for the community social workers had failed to allocate Ivy to one of the staff. If existing procedures had been followed, she would have been safe.

Human error. My thoughts kept spinning back to Naomi. Was it simple human error that had caused her to accelerate when she should have slowed, to misjudge the curve of the bend and find herself on the wrong side of the road, wrench the steering wheel in a jolt of shock then, too late, see the figure on the bicycle, feel the thump of impact, the punishing lurch as the car tumbled over, hanging upside down, flung about, the force breaking bones and rupturing soft tissue?

After the hearing concluded, I called into the office. I'd arranged to go for a bite to eat and a catch-up with Evie. She waggled her fingers at me, phone pressed to her ear, and I waited for her to finish the call.

'How was it?' she asked.

'Grim, glad it's done.'

She retrieved her bag from her desk and we walked across the square to a little deli with a few tables outside. The city was bathed in golden heat. It seemed peculiar that there was this balmy, bright backdrop to the misery of the accident, to the fate of Ivy Cottesloe. I said as much to Evie, who nodded. 'Yeah, should be pissing it down really. Oh, yeah!' She feigned surprise. 'Usually is.'

I laughed.

'Look at this.' She stabbed her finger at the freckles on her arm; Evie's fair-skinned, red-haired and the sun really brings her freckles out. 'Few more days and they'll all join together and I'll look like I've got a tan.'

She asked after Naomi again and I told her about Don. Every so often a bus or a taxi lumbered past, making it difficult to hear.

'It's hard on Suzanne, too,' I said. 'New baby and all. It's a tough time and suddenly all the attention's on her little sister. And Jonty's away again. Of course Suzanne says she's fine with Ollie – doesn't know what all the fuss is about.'

'You believe her?'

'Well – you know Suzanne: Mrs Capable.' I groaned. 'Oh, that sounds mean. It's just she never puts a foot wrong.'

'Which might not be such a great reputation to have. Lot of pressure living like that, trying to be perfect all the time. Can't let your guard down.'

I put my glass down. 'You think we fucked her up?'

'Course you did,' she teased me. 'It's what families are for. But honestly,' she sat forward, 'there she is being so great at everything, getting praise and respect from all quarters: how can she ever fail? How can she ever ask for help?'

'I know. I'm run ragged with Naomi and hospital and the lawyer and I'm not giving Suzanne as much time as I want to.'

'Make it clear. Tell her. Unless you'd rather write,' she added flippantly.

'Ha ha! Will she listen?'

'That's up to her, but you'll have said it.'

'It's you and Russell, isn't it?' Evie had been the well-behaved big sister to her wayward brother Russell. Their parents were always getting drawn into helping Russell with the endless mishaps and mistakes that dogged his life. Evie was left to get on with it. When she actually did crave their support – going through months of infertility treatment with IVF and failing to get pregnant – they were too wrapped up in Russell's latest melodrama – an ill-advised and tempestuous marriage to a Estonian waitress – to respond to her.

'Yes,' she said, mockingly, 'I have lived the dream. Look, Suzanne isn't me and you're not my parents.' She shivered. 'And no way is Naomi anything like Russell. But just because Suzanne is so adamantly self-reliant doesn't mean—'

'I know,' I broke in, 'and you're right. We can't just be fixated on Naomi; we need to try and create some sort of normality.'

As I walked back to the tram, I thought about what Evie had said. Even as little kids it was Naomi who demanded most care, a keener eye. She'd wander off, caught up in the moment, forgetting rules and cautions simply because of the novelty and excitement. When she was seven, we'd been at Glastonbury, camping. It wasn't as big a festival back then, but still not somewhere you'd want to lose a child.

It had rained all night, so there was mud everywhere. We'd come equipped with wellies and waterproofs. The kids actually had all-in-one waterproofs, little PVC boiler suits, which had been a boon and also helped us keep track of them; Suzanne's was red and Naomi's

118

bright yellow. We'd had breakfast and managed the toilets, although Suzanne was outraged at the state of them and said she was not going again until we were safely home. We spent a few hours exploring, then went back to the tent to eat. I fancied seeing Gil Scott-Heron, who was on the NME stage, and we told the kids we would walk over there in a few minutes.

The next time I put my head out of the tent, Suzanne was sitting on a folding stool, her head in a book, and there was no sign of Naomi.

'Where's your sister?'

She glanced up, looked right and left, then shrugged. 'Dunno.'

'Naomi?' I called, panic nipping at the back of my neck. 'Naomi?'

Phil got back from the toilets then, loo roll in hand. 'What's up?'

'Naomi, don't know where she is.'

He blanched, ran his hand through his hair. 'You wait here in case she comes back, I'll find the lost children's tent.'

He seemed to be gone ages. Suzanne got snippy when I pressed her to remember exactly where she had last seen her sister and which way Naomi had been facing.

'I don't know. Don't you think I'd have told you if I had any idea?' Sounding like some grumpy fifty-year-old rather than a child.

Reassurances flitted though my mind: they were a nice crowd here, someone would be looking after her; she'd be back any second. Behind them, swelling with menace, were my dark fears: abduction, molestation, murder.

Phil came back alone. He had alerted the festival staff and some were already actively searching. They suggested we split up and look for her.

'One of us should stay here,' I said.

'Take turns then,' he agreed. 'You might as well start at the stage.'

I pulled a face. I was hardly going to be taking in the music.

'Go.'

'Suzanne, do you want to come, or stay with Dad?'

'Stay,' Suzanne said. She wasn't worried. *Why* wasn't she worried?

Weaving my way through the campsite and the fields, my eyes seized on any scrap of yellow. And there was plenty of it: oilskins and hats, pennants and balloons, scarves and jumpers.

There was a sizeable crowd in front of the stage, the band already playing, and in spite of my anxiety, my heart warmed as I made out a song. I'd got the binoculars and I scanned the audience, sweeping slowly from one side to the other, trying to be systematic. It was fine weather, the air warm, the sun high, just a few streaky clouds melting away. There! No – it was a man's jacket. I swept on. Nothing.

I lowered the binoculars, my throat aching, eyes stinging, and had turned to retrace my steps when something bumped my knees.

'Mummy!' She grabbed me round the waist. 'You were ages.'

'Where've you been?'

'Here, you said come here.'

'We were all coming together.' I stooped and picked her up. 'You're not meant to go anywhere on your own, you know that.'

Her smile fell, her eyes dimmed. 'Oh.'

'We were worried. You were lost.'

'I wasn't lost,' she said. 'I was here. It's all right.' She nodded.

'Yes,' I said, stupid tears blurring my vision, 'it is.'

120

'Put me down,' she said. 'You like this one.' The band had launched into the intro to 'The Revolution Will Not Be Televised'.

'I know but we have to tell Dad and the festival people that you're okay.'

She sighed.

'Here.' I held out my hand and she grabbed it and we ran all the way back. Outpacing the monsters and the ghouls and racing to claim the day.

Naomi

A flash of red. A thumping, then a squeal. One thump, then another, *boom pause boom*. Like a slow heartbeat. And then the shriek.

It's coming back! Is it? Oh God.

It's night on the ward and the woman opposite has a dreadful cough. Much worse than mine. She coughs so hard she starts to choke. She's fallen quiet now but it won't last long.

A flash of red. I try and find a shape to it, and when that fails I focus on defining the colour. Crimson. Not red like fire, not orange, but deeper, bluer, closer to dark pink. It could be anything: the colour from the inside of my eyelids, or some of the food at the party. Cherries or beetroot. But before now, that flashback to the food, if it was a flashback, has always been lots of different colours, not just crimson. I'm not sure if it's significant.

But the thump and that shrieking sound, surely that's from the moment when we crashed. The thud that drove through me like a jackhammer. *Poom!* Then again. *Poom!* One for the first impact, and the next when we hit the school gatepost and flipped over. And the shrieking, that must be the car roof as it scraped on the road.

The red. Did she bleed? Was there blood on the windscreen? It's a horrible thought, but I force myself to consider it. After all, flies and things leave little smears like that on the glass. Oh God. My stomach churns. Alex must know; I'll ask him next time he comes. But if I've remembered this, then maybe I'll remember more. I feel a flush of excitement. I want to tell someone, wake someone up and tell them.

What if I forget again? Could that happen? My blood turns cold at the thought. Surely memories wouldn't just come and go. If these are memories – and I'm pretty sure they must be.

CHAPTER TWELVE

Naomi

I t's awkward asking him about the accident. He doesn't really like to talk about it because he knows how ashamed and horrible I feel about it and he doesn't want me to feel bad. So we avoid it a lot of the time. Now I come right out and say it: 'I need to ask you something about the crash.'

'Okay,' he says, and waits for me to go on.

'I think I remember the noise, the sound, when I hit her and when we went into the gatepost and turned over: a bang then another and a horrible screeching. Is that right?'

'Something like that. It was all so fast, but you're right about the screeching.'

I nod, thankful, even though it's such a small fragment.

'And there was something else. Well – I'm not sure if it's from the accident or not.' I feel so clumsy saying this. 'Did she hit the windscreen, was there any blood?' I bite my lip, suddenly shaky again; it's important to talk about this and not collapse in tears. I sniff hard.

'No.' He shakes his head.

'I think I remember red, dark cherry red. Her bike?'

'No.' He shakes his head again, and his green eyes hold mine. He blinks. 'She was wearing a red dress.'

I gulp, my neck burning, my pulse bumpy. 'A red dress?'

'Yes.' He looks at me.

'That must be it,' I say. *Oh God, I have remembered.*
Oh God.

It's hard to talk much after that, but I do make an effort, asking about the rest of his day and how he's managing with the crutch. And he asks me how I feel about him starting to look for a flat for us soon. The notion of me leaving hospital and our lives going on seems totally unreal. The police might press charges. It's likely they will. But I say that's fine and to get somewhere near a tram stop because it would be good for work. His work. The firm are based in town, off Deansgate.

That night before I sleep, I centre my thoughts on that glimpse of red, poring over it, willing it to evolve, unfold and show me more.

I will remember.

I will.

Carmel

I uploaded the pictures from Phil's camera and the ones Jonty had copied for me and then made a selection of those that I thought might best help Naomi. There's a lovely one Phil took of Naomi holding Ollie. She is staring down at him, solemn-faced, and he's gazing back up at her. Both their faces are in profile and Phil has just caught the moment.

And I continued to work through the list of barbecue guests. I met Gordy at a café in Prestwich, up in north Manchester, close to where he lived. He was my sort of age and had a substantial paunch and sounded breathless all the time. I asked him to tell me everything he could remember about Naomi at the barbecue, and took notes as he spoke.

'We talked for quite a while,' he said. 'My middle one,

Laura, is applying to Newcastle. Naomi was raving about it. She's a lovely girl.'

'Yes.'

'We sat on the swing seat,' he said. 'Some of the time Pip was with us. Have you spoken to Pip yet?'

'No.'

'What do they think the chances are of her remembering?' he said.

'No one will even hazard a guess,' I said. 'When something like this happens, you find out how little we still know about the brain.'

'Poor kid,' Gordy sighed. 'And the other family, of course.'

'Yes. I still can't really imagine what they're going through; just this generalized notion of how horrendous it must be.'

'There was a toddler at the party,' Gordy said, 'little boy in blue dungarees.'

'Oh yes.' Alan, or Adam.

'Naomi read him a book. He was getting tired and his mum had given him this book and he chucked it on the floor. Naomi pretended she wanted to look at it and began reading it out loud making deliberate mistakes, and that drew the boy in. He clambered up on to the seat and she read it to him. I left them to it then. That was around quarter to six.'

'Did you notice if Naomi was drinking?'

Gordy shook his head. 'Sorry, no. You think she . . .'

'I don't think so, but Suzanne does. Did she seem tipsy?'

'Not especially, no. I might have been, though,' he said. 'Kids – you think once they're adults it might get easier, and then something like this happens. My eldest, Jordan, passed his driving test first time, twenty he was. Two months later he was sent on one of those courses for speeding drivers. Sometimes they seem to think they're invincible, that nothing can touch them, that it won't happen to them.'

I nodded. 'If you think of anything else . . .'

'I'll call you, I've got your number.'

Gordy hadn't seen her drinking, I thought, as I walked to the car. That was good. And there were several little moments in what he'd told me that were worth passing on. Given that she'd begun to remember other fragments, I was hopeful that her amnesia would lift.

We asked the staff if there was anywhere private we could meet with Don on the Monday. They let us use a small side room near the ward and confirmed that Naomi was fit enough to be taken there in a wheelchair.

Don is a lovely man, his softly spoken manner at odds with a dirty, raucous, infectious laugh which turns his eyes to tiny lines in his plump face. He's virtually bald and keeps any remaining hair shaved close to his scalp.

I don't remember seeing him in a suit before, but when he arrived at the hospital he was in the full kit, shirt and tie and shiny shoes with long pointy toes. Italian at a guess. He certainly took more care with his wardrobe than Phil ever did. Or me, come to that.

Don shook hands with Naomi before sitting down and asking her to tell him about the accident. He had a tablet with him, prepared to type in notes.

She shook her head. 'I can't really remember any of it. Just a noise and a flash of red.' Her voice dipped. 'Alex says she was wearing a red dress. So, I only know what Mum and Dad told me, and Alex.'

'Okay.' Don glanced at Phil.

Phil went over what we'd learnt from the police and what Alex had said. Don didn't talk very much, just stopping Phil when he needed to clarify points. 'Were there any eyewitnesses?' he said.

126

'Monica, Alex's mum; she passed them on Lees Hall Road, a few minutes before.'

'What about at the actual crash?' Don said.

'I don't know,' Phil said.

I thought about it. 'Alex didn't mention anyone, but you'd have to ask him.'

'He rang the ambulance himself,' Naomi added, 'so I don't think so.'

'What about CCTV?' Don said.

Phil and I looked at each other and both shrugged. I couldn't recall any cameras at the scene, but then I hadn't been looking for them.

'Is Alex likely to give a statement to the police and appear in court if charges are brought?' he asked Naomi directly. 'He'd cooperate?'

'Yes, I think so,' she said.

'He's training to be a lawyer,' I said.

Don thought for a moment, then scrolled over his notes, rubbing the palm of one hand over the top of his head.

'I can tell you what is likely to happen,' he said, 'but until the police bring charges – *if* they bring charges, and in a case this serious that is highly probable –there's nothing I can actually do yet. Without knowing what their case is, we can't usefully look at a defence. You understand?'

Naomi nodded.

'So, it all rests on what evidence they have. They are likely to be using a road traffic investigation unit and they'll examine the car, the scene, the forensic and medical evidence before considering charges.'

The charred chassis of the car, the bent gatepost, the child – her injuries.

'They won't make an arrest while you're in hospital; you have to be medically fit for questioning. They'll need time anyway for the various tests to be done and the results assessed.'

'Will it be causing death by dangerous driving?' I asked.

Don placed his hands on the table. 'The CPS will always go for the most serious charge that has a realistic prospect of conviction. For that offence they would need to prove that the driving was dangerous rather than careless and that is something we would seek to challenge. If we cast doubt on the driving being dangerous, they might then seek a lesser charge of careless driving, which carries lower penalties. It's reasonable to argue that temporarily losing control on a bend is careless rather than dangerous. Then there may be aggravating factors. Had you been drinking or taking drugs?'

'I can't remember,' Naomi said.

'She did have some champagne,' Phil said.

'Earlier in the afternoon,' I added. 'We don't know about later. Suzanne says she was drinking, but Alex says the opposite.'

'They'll have taken a blood sample, won't they?' Phil said.

'Yes,' Don replied. 'The police will have to furnish proof if they wish to introduce it as evidence. The thing to bear in mind is that the prosecution have to be able to prove every single point of their case in order to take it to court. So to successfully prosecute causing death by careless driving, for example, they have to prove (a) that you were driving the car that evening, (b) that your driving was careless and (c) that the death was as a direct result of that careless driving. Our job is to undermine their case by challenging the evidence and raising doubts. If there are any reasonable doubts, there can't be a conviction.'

'So what happens next?' Phil said.

'If Naomi is arrested for questioning, I will then be given a summary of the case against her.'

Just the word *arrested* made my stomach turn over.

'I would then talk to Naomi before she was questioned and we'd agree how to proceed, what she would be saying to them.'

'What could I say?' Naomi protested. 'All I can say is I can't remember.'

'That's true,' Don said. 'If the amnesia persists, we'll decide whether to sit through the questions or whether to give a prepared written statement instead.' He went on, 'If the police then decided to charge you, they'd do that and release you on bail to appear in the magistrates' court in a few days' time. Because of the gravity of the incident, the magistrates would automatically set a committal date, usually a month or two ahead, and that's when they'd refer the case to the Crown Court. About six or eight weeks on from that, we'd have plea and case management hearing. That's when you enter a plea of guilty or not guilty, if you've not already done so, and the arrangements are agreed to schedule a case.'

Something struck me forcefully, 'She can't plead guilty if she can't remember anything about it, can she?'

'That's right. Not that I'd advise a guilty plea anyway, but it would be nonsensical. At the committal stage, once I receive the complete bundle of case notes from the prosecution, I apply for legal aid on Naomi's behalf and start looking for our own evidence to contest the prosecution case. That's when the real work begins.

'The defendant's character is of great significance in this sort of case,' he went on. 'Any previous convictions?'

'No,' we all said in unison.

'I didn't think so,' he said. 'Any history of careless driving, driving under the influence, anything of that nature?'

'No,' Naomi said. 'We share the car but it belongs to Alex. I've always been careful with it.'

'What about speeding? Any penalty points?'

'No,' she said.

'Good. And what about Alex?'

'The same,' Phil said. 'He's a responsible lad.'

Naomi nodded.

'You mentioned he was going into the law?' Don said.

'Yes, he's just got a training contract with a firm here. Hasn't started yet.'

'Do you know who?'

'Vincent and Kaplan.'

Don smiled. 'Good firm.'

'What if there was a problem with the car that meant Naomi couldn't correct her speed?' I said.

'We'll certainly be looking for anything like that, as will the road traffic investigation unit.'

'The car was completely burnt out,' Phil said.

'Makes it harder. All we can do is wait and see what they put in their report. It's a lot to take on board. Is there anything you want to ask me?' Don asked Naomi.

'Yes, can I write to them – Lily's family? Say how sorry I am.'

Don pulled a face. 'I really wouldn't advise it. You're pleading not guilty. Any communication like that, no matter how neutral, could be used against you – the prosecution could argue it signifies an admission of guilt.'

She looked crestfallen.

'Could I write instead?' I asked. 'Send a card or something?'

He shook his head. 'It would be very unwise.'

'Okay,' I said.

'I'll take you back through,' Phil said to Naomi.

'See you in a minute,' I promised her.

'Is there anything else?' Don asked when they'd gone.

I hesitated. The trouble we had with Naomi during sixth-form college. Should I mention that? It was years ago, but . . . I dithered and then told Don all about it.

The first we knew about Naomi's trouble was a visit from a pair of community support officers to inform us that Naomi and another girl had been apprehended drinking in the local park. The other girl was Georgia. Naomi stood with a sullen look on her face while they spoke to us, and when they'd gone and I tried to talk to her about it, she told me to mind my own business and flounced off upstairs. She was slightly more amenable by teatime, told us not to have a fit about it, it wasn't like she'd killed anybody or anything. She promised that she wouldn't play truant again. I was more worried about her drinking in the middle of the day.

Next thing, we got a letter from her tutor. Naomi had been found with alcohol in college. It was a disciplinary matter, this was a final warning, and if it happened again she would be expelled.

I went numb, my head cloudy and muddled. I waited until Phil got back to talk to him about how to tackle it. He read the letter, raked his fingers through his hair. 'Well, she has to take it seriously or they'll kick her out,' he said. 'Don't know that anything we say will make a difference.'

'That's it, think positive,' I complained.

'Talk to her after tea?'

By then Suzanne was at Bournemouth, emailing us every Sunday and enjoying the course. Just the three of us at home.

'Wait a minute,' I said to Naomi later as she got up to leave the dinner table. 'We have a letter from college. See?' I pulled it out of my pocket and opened it, set it down for her to read.

She flushed and a mutinous glare rolled through her eyes.

'What's going on? What were you thinking of?' I said.

She shrugged.

'How often have you been drinking? If you've got a problem with it, you need to—'

'It's not like that,' she said.

'It's not healthy,' I said. 'You're seventeen, you shouldn't be drinking at all, let alone at college.'

'Get real,' she sneered.

'No! You don't get to have that attitude. This is serious, it's dangerous.'

She sighed.

I changed tack, I knew shouting at her wasn't going to be productive. 'Aren't you happy at college?'

'No.'

'You want to leave?' Phil said.

'Maybe,' she said, sounding utterly miserable.

'Why?' he said.

'It's boring and they treat us like little kids.'

'What would you do instead?' he said.

'I don't know.'

'C'mon,' Phil chided, 'you must have some idea.' At her age he was already planning the shop, already playing in the band.

'Well I don't,' she said.

'Is there anything you do like there?' I was searching for a positive morsel to focus on, to build a strategy with. 'Dance,' I said, 'you love dance.'

'Not with Miss Gaffney, she's crap.'

I sighed. 'If you leave, it won't be easy to get work; you're not eighteen so lots of places won't consider you. You've hardly any experience.'

'I'll sign on, then.'

Oh great. 'Look, you need to think about what you

want. I know it's not that easy, but it's no fun being on the dole. You get fifty quid a week and you'll be filling in great long forms and having compulsory interviews with the jobseekers people to see if you are trying hard enough. Do you want to go to university? Because if you do, then you have to have A levels.'

She shrugged, bit at her thumbnail.

I had a sudden thought. 'Is Georgia doing all right there? Does she like it?'

'She left.'

Ah. 'What's she doing?'

'Nothing.'

'That going well for her, is it?' Phil said.

'Don't be mean, Dad,' Naomi said.

'Just because she's jacked it in—' I began.

'It's nothing to do with that. I told you, it's boring.'

We didn't get much further. I told her we'd discuss it again the following evening, by which time she should come to a decision about whether to make a renewed effort or to give up her place.

'I'm not going back,' she said the next morning.

It wasn't the end of the world, but it was a pretty dreary place to be. The next few months were not happy times. Phil and I tried to keep positive; we didn't want to put her under any more pressure and add to her sense of failure. She claimed jobseeker's allowance for several months. Georgia's brush with alcohol-related illness and their combined lack of funds didn't seem to have had much impact on their socializing (though Georgia had never set foot in our house again after the fire), and they continued to party with the best of them and sleep the day away. Any attempts to discuss Naomi's behaviour met with a wall of indifference punctuated by outbursts of anger. She was demonstrably unhappy, but we were the last people on earth she wanted any support from. Or so it seemed.

133

I remember comparing it to my own adolescence. It had helped that I knew what I wanted to do with my life, starting with becoming independent. University was the route to that and so it made sense to work for it. As for under-age drinking and the like, that all went on but I never got caught and I spared my mum and dad any confrontations. In my last two years at home, I'd often wait until they were in bed and then sneak out to meet up with people, or I'd pretend to be going to bed and actually leave the house. What they didn't know wouldn't hurt them.

Early summer things seemed to change. Naomi began seeing more of her other friends, and Georgia was in a heavy relationship with some lad and apparently besotted. Then Naomi got a part-time job in a restaurant, washing up and running errands. Like someone emerging from sleep she seemed brighter and had more energy, she regained her equilibrium and her confidence grew. She no longer had to pout and bluster to disguise her faltering self-esteem. And she raised the prospect of going back to college.

She altered the mix of courses to avoid the dreaded Miss Gaffney, who she really did dislike, and she had to have a meeting with the staff, who did not want a repeat performance and needed convincing of her commitment.

We never looked back – well, only with a grateful laugh and a shudder when Phil and I recalled that time and related it to friends having traumas with their own teenagers. Naomi got an A and two Bs in her exams. Surprised us all. Miffed Suzanne, who always considered herself to be the brightest child.

Naomi had tested us significantly as a teenager, but in the intervening years, in the recent months, I'd seen no sign of her reverting to that risky, out-of-control behaviour, though she knew how to have fun still. She got tipsy sometimes when she and Alex went partying, but she'd not given us any cause for concern.

Don heard me out. He believed it had very little bearing on the case or any potential prosecution. What was more significant was that Naomi had a clean licence and no record of any drink-related offences, antisocial behaviour and so on. And as yet we had no way of knowing whether alcohol was even a factor in the accident.

CHAPTER THIRTEEN

Naomi

Today they got me out of bed and made me stand on my good leg, holding on to a frame, for a few seconds. My leg was shaking, weak as a kitten. Like in dreams where you can only run in slow motion, or when you can't run at all even though there's some bear or wolf or a psycho serial killer hurtling after you.

The physio will come back and in between I have to do these stretching exercises. It'll be another couple of weeks before I can put weight on my broken ankle. The other women in the ward are so cheery and chatty and they're always sharing their symptoms, but I feel awkward joining in. I don't want them to know what I've done. When the rest of them talk, I pretend to read, or to sleep. They know I was in a road accident, but that's all, I think.

They've moved me to a bed near the window because I don't need any attention in the night. I can look out on to a service road with double yellow lines all along it. I see the vehicles going up and down and sometimes a smoker will walk by, puffing away. There is a building on the other side, a vast brick wall without any windows. It is impossible to count the bricks but I try, hoping it'll lull me to sleep. There is a corner of sky at the far side of that roof. A little patch, just enough to see whether it's cloudy or blue or night.

Mum paid for a TV for a few days but I told her I wasn't fussed. It's hard to explain: stuff that used to be a laugh even because it was so dire, like *Come Dine With Me* or *Jeremy Kyle*, well, I know it's trivia, always did; I could poke fun at it, chat about it later. But now I glaze over. I can't connect any more.

Not just with telly. With anything.

They try and jolly me along, Mum and Dad. They take turns coming now. Today it's Dad. I always feel this pang when I see him. That I've let him down. He never asks about it, the accident, doesn't go on about remembering like Mum does.

'Hello.' He kisses my head and puts a bag on the tray table. 'Chocolate flapjack.'

'Thanks.'

He takes off his coat and hangs it on the back of the chair, then shifts the chair about till he's facing me. 'Tickets will be out soon for Leeds Festival,' he says, 'if you and Alex would like to go? Or Sziget in Budapest if you fancy going further afield. Go with Becky and Steve, maybe? I can get some tickets. I could treat you.'

I can't look at him, and he says, 'You'll be up and running by then,' to chivvy me along. But that's not why I'm skirting round it; it's that I don't want him to waste his money on something that I don't think I could face. I can't see myself in a field with a load of people, jumping about pretending things are okay. Can't imagine ever doing anything like that again.

'The police,' I say. 'Who knows what'll happen?' Because it's easier to make an excuse about that than to tell him I couldn't cope with his treat.

He sticks his lip out and sighs. His whiskers are grey now, eyebrows too. He looks old. I never noticed that before.

He's downloaded me some more tracks, for my MP3 player. I let him load it up. All these lovely things; he's trying so hard to make things better and I just feel like crying.

137

He's got the paper with him, the crossword, and he reads out a clue. I never, ever get them, they're way too hard for me, but it's not a bad way for the two of us to spend visiting time, because the silences aren't awkward while he's working out an anagram and I can get away with the odd question like 'What does it mean?'

Alex texts me: *Hey u good babe? x* There are signs on the wall about not using mobile phones, but everyone ignores them. I text back: *K, dad's here, sleepy l8trs x*

Dad folds his paper up and gets his jacket on. The leather is so cracked now, the whole thing is dropping to bits. I can't imagine him ever getting a new one; he'd look so weird in something neat and shiny.

He kisses me again. 'Need anything bringing?'

'No, ta,' I say.

I lie down and close my eyes, but before long they insist on doing my checks. Then the expedition to the toilet. Then comes the night.

I dream of her a lot – Lily. I dream all sorts about her. Sometimes she's fine. I dream, but what I need to do is remember.

Carmel

I was returning books to the library, unread and overdue, abandoned in the upheaval, just paying the fine, when someone called my name. Julia, Suzanne's neighbour, the ones who came to the barbecue. I couldn't remember exactly what she did, something with disabled children; she had a young woman with her, a girl with Down's syndrome.

'How are you?' Julia said. Then pulled a face. 'Sorry, stupid question. I'm so sorry, what a nightmare.'

'Yes,' I agreed.

'Have you time for a coffee?'

'Yes, if . . .' I looked at the girl.

'I'm leaving Lauren here, work experience,' Julia said.

I waited while she said her goodbyes to Lauren, then we crossed to the nearest coffee shop further down the high street and took our drinks to a quiet corner at the back.

'How is Naomi?'

Broken, I thought. But I tried to be less pessimistic. 'Still reeling; she was quite badly injured.'

Julia nodded. I imagined Suzanne had told her some of what was going on.

'And of course with, you know . . .' It was still so hard to frame the words, to release them into the air, stark and forbidding. *With the death . . . with the little girl dead.* I shook my head, 'She still can't really remember anything,' I said. 'I'm hoping to find out stuff for her, talk to people who were at the barbecue and see if I can help her get her memory back. Did you see much of her?'

'A bit. We talked about festivals,' Julia said. 'She and Alex couldn't afford to go to anything and she was telling me how you and Phil took the two of them when they were younger.'

'For years. I'm getting a bit past it now. I like my own bed. But Phil would sleep on a bed of nails if he got to hear some decent bands. Do you remember anything else?'

'Her arriving with the champagne?'

But I'd seen that myself.

'What happens now?' Julia said.

I told her about the legal stages. She was sympathetic and non-judgemental while other people were avoiding us. I wondered where that came from.

I returned to the party. 'What time were you there till?'

'About half four. Collette was getting ratty and Fraser

had promised to give Neville over the way a hand. Did you ever meet Neville?'

I frowned, not sure who she meant.

'The dog people.'

I smiled. 'Oh, right.' The neighbours immediately across the road, in one of the new houses, trained dogs and had a kennels half a mile away.

'They were moving, Fraser was giving them a lift.'

'What are the new people like?'

'Not seen them much yet. Youngish, out at work all hours. Makes you wonder if we've got it all wrong. There's millions with no work and those that have jobs are working themselves to breaking point.'

Walking home, I considered who to talk to next, who else Naomi might have socialized with between five, when we'd left, and eight, when she had.

Naomi

There's a saying somewhere, China or India, that if you save a person's life you are responsible for them for the rest of your days. Which seems a pretty heavy-duty burden and might put you off in the first place. And it's beginning to feel like that is how it is between me and Alex.

He visits and it's as if he thinks we can go on like before. I don't know. The accident has poisoned everything. It's this horrible event that's there, a dense shadow over our heads.

I can't shift the guilt inside me, and the nicer Alex is, the worse I feel. I don't deserve it. I don't deserve him. Why did I ever think we were right for each other? He's got an amazing degree, he's got ambition and a job to go to, and I'm just not in the same league. Imagine it, when

140

he's hanging around with all the legal types, going for drinks after work and staying up late cramming his textbooks, and I'm in a call centre or stacking shelves (if I'm lucky) or behind bars in prison (if I'm not).

Carmel

As I was starting work, an evening shift, one of the community social workers I'd not met before called in to follow up on a client.

The social worker, Ricky Clarke, had an easy way about him. Late twenties, a local lad, he was relaxed and friendly. I warmed to him. We covered what we needed to, then as he was leaving he paused and said, 'Hope you don't mind me asking, but I think you used to know my mum. Geraldine Clarke, was O'Dwyer.'

Good God! Petey's sister. 'Yes!'

'And my uncle—'

'Petey.'

'Yeah, he was in a band . . .' he said, sounding uncertain.

'That's right, the Blaggards, with my husband Phil.' Geraldine, known as Dino. This was her son. Oh God. I was smiling, but suddenly I found it painful to remember and I didn't know how much he'd been told. He was tiny when it happened. 'Say hello to your mum,' I said. 'How is she?'

'She's good, yeah. I will.' He grinned, and I saw a sudden flash of Petey in the way he tilted his head. Then he left.

Petey. Feeling shaken, I sat down.

He'd moved in with Dino in 1983. She was the one member of his family we'd all met, as she was closest in age to Petey and came to quite a few gigs. But she

141

wouldn't give the drums house room. She had a new baby. So the kit stayed at the shop.

He'd been living with her almost a year when it happened. We'd seen him on the Saturday. The Smiths were on at the Hacienda and we'd had a brilliant night. Phil and me, Ged and his girlfriend, and Petey. We walked partway home, oblivious to the steady rain, and stopped for a curry on the main drag in Rusholme. Ged and his girlfriend left and the three of us went back to Platt Lane. We stayed up another couple of hours, drinking and smoking and talking about all sorts. Phil was excited by the idea of setting up a gig for the Blaggards at the Capri Ballroom further down the road.

The next day was dry but clouded over, a hangover-type day. We ate sausages and beans for breakfast, drank loads of coffee and got smashed. Petey came to the park, where we had a chaotic game of frisbee and got stared at and called names by a bunch of scrappy kids.

He went off to get the bus from there. He had a loping walk, always had his hands in his pockets and leant forward as if he was struggling into a headwind. When he reached the end of Platt Lane, he turned and raised a fist, an ebullient wave, and we waved back, jumping and larking about. We were still kids, really, twenty-three and twenty-four. So young.

Dino rang the shop on the Monday morning. I was upstairs getting ready for work, on the rota for a double sleepover at the children's home and intending to go shopping for some food before then.

Phil came into the room, his face ashen.

'Phil?' A shiver ran through me.

His mouth trembled as he spoke. 'It's Petey, he's dead. Been killed.'

'What!'

'Run over.'

142

'Oh my God. Where . . . when?'

'Last night, Regent Road.' One of the major roads in Salford. 'The guy stopped. They breathalysed him, apparently. He was drunk.'

'Petey. Oh, fuck.' I dropped the top I was ironing and began to cry.

The shock was overwhelming.

I wondered who the driver was. Some flashy business guy who'd been drinking at one of the private members' clubs or entertaining clients before leaving for home? Or a local lad tanked up on cheap cider? Was the driver on his own? Was he hurt? The lack of any detail was infuriating.

I still went into work, muddled through in a daze.

A couple of days later I rang Dino to ask about the funeral arrangements. 'I'm so sorry,' I told her. 'We all are.' The news had spread quickly around our circle of friends and acquaintances.

'We've had the police round again,' she said. 'They say Petey walked into the traffic on purpose.'

'What?' I thought I'd misheard.

'He walked into the road and just stood there. He wanted it to happen.' Her voice was ragged, tired, hopeless.

'No,' I said, my stomach twisting and a shock of cold dropping through me.

'There were witnesses; they've got it on camera, too.'

'Oh, Dino.'

'Why would he do that?' Her voice broke and I got a lump in my throat. I had no answer.

Apparently several cars had swerved to avoid hitting him. But he stood there, unmoving, facing the flow, and eventually the driver, an engineer with a family and no history of driving offences, ploughed straight into him.

It was so tempting to grasp for other explanations: was

143

Petey high, tripping on something, or sleepwalking, oblivious to the peril? Each fiction, thin as tissue paper, tore under the slightest examination.

He hadn't left a suicide note, and that gave us hope that he'd had no set intent to end his life when he left home and walked to Regent Road in the rain. Perhaps it was a whim, a bad few hours, and if the car hadn't struck him or the traffic had been lighter, or it hadn't been raining or someone had stopped him for a light, he might have changed his mind.

We were looking everywhere but at the truth. Plain and stark and mystifying. Petey had deliberately stood in a road because he wanted to die. We never knew why he wanted to die, presumably because carrying on living was unbearable. It's hard to accept that someone you love can feel so desolate, that you are incapable of providing what they need to make life tolerable.

Over the weeks that followed, we tried to make some sense of it, going over what we knew of him, what we'd seen, how he had been. We failed.

There hadn't been any cloud of depression like a black halo over his golden hair that final weekend; he had not been surly or angry or anxious in our company.

He'd barely seen his father since moving out, so it wasn't as if he'd been attacked again recently. We could find no explanation, no justification. His death was like something random, wicked, fickle. It took me years to be able to think about Petey without the cramping pain of grief and guilt.

And of course what hurt more than anything, a sting in the heart, was that he hadn't been able to tell us; we hadn't been able to help him.

The funeral was ghastly. A Catholic service with lots of prayers and hymns and communion. It had nothing of Petey in it. Not in what was said or the music or the flowers. We could have been burying his grandmother; apart from the name and the reference to *this young man*, it would have been exactly the same.

We sat at the back, a gang of us, his mates, like interlopers. Dino, her face softened by sorrow, holding the baby on her hip, was the only one who even spoke to us. Their mother had to be helped to walk, so distressed was she, and their father, a big beefy man with a large head, was like an ogre in my eyes.

I fantasized about exposing him, laying bare the truth of how he used to terrorize his son. Cloud cuckoo land; besides, I didn't really know the hard facts about his mistreatment.

After the cortège left to go and bury Petey, we all got the bus to the Grant's Arms in time for opening hours and held our own version of a wake. Drinking beer and putting our favourite tunes on the jukebox. I kept expecting him to join us. Someone would come into the pub and I'd glance across, my heart rising in hope, thinking I'd see his flare of hair and his sweet face; that he'd pull up a stool and drum on the table or scrawl a picture on a beer mat or print the opening line for a new song. Beat me at arm-wrestling.

We've a few photos from those days. My favourite, the one I got blown up to A3 and mounted for Phil's fortieth birthday, is one of the band after they had played a little club off Shudehill behind the Arndale Centre. It's dark and it's been raining and the four of them are outside, with the gear, waiting to load it into the van that Ged had borrowed. It's in black and white, and the flash picked up silver drops on the brickwork behind them. Lorraine and Ged are to the right, then Petey in the centre and Phil on the left. Someone has said something funny and the other three, their faces bright with amusement, are all looking at Petey, who is finding it absolutely hilarious. His head is flung back, he's got this great smile on his face, one hand clutching his chest as though he'd die laughing, the other half raised in a little fist of triumph. I can't remember the joke, but that's how I like to remember Petey: happy, helpless with laughter, with his mates, loved.

The Blaggards never played again.

CHAPTER FOURTEEN

Carmel

The next couple of party guests only added a little to the picture. Francine Moorhead had talked house-hunting with Naomi. Apparently Naomi was already fantasizing about getting a place with Alex, now that he had a job, and Francine had bought a flat in the Northern Quarter in the city centre. But Francine had left after that conversation, so there was not much point in meeting her. Stella Connor was vague on the phone, struggling to remember Naomi, but finally recalled that they had talked briefly about club nights while getting food from the buffet soon after Naomi arrived.

'You can't remember for her,' Phil said, one day. He thought I was becoming obsessed. 'It's futile.'

I didn't argue. I didn't want to get him any more stressed. He may have taken my silence for consent, assuming that I agreed with him, but I went on in my own sweet way.

Pip Shiers and I had talked a bit over the buffet. Jonty's colleague, she was getting used to life outside London but admitted she still missed living there. 'I'll give it another couple of years,' she said, 'and then decide whether to move back. Depends if I can get any work, of course.'

When I rang Pip, she said she had spent some time with Naomi at Suzanne's. 'We got the dancing going,' she said. 'Not at all easy on gravel.'

Another nugget of information to tell Naomi –

you were dancing. I could just imagine it, her dancing her heart out, arms raised and waving above her head, grinning at everyone. I hadn't yet sat her down and laid out all the memories I'd been collecting for her.

I asked Pip if she'd meet up with me.

'Not sure when – I'm up to my eyes with pre-production for Aberdeen.'

'I could come to you, if that makes it easier?'

'Great.'

Pip lived in one of the new flats in the developments at Harbour City, where Salford's docks have been transformed. Her instructions for parking and finding her place were complicated but precise, and we met after she got back from work late one evening.

'Sorry to drag you all the way out here,' she greeted me.

'No problem,' I said.

'How is Naomi?'

'Still in hospital. Should be home in the next couple of weeks, we hope.'

Pip just shook her head. She offered me coffee but I didn't imagine I'd be there all that long. She had a mesmerising view from her window, over the tramlines to other tower blocks and one of the canal basins. It was beautiful, a clear, still night. Lights reflected on the black water. There was an amazing number of stars visible. When I commented on the view, she said, 'Yes, though I neglect it terribly. Too busy staring at the television. Comes with the job.'

'So, you and Naomi started off the dancing?'

'Yes, she'd got a party mix and she put it on. Jonty had speakers rigged up. I agreed to dance if she did and we got a few people up eventually.'

'Can you remember any of the music?' Music was supposed to be good for evoking memories, like smells, acting like a direct line to the part of the brain where they are stored. Maybe I could play Naomi the music?

'Ooh, a real mix, "Dancing in the Street", "Simmer Down" and that Smokey Robinson one . . .'

'"Tears of a Clown",' I suggested.

'Yes, and "Candyman". What else? Oh yes – "Jump Around", "I Got You Babe" . . .'

I recognized all the tunes she mentioned. 'Did you talk about anything in particular?'

'The job market, Alex getting his job. And Naomi told me about her interview. For a teaching assistant?'

'Yes.' I stopped writing. If they'd only left five minutes earlier or later, if she had driven just that little bit slower, she might have a job now. Lily Vasey would still be alive. Alex and Naomi might be moving into a place like this.

'And apps,' Pip said, 'for phones: what we've got, what we like. She was into Angry Birds.'

Not any more. I suspected she was not allowing herself to do anything that could be considered fun or pleasure.

'Was she drinking?'

Pip's face fell, 'Some,' she said. 'White wine.'

My stomach turned over.

'When was this? Can you remember?'

'When we were dancing. So sometime between seven and eight? Jonty said you don't know yet if she was over the limit?'

'That's right – they couldn't breathalyze her and the blood test they do takes a few weeks for them to get the results. Did she seem drunk?' I was apprehensive about the answer.

'Bit merry, perhaps. Not pissed, though.'

Sober enough to drive? 'Did you see them leave?'

'No. I'd gone to the loo, and on the way back I got talking with Jonty.'

What Pip said echoed Suzanne's account. They'd left

at eight, so Naomi hadn't had time to process anything she had been drinking. *Not pissed, though.* Was that enough? *Oh God. Please, please, not pissed.*

'I Got You Babe'. I thought about it as I drove home, I'd played it non-stop, the UB40 and Chrissie Hynde version, when Suzanne was tiny. For the next twenty-one years, Phil and I were no longer just a couple, but a family. Then Suzanne left home, followed by Naomi. I'd been anxious about how I might feel, but I didn't really suffer with empty nest syndrome when Naomi went off to uni. Yes, the house was quieter, there was an absence of interaction, a period of getting used to there only being the two of us, but my relief at her getting into university was the dominant feeling.

All the little chores felt easier too, the shopping and cooking, washing. Naomi, the girls between them, had generated a disproportionate amount of housework. With only Phil and me it was a doddle.

We began to rediscover some of the freedom we'd had before becoming parents. Spontaneity returned. We could decide to go and see a film or have a meal at the last minute, go to bed on Sunday afternoon if we fancied it, book a weekend away without having to worry.

I had more time too. I was still doing my shifts with the emergency duty team and of course I had my regular visits to Mum to fit in. But there was space in my week to take up new interests. I began to learn massage. I'd a vague idea that if social work got too grim, if I became burnt out, which I'd seen happen to many colleagues of mine, it would be useful to have some other skill. Something I could trade where I'd work for myself.

We didn't get too complacent. Naomi came back at the end of each term and her summer breaks lasted several months. Nevertheless, it was a shock to the system when she and Alex first moved in with us.

They had stayed on in Newcastle for almost a full year after graduating. She had a part-time job in a video rental shop and he was working in a bar. Then the video shop closed and they couldn't manage their rent any more.

They spoke to both Monica and then us, sounding us out. If they split their time between the houses, would we be happy for them to live with us until they found work? Well, we weren't going to say no, though I did wonder whether it might be simpler all round to just base themselves in a single place instead of toing and froing all the time.

But once they'd come back, I saw that we would have struggled to accommodate all Alex's possessions as well as Naomi's. This way, most of his stuff was at Monica's and most of Naomi's at ours. They kept their old postal addresses and we gradually got used to the situation.

Naomi had a TV in her room and they made their own food. There were some niggles: their version of tidying the kitchen after having a meal was a long way from mine. Our fuel bills leapt up; they were in much more of the daytime and there were all the extra showers and loads of washing. But we rubbed along all right and we didn't think it would be for ever.

Now for the first time I wondered whether Naomi would ever be able to build an independent life. If she did go to prison, securing work afterwards would be even harder. It was still unclear whether she'd have any long-term health issues as a result of her injuries. The biggest risk was infections; without a spleen, her immune system was compromised, and being in prison was a terrible place to be on that score.

I tried not to dwell on it, not to worry when it was all uncertain and unknown, but it was hard.

Naomi

Monica brings Alex to the hospital. She came in with him the first time, after he'd been discharged and was visiting. She was friendly and everything but sort of professional – I bet she's like that when she's dealing with her passengers. No real connection. Not that we ever did have much of one, anyway. She used to try and pass clothes on to me. I know she was being kind because Alex and I were really skint and Monica's my size. But I like boho stuff, or skate/surf-type clothes. There are little stalls in town where you can get recycled clothes and I like some of those. She wears completely different things, smart and tailored. At first I just used to thank her and put the things in my drawers, but then one time, when she had a roll-neck mustard sweater and a tweed pencil skirt, I said, 'Aw, thanks, but I'm not sure they're really me. I could take them to the charity shop unless there's anyone else you know who would like them.' I was blushing like mad; I really didn't want to upset her, but I had to find a way to stop her doing it. Because sooner or later she'd see I wasn't wearing any of it.

'If you really don't want them . . .' she said.

My cheeks were on fire. 'No, sorry, thanks, but . . .' I said in a rush.

'I've a friend might like them,' she said. And she smiled.

We left it at that. It felt awkward but I think it was better than never saying anything.

Alex is her only child and there's probably no woman out there who's good enough for him. But I bet she'd rather he found some clever lady lawyer to date instead of the no-hoper who totalled her son's car, broke his bones and killed a little kid.

It's getting so I dread his visits, because it's like this massive reminder of the mess I am in, the terrible thing I've done, the thing we can't talk about because what is there to say? And so we talk about stuff that means nothing. Each time he goes, there are angry red arcs on my palms where I've dug my nails in.

How long will it take for him to come to his senses, to go off me? To realize that I can't be cheered up? That I'm hard work and could get harder? That I might be left with health problems as well as a criminal record? He won't dump me, you see – he's loyal. He feels sorry for me, he wants to show he forgives me for the accident, for the nightmare I set in motion. But I don't want any of that. I haven't earned it. I don't want him visiting me in prison.

And if he won't leave me, then I'll have to leave him.

He's talking about our friends Becky and Steve, who are planning a wedding and can't agree on a venue. I cut across him, interrupt, no preamble or anything, straight to the bone. 'I don't think we should carry on.'

He's confused, a half-smile flickering around his lips, and I put him straight, stop him trying to find a way to reinterpret my statement: 'We should stop seeing each other.'

His eyes cloud over and for a second his mouth hangs open. He never expected this. My heart goes out to him and I'm close to back-pedalling. I love him so. Maybe there is a way to work it out?

My toes are curled rigid under the sheet, my spine set. I must not cry; no weakness or he might talk me round. 'I'm sorry,' I say quietly, 'I can't go on any more.'

Something flickers through his eyes; it takes me a moment to work it out, but it's relief. He's glad! Deep down he wants this. I'm letting him off the hook and he can taste the sweet release of it. The freedom, the fresh start. As quickly as it came, the hint of relief vanishes and his eyes glitter. 'Why?' he says, his voice wobbling.

'Everything that's happened . . . it's never going to be the same now and it's no good like this.' I plaster my tongue hard against the roof of my mouth to stop any tears arriving.

Alex wipes his face with his hand, gives a sigh. He doesn't know what to say. Not that he needs to say anything. He just needs to go.

'Please,' he begs. The blood has drained from his face and he looks frightened. 'Don't.'

I sniff hard. I feel lousy, I'm shaking and I can't get it under control. 'It's what I want. I don't want to be with you any more. I'm sorry.' The sentiment is brutal and he whips his head away, his throat tensing, his hands balled. I pray he won't argue, or declare his love or propose marriage or make any other attempt to save the relationship.

Memories we shared, moments of connection, my love for him hover on the sidelines, just out of view, and I keep them at bay. Trapped behind the fences in my heart.

He swallows and gets up. I can't watch. I listen to his footsteps on the hard floor, to the sigh and thud of the ward door as he leaves.

When I am sure he's gone, I let go. Pulling the sheet over my head and weeping silently so no one will say anything. Already I ache for him, for the time we had and for the future we won't share. But I have only myself to blame.

CHAPTER FIFTEEN

Carmel

One afternoon when I visited, I could see something was up. Naomi's eyes were pink. She had been crying. I was allowed to wheel her to the canteen. She was desperate for a change of scene, a few minutes away from the ward. She said she wanted to go home, when could she go home? I promised to ask and add my voice to hers. In the canteen she stirred sugar into her tea, round and round, as though she was trying to drill through the bottom of the cup. I reached out my hand to rest on hers. She gave a small shrug of her shoulders, put the spoon on the saucer by the used tea bag.

'I've broken up with Alex.' She blurted it out.

'No!' My heart kicked with the shock. 'But why? What—'

'It won't work, Mum. Not after all this.'

'You still love him?' I tried to grasp where this had come from, what her reasons were.

'Of course.' She fought tears, concentrating on the spoon, mashing it into the tea bag, dark orange liquid seeping out and circling the saucer. 'But I can't face him. This is so awful. It's spoiled everything.'

'But if you love him . . .' I said lamely. 'If he loves you . . . I know it's hard, but together . . .'

She shook her head, her nose reddening and a tear falling on to the table. She wiped her eyes with her fingers.

'Have you told him? What did he say?'

'He was really upset,' she said. 'He was gutted.' She looked at me, her face crumpling.

'Oh darling,' I moved to sit closer and held her. She was stiff, even with the release of tears, her back and shoulders tense. After a few moments, I let her go, found some tissues in my pocket.

'I can see why you might feel like ending it with him, but you've been through a terrible thing, it's not a good time to be making big decisions. Not when you're at your lowest. And if you still love each other . . .'

'That's not enough, though,' she cried. 'I look at him and see his arm and leg in plaster, and then there's the little girl. That's all I think about when I see him – nothing else . . .' She broke off.

I was so saddened at her decision. She was cutting off one of the few people she loved who could have supported her through the days to come. They had been such a perfect fit.

'I hope you'll change your mind,' I said eventually.

'I won't,' she said.

'I think you're wrong, I think you're making a mistake.'

'Another one?' she said harshly.

'Just don't write it off, the relationship; you might feel very different in six months' time.'

'I could be in prison,' she said.

'I hope not,' I said. 'Don will do everything he can to try and make sure that doesn't happen.'

'Alex should just get on with his life.' Her breathing was fractured, the words coming out one at a time.

I felt she was being destructive, punishing herself, but she was in no mood to listen to me.

The news troubled me for the rest of the day. Phil too was disappointed to hear it. 'You're joking!' he said. 'I thought they'd make a go of it.'

'He saved her life,' I said. 'How's he going to feel now?'

'I guess something like this – it changes things,' Phil said.

'Yes, but it's too soon to really see how. Okay, in a year's time it might be clearer: are they still in love, are they still happy, has it driven a wedge between them? But she's not even giving it a chance.'

'If she thinks it's the right thing to do . . .'

'She's not thinking straight,' I told him.

'It's her life, you have to let her get on with it. You can't interfere,' he said.

'I know.'

But I did.

Monica answered the door. 'Hello,' she said coolly, no smile. Probably as upset as I was that Naomi was ditching Alex.

'I've got some of Alex's things, clothes and trainers. And I was hoping to have a word with him.'

'He's not here,' she said.

'Oh.' I hovered on the doorstep. There was a soft grey rain falling, which brought out the scent of the roses in her front garden and the tarmac on the path.

'When will he be back?'

'I don't know.'

'Right.' I handed her the bag. She took it and clutched it to her chest defensively. She didn't invite me in.

She's a striking-looking woman: the green eyes that Alex has inherited, a deep golden tan, sun-streaked hair. She was wearing make-up, carefully done, but still she looked tired.

'Did he tell you Naomi had broken up with him?'

'Yes,' she said. That was it. *Yes.* No elaboration.

She wasn't making it easy for me, but I ploughed on.

'That's why I'm here. I wanted to tell Alex that I think she's making a mistake. With everything that's happened, the state she's in, she can't see sense. She still loves him, she's told me that.'

'I think it's for the best,' Monica said quickly, a flare of red blotching her neck. Had I misheard? 'She could have killed him, killed them all, not just . . .' Her eyes were simmering with heat. She was furious.

'It was an accident,' I said, trembling. 'She's never done anything like this before.'

She stepped back, shaking her head, her lips clenched in a bitter line. Preparing to close the door.

'She didn't do it on purpose,' I said. 'Please tell Alex—'

'Alex told me she was thrown out of sixth-form college for drinking. If she was drunk, that explains a lot, doesn't it?' She shut the door.

A flash of temper forked through me, sharp as lightning. I wanted to kick the door down. Shake her till she understood.

I wrote a note to Alex while I was at work that evening. Explaining my fears and asking him not to assume that there was no chance for reconciliation. Telling him that Naomi still loved him and that perhaps in time, if he felt the same, they could try again. I didn't talk about the accident or blame or the police or any of that. But I said I was really sorry about all that had happened and thanked him again for saving her life. I posted it first class so he would get it the following day.

I never told Naomi or Phil that I'd sent it, but I did tell Evie, who said she'd probably have done the same.

Naomi

As Mum talks, I imagine it as a movie. Me in my blue dress and spotted shoes in the garden. Some of the background I can fill in from the photos she's printed out – like where they'd put the buffet in the shade under the canopy and where the chairs were, the faces of the people I talked to.

'Straight after you arrived, Alex opened the champagne,' she says. 'You made a toast. After that you cuddled Ollie.' She hands me the picture of us together. 'Then you had something to eat. Francine, this woman with Suzanne,' another photo, 'had just bought a flat in town, so you discussed the pros and cons of being in the middle of things. There was a girl there called Stella, she had a poncho on, one of those floaty ones, and she asked you about clubs in Manchester . . .'

As she talks, I wait for a prick of familiarity, for some word or phrase or image to puncture a way through to my memories. To tear through the screen and let them all come spilling out.

'. . . You had a tuna kebab. That was just after we left, and you talked to Gordy about Newcastle,' she says. 'His daughter's thinking of applying to uni there. There was a little boy, a toddler in dungarees called Adam; you read him a book on the swing seat. And you helped get the Chinese lanterns ready; that was just before seven. Pip, she's the one from London who works with Jonty, discussed phone apps, and when you put the music on, she danced with you.'

I wait and listen, but the words have no resonance; there's no echo in my head, no spark or tingle.

'Pip said you drank some wine around then.'

I swallow. Mum's told me that Suzanne reckons I was drinking a lot, but Alex says different. It's something else

159

I can't recall. But I can't imagine getting drunk and driving the Honda. I never drive when I've been on the booze.

'I've not been able to find anyone who saw you leaving,' Mum says, 'but you waved goodbye to Suzanne at about eight. She was inside then; only a handful of people were left.'

Mum stops and looks at me. When I shake my head, I see her shoulders dip in disappointment. But she rallies and touches my arm. 'Give it time, darling. After all, you've had a little bit come back; maybe it'll be a gradual thing. You can always try listening to the playlist.'

'Yes.' I try to sound positive.

When she's gone, I go through the photographs again, try and knit the pictures to the stories Mum has brought. Perhaps if I keep looking, keep trying, something will happen.

The brain can repair itself, I've read that; pathways are made in other areas when there is damage. I just have to keep trying. Find something more than that kiss and the buffet and Lily's red dress and the sound of the collision.

Carmel

Six weeks after the accident, Naomi was discharged from hospital. She was still convalescing, with a range of outpatient appointments to attend in the future. She was not supposed to lift anything heavy, no manual labour, no driving. She slid her eyes sideways and gave a sad little snort when the nurse said that.

I was on tenterhooks as I drove her home, anticipating that the experience of being in a car again, the motion, the noise, the smell of the interior might be the key that would unlock her memory. But she sat passive and silent all the way home. She looked washed out, her hair greasy, the layers grown out, her dark blue eyes ringed with deep shadows, the scar on her cheekbone a patch of puckered, shiny red skin.

I had cleaned her room up, asking her what she wanted to do with the photographs on her wall – mostly of herself and Alex. She asked me to take them down. Any attempt I made to talk about him, she stopped me dead.

Naomi

'I want you to take me to Suzanne's, drive me home, past where we crashed.'

Mum looks alarmed. 'Are you sure?'

I feel a bit wobbly about it, to be honest, but I won't let that put me off. 'Yes.'

'I've got the dentist now . . .' she begins.

'Not now,' I say, 'later. After tea.' A similar time of day to when it happened – part of me thinks that might increase the chances of it working. The weather's different today, though, dull and overcast and warm. No sunshine.

I have to remember! Mum's been bringing me morsels of information like a cat bringing dead birds into the house. I know she's been trying her best, doing what she can, but it's not enough.

Dad offers to come too, but I tell him it's okay. The prospect of me freaking out is at the back of my mind, and they don't both need to see that.

'Don't tell Suzanne,' I say to Mum.

'Okay, but if she sees us . . . ?'

'Only then.' I can imagine her mocking me, and I don't want to be distracted by that. Her default setting is

161

finding fault; she always looks for the negative. It drives me mad. I don't know how Jonty stands it.

When we set off, I think Mum's as nervous as I am. She talks too much when she's anxious. She's going on about the dentist, how much the treatment costs, but eventually she shuts up.

Of course we have to drive past where it happened to reach Suzanne's, so I try to recall Alex and me in the Honda on the way to the barbecue. I know we took champagne. Alex told me we bought it from Safeway. I know from what Mum's said that we arrived at four. But nothing emerges. The only memories I have from immediately before we got there are Alex breaking the news when we were at home and me jumping at him, and then the kiss at the side of Suzanne's house.

My stomach swoops when we get to Mottram Lane and drive past the school, but the images in my head are the second-hand ones I've been given. I try not to get too disappointed and tell myself it might be different coming in the other direction.

The sky is still clouded over and there's a sewagey smell in the air. Lots of the houses have Union Jack flags flying high for the Queen's Jubilee. Becky and Steve went to a street party; his mum's a keen royalist, apparently. My folks are the opposite. When they were still at school, it was the Silver Jubilee, and the Sex Pistols were at number one with 'God Save the Queen' and it was banned from the airwaves.

At Suzanne's street, Mum does a three-point turn and stops. 'This is where you were parked,' she says. 'We saw your car when we were leaving.'

I nod. I close my eyes to see if that helps and run through the sequence Mum has discovered: handing out champagne, cuddling Ollie on the swing seat, eating, talking to Julia about festivals, taking photographs on

Jonty's camera, the conversation with Gordy, reading to Adam, the Chinese lanterns, dancing with Pip.

'Okay.' I clear my throat, nod to Mum that we should set off.

She drives to the dual carriageway and along to the junction with Mottram Lane. The lights are red. My knees are pressed tightly together, my hands between them. There's a sickly taste in my mouth. A magpie pecks at something at the side of the road. I look away.

The lights change and Mum turns right. I try to relax, to let my body settle and my mind loosen so I'm more open to the chance of remembering. It's not easy, though; my back is stiff and my guts are knotted up still.

Mum drives slowly to the bend; there are no cars behind us. 'This is where you went too fast,' she says, 'and here,' as we round the first curve of the bend, 'is where you swerved back in.'

I imagine it. That's all I do.

I see the railings by the river on the left and the bushes and trees there, the school over to the right. The glimpse of red, Lily's dress, the thump and screech; they fit here but that is still all I have. Free-floating elements, isolated and incomplete.

'Can you stop?'

'Hang on.' She drives a little further until we are on the straight stretch and parks at the side of the road.

'I'm going to get out,' I say.

She nods.

'I won't be long.'

A couple of cars drive past as I walk along the pavement back to where it joins the grass verge on the bend. I'm still using a stick to take the stress off my ankle. I walk across the grass to where the railings are broken. Alex said they smashed through the rear windscreen. The trees are blackened, fire-damaged. On the ground, new shoots of green have grown up through the scorched grass. This is where we ended up, hanging upside down, rammed against the railings. I look over towards the school. Lily's body landed somewhere in the middle of the road. I try to picture her in different poses, on her back or curled in a ball. Here Alex pulled me out. Here he called the ambulance. Here Lily died and my heart stopped too. But I was lucky. Tears sting the back of my eyes. Why, why can't I fucking remember?

I see Mum coming.

'Anything?'

Shake my head.

'Lie down,' she says, 'if you can manage it.'

Oh God.

'Try it. You never know.'

And I do, with her help. Because I'll try anything that might work. I lie on the grass after checking it for dog dirt and shut my eyes. I can hear birds somewhere, chirping, and traffic, and an ice cream van's chimes suddenly cut out. I hold the red in my mind for a few moments. Then I think about the thumps and the screech.

Another car goes past fast, rap music pulsing out for a couple of seconds.

I open my eyes and see the shattered branches of the burnt trees reaching towards the vast sky. The sky is grey, blank like my memory.

I lift my arm and she helps me up. I brush the bits of twigs and cinders off me. My throat aches, a tight ring of frustration.

I don't want to cry, and try not to, but tears run down my face anyway.

I'm so sorry, I think; I wish I could just go and tell them. Over and over and over again. Find a way to show them how dreadfully, dreadfully sorry I am.

Mum hugs me and we walk back to the car.

I'm not going to give up, I'm not going to stop trying. I'll try hypnosis –anything else I can find that might help.

I owe it to them, to Lily's family. The loss of memory makes me feel like I'm hiding from what happened. I don't want to do that. I want to take responsibility and remember every fucking second and every detail. I want to remember it every second of every day for the rest of my life. I want to be unable to forget it.

That's what I deserve. I have to find a way to make it happen.

We're finishing lunch the next day and Mum is asking me if there's anything I want to do in the afternoon when the doorbell rings. It's the police. Come to arrest me.

I freeze, outwardly numb but my mind shrieking with fear. I don't want to go to the police station. Of course, I have no choice.

Mum's saying how they'll get Don, telling them I have a solicitor. And then we're going. My legs tremble as we walk to their car and there's a roaring sound in my head.

At the police station I'm taken to the custody suite and have to answer questions about who I am and my health; they take my fingerprints and a mouth swab. They ask me to hand over my phone and keys and everything in my pockets. They want my belt, and my necklace too.

They lock me up. A cell with a hard bench and nothing else. Graffiti scratched into the walls. With what? Fingernails? It smells like disinfectant and something else, something cheesy. I'm cold but I'm sweating too, I can smell it. I want to wee but I don't know if I'm allowed to or how to ask someone. If I'm supposed to call out or what.

It's hard to judge how much later a police officer

unlocks the door and says, 'Your solicitor's here. Come this way.' I do as I'm told.

I nearly cry when I see Don. He's got me a drink of tea in a paper cup. He arranges for me to go to the ladies' – a police officer waits for me in the corridor outside.

'I've spoken with the police,' Don says, 'and they want to interview you on suspicion of causing death by dangerous driving. You understand?'

I nod. My heart contracts.

'They've got the blood alcohol results from when you were admitted to hospital.'

I can hear a rushing sound in my head, and from his expression I can see it's bad news. *Please, no!*

'You were almost one and a half times the legal limit for driving.'

It's like the ground's opened up beneath me and I'm plunging straight down. *Oh God, no!* How could I have done that? I can't believe it. What the hell was I playing at?

I can't talk; I'll just blub if I try.

'Still no recall?' he checks.

I shake my head, my mouth all wobbly.

'Right.' He picks up his iPad. 'There's nothing to be gained by sticking you in an interview where all you can say is "I can't remember", so I'd advise you to offer a prepared statement. Yes?'

When I agree, he goes on, 'All we need is to explain to them that you've no memory of the accident and the hours preceding it.'

He helps me word the statement, keeping it short and to the point.

Then I have to go back in the cell again.

Eventually they come for me, and they read the charge. I try not to cry. I will be released on bail, to appear at the magistrates' court in a few days' time. At the custody desk I get my things back and have to sign some forms, and then Don takes me home.

It's official. It's not going to go away or get forgotten about. I'm not going to wake up and laugh about it. I feel so dirty. So rotten. To the core.

CHAPTER SIXTEEN

Carmel

Naomi had been petrified, monosyllabic before they took her away. Her face, already pale from being inside so much, was now white as chalk. Don met us at the police station. We weren't allowed beyond the front desk. They took her down to the custody suite. My work had brought me to police stations on several occasions. I knew the drill. But the fact that this was my daughter being booked in put a completely different slant on it. Phil had closed the shop and come to be with me. We were grateful to see Don, to have someone take charge.

'I'll have a pre-interview meeting with the police first,' he said. 'They are aiming to talk to her on suspicion of causing death by dangerous driving and they have the blood alcohol results.'

I swallowed, watching Don's lips, trying to second-guess what he'd say. Wanting the result to be negligible, below the limit, to exonerate Naomi, lift the cloud. To demonstrate that it was an accident, nothing more. Her greatest sin taking the corner too fast. An accident, pure and simple. If she had been drinking, the purity vanished, didn't it?

'She was over the limit.'

My heart swooped. *Please no. No.* The hope melted away. I felt everything get darker.

'They'll tell me what they've got – the bare bones. Then I'll see Naomi, advise her and take it from there. We could be a couple of hours. I can ring you?'

We hesitated, but he encouraged us to go. 'There's nothing you can do here,' he said.

Phil was too strung out to go back to work, and my shift didn't start until four. I rang Suzanne and we went over there.

'Alex told us she was fine,' I said to Phil when we were on our way. 'Oh, Phil. Perhaps she's got a drink problem? With all that stuff in college and now this. She could have been hiding it from us. From all of us.'

'She hasn't the money to drink all that much. We'd have noticed. We'd have seen the evidence, smelled it on her. It's more likely she just made a serious misjudgement, thinking she could drive having had more than she intended.'

Back then, when she had been drinking in college, I'd tried to work out whether we'd contributed to her unhealthy use of alcohol. Had we not sent clear enough messages, been too tolerant of stories about drunken folly or set a bad example? Alcoholism runs in families, but there'd been none of that as far as I knew in either Phil's or mine. We didn't drink to excess, we didn't drink every day, but booze was a pleasure and part of our socializing.

'Suzanne was right,' I said. Oh God. I could feel a band of tension around my skull, and my eyes ached. 'What's going to happen, Phil? If she's convicted?' I thought of the prisons I knew, of how grim life was inside them. 'The drink – that'll add to any jail term.'

Why? demanded a voice in my head; *why, why, why?* Why had she been so stupid? To risk everything, to take a life for the sake of a couple of drinks.

We were all subdued, our talk desultory as we wandered around the country park near Suzanne's house, taking turns to push Ollie in his pram. Suzanne hadn't said much when I told her she'd been right about

Naomi drinking, that she was over the limit. Just dipped her head once in acknowledgement, drew in her lips in a little moue of disapproval. I was glad she hadn't launched into any attack or analysis; I don't think I could have stood it.

The time stretched out, painfully slow. Phil kept checking his phone as if we'd not all hear it when it rang. Back at Suzanne's we had a cuppa and some fancy ginger cake she'd bought, and Phil's phone finally went off, making me jump, splashing some of my drink over the side of the cup.

Phil answered, listened. I saw a spasm of disappointment tighten his face, and then he said, 'We'll see you there.' He put his phone down. 'They've charged her, causing death by dangerous driving.' He cleared his throat. 'Released her on bail. They're going back to the house now.'

'Oh God,' Suzanne sighed, and fetched a cloth to mop up my spill.

I got up. There was a roiling sensation in my stomach.

As we reached Mottram Lane, it was afternoon break and the children were running around in the school playground, busy knots of them in powder-blue uniforms.

Charged and released on bail. Words that I'd never imagined hearing in connection with one of my kids.

We reached home at the same time as they did. Phil made tea; we were drinking an inordinate amount of tea. I had switched from coffee not long after the accident when I found myself speeding and jittery and having trouble sleeping.

'The basis of their case against Naomi is Alex's eyewitness statement,' Don said, 'in which he describes her as driving too quickly and losing control of the car.

They also have statements from other witnesses who saw Naomi drinking at the party.' *Suzanne would be one of them.* 'And the results of a blood alcohol test. Naomi had one hundred and fifteen milligrams of alcohol per hundred millilitres of blood – the limit is eighty, so she was almost one and a half times the limit.'

I saw Naomi set her jaw, head down, staring at her hands.

'That doesn't alter the charge,' Don explained. 'It will be taken into account for sentencing, but I hope we will not reach that point. We gave the police a prepared statement explaining Naomi's persistent amnesia. We go to the magistrates' court sometime in the next couple of weeks, but that will simply be adjourned. The prosecution need time to get all the committal papers together. The committal hearing at the magistrates' is usually within four to eight weeks after the preliminary hearing. If you know all this, with your job, stop me . . .' Don looked at me.

'Some,' I said.

'But it's all new to me,' Phil said, 'and Naomi.'

'Their case rests on Alex's account, but I don't know that there's anything in there that *proves*,' and he stressed the word, 'dangerous rather than careless driving. The amnesia means it isn't an easy case to fight, but I'd argue it's not an easy case to prove, either. I'd be very hopeful of being able to reduce the severity of the charge or even get a not guilty result. Though there are no guarantees.' His confidence was a lifebelt to cling to.

'There'll be a jury?' Naomi asked quietly.

'That's right.'

'Will Naomi be cross-examined?' I said.

'It's up to us in consultation with the barrister who will take the case – I've someone in mind for this, he's excellent. But given that she has no recollection of the

171

incident, I can't see that there's anything to gain from putting her on the stand.'

'What if they think she's faking it, the jury?' I said. 'If she just doesn't say anything, won't it look bad?' Naomi's amnesia might be seen as very convenient. A deeper, more elaborate version of the replies used by defendants when they don't want to admit culpability or incriminate themselves. *Did you attack first? Can't remember. Did you use a knife? Can't remember. Did you shake your child? Can't remember.*

'The judge must instruct them that nothing adverse can be inferred from her not taking the stand,' Don said.

But they're only human – they're bound to think less of her, surely? I thought.

Don went on, 'As for the amnesia, we will get expert testimony to speak about this as a medical condition.'

'We know she's not making it up,' Phil said. 'We just have to make it clear to them that she's honest.'

'If they don't hear from her, how can they see what sort of person she is?' I asked.

Don nodded. 'We'll be calling witnesses to testify to Naomi's good character, her previous good record and so on. People who will describe her as a diligent driver, a responsible citizen.'

Naomi shuffled at this, a little awkwardly.

Naomi

'Alex said I was okay to drive.' I am still muddled, finding it hard to keep up with the discussion.

'Well, there are two possibilities,' Mum says. 'Either you managed to act like you were sober and Alex never gave it a second thought, or . . .' She hesitated.

'Or what?' I say.

'Or he got in the car knowing you'd been drinking and took a chance, and then he lied about it.'

'Why would he lie?' I say.

'To protect you, hoping no one would know you'd been drinking, that you'd not actually be over the limit.'

'Or to protect himself,' Dad says. 'Passengers can be charged for that, can't they?' He looks at Don.

'Yes, he could have been prosecuted if he knowingly got in the car with a drunk driver,' Don says.

'He wouldn't have done that,' I say. 'He wouldn't risk it, not when he's going into the law.'

'So you put on a good act, then,' Mum says.

A wave of anger pours through me, anger at myself. 'Why can't I remember?' I hit the table and put my head in my hands. Why did I do it? 'I wish . . .' Oh God. There are too many things to wish for. A whole world of them. 'Will you ask him?' I say to Don. 'Is that part of what you'll be doing?'

'Yes, if not before the trial then once he's on the witness stand. Because if he knew you were drunk, then he is partly culpable: why didn't he dissuade you from driving? Did he actively encourage you? At the committal hearing we'll get the whole case file from the prosecution, so at that stage we'll be looking at where to direct our efforts in building a defence. There's no point in doing anything very much until we know exactly what they've got both from the witnesses and from experts, forensics and so on.'

Whether Alex knew I had been drinking or not, whether he lied to protect me or lied to protect himself for not having the sense to stop me doesn't really matter compared to the fact that I was drunk and I was driving. Whatever Alex did or didn't do, I'm the stupid fucker who kept on drinking and then took the wheel. How could I? How could I be so stupid? Why? We could have gone out and got drunk later if it was about celebrating his job. We could have gone to the pub, or bought something to have at home, or gone clubbing even. Why couldn't I just wait? I am so angry at myself, and not being able to remember the horrible sequence of events, not being able to relive it, leaves me feeling helpless and half mad.

It's like a storm building inside my skull with nowhere for it to escape. When I finally go upstairs, I thump the bed again and again, cursing myself. Ignoring the physical pain. Full of fury and shame.

Carmel

I rang Suzanne and gave her a quick summary. Then tried to change the subject, invited her to tea one day to suit her. Determined to maintain some semblance of normality.

'I can't do it,' she said. A peculiar tone in her voice.

'What? What's wrong?' Ollie? *Can't* wasn't in her vocabulary.

'Play happy families, pretend everything's all right after what she's done.'

My cheeks burned in a sudden wash of resentment. 'Nobody's pretending anything. I'm coming over.'

'There's no need,' she said.

'Suzanne, we need to talk about this properly,' I said firmly. 'I won't be long.'

Ollie lay on a cotton baby blanket on the living room floor. Eyes alert, darting here and there, then stopping to drink in some fascinating object. She had dressed him in a navy and cream all-in-one.

I knelt down to greet him, feeling a warmth that hadn't been there before I laid eyes on him. He stiffened with excitement, his eyes gleaming, then waved his feet round, dancing as I made baby noises and told him what a wonderful creature he was.

Suzanne was a little guarded, sitting at the table. When I joined her, I didn't need to start the ball rolling. She kicked it straight at me. 'I don't want to see her.'

'She's your sister.'

'And she's done something unforgivable. Which she won't even own up to.'

'Don't be stupid!' My voice rose dangerously. 'How on earth can she own up to something she can't remember?'

'Yes, that's a great get-out, that is.'

My look must have penetrated, because she hesitated, gave a little toss of her head, as though she was on the defensive, then said, 'She got drunk and she killed a child. And I look at Ollie and—'

'Don't you think she's being punished enough? She's being taken to court, her relationship's over, her health . . . well, God knows . . . She might end up in jail. The law is punishing her and we don't need to.'

'When I see her . . . when I look at her . . .' Suzanne spoke very precisely, her palms together, fingers pointed at me, resting on the table, moving up and down to the rhythm of what she was saying, 'I'm just so angry, like I want to hurt her. I don't like being put in that position, and I won't do it,' she said tightly.

'She's your sister, we're all she's got.'

'*You're* all she's got.'

'Suzanne, please.'

She stood up abruptly. 'No,' she said. Ollie began to whimper.

'People ignore us in the street. We've enough enemies.'

'I don't want to see her and I don't want her here.'

'That is so hard.' I wanted to weep. 'Have you any idea what this will do to her?'

'She should have thought of that before she drove the car.' Suzanne crouched to pick Ollie up. 'You can make all the excuses you like.'

'And Ollie? Does she get to see her nephew in this brave new world of yours?' I wish I hadn't said the last part, but I was shivering with rage by then, close to losing control.

'I don't know,' she said.

'Oh, Suzanne.'

'You and Dad can always come here, if you like.'

I knew I was going to cry then, and I didn't want to do it in front of her, have her accuse me of emotional blackmail or whatever into the bargain. 'Right,' I managed, 'I'll go then.'

'I'm sorry,' she said at the door, but her expression was defiant, not sorrowful.

'Yes,' I said. My throat was dry and swollen; there was terrible pressure behind my breastbone.

I'd hoped things would improve between Suzanne and Naomi once they were grown up and independent. In fact I'd dared to believe they had, especially when Suzanne asked Naomi to be her bridesmaid and Naomi agreed.

When they were little, I'd often pick over their antagonism and rivalry with Phil, with my mother, with Evie, with anyone who'd listen. Was it normal for siblings to be so at loggerheads? Was it because they were girls? Because they were so close in age? What were we doing wrong? How could we reduce the animosity, the incessant squabbling and tears.

We tried various tactics: praising good behaviour, rewarding cooperation, striving to be consistent in how we dealt with their shouting and fighting. We organized it so they could have time with us apart from each other, when they'd enjoy our undivided attention. There was no dramatic improvement.

I could see that as the older child Suzanne was naturally jealous when Naomi came on the scene. But it seemed ridiculous that she'd let that colour the rest of her life. She clearly resented the attention Naomi got through her bad behaviour in those teenage years. But still to maintain that position seemed so churlish. Had I contributed to the dynamic? Reinforced it? Even now, in supporting Naomi as best I could, did Suzanne see that as me taking sides? She was a grown woman; surely she was mature enough to distinguish between support and approval? To understand that trying to help Naomi through the mess she was in was not acting to spite Suzanne. None of it was about Suzanne. Maybe that was the problem.

I drove the car out of their cul-de-sac and then pulled up at the side of the next road to cry. How on earth would Naomi weather this on top of everything else? I felt so sad, deeply sad, like something had been taken from me, leaving me aching and hollow.

CHAPTER SEVENTEEN

Naomi

At the magistrates' court, Don talks me through the papers, the advance information from the prosecution. I see Alex's signature on his statement and I think how I miss him, his company and humour and waking up with him. All that love and excitement we shared, just snuffed out. But I still think I did the right thing.

There are other statements – Suzanne's, and ones from two other guests at the barbecue, neither of whom I know, and my prepared statement from the police station – as well as a summary of the accident with diagrams. And the blood alcohol results.

'No surprises here,' Don says, 'so my advice remains the same: you enter a plea of not guilty. Yes?'

'Yes.'

'Okay.' He gathers together the file. 'When you go in, you should remain standing up till you're asked to be seated.'

I hope I don't mess up.

'The only things you'll need to say are your name and address and date of birth. The rest, entering your plea, I'll do as your representative. Any questions?'

'No.'

'Anything you're not sure of you can just ask me, okay?'

I feel dizzy waiting with Mum and Dad and Don to go in. What will happen if I keel over? My face is so hot, burning up, and my mouth is dry; even when I sip water it's still dry, like it's lined with chalk.

I know that all that today is for is to send me to a higher court because the charges are too serious for the magistrates. It's a formality but it's still nerve-racking.

An usher calls me in and Don shows me the way to go and Mum and Dad sit down.

There are three magistrates, two men and a woman, and they are looking at papers, occasionally leaning over to say something to each other. Talking about me?

In the dock, I'm still hot and my pulse feels so strong it's almost like I'm growing and shrinking with each beat. Like *Alice in Wonderland* speeded up. My hearing feels muddy but I try to follow what's going on and answer, to confirm my name and address and date of birth. My voice sounds weedy, like I'm putting it on.

They ask Don if I'm ready to enter a plea. He tells them I am pleading not guilty.

Then one of the magistrates says something quickly which includes the words *adjourned* and *Crown Court*, and then I can go.

I thought the Vaseys might be there, but when I ask Don about it, he says, 'No, they'll almost definitely be at the trial and possibly the plea and case management hearing, but . . .'

I'm fixed on the word *trial*. It's definite now. I am to be tried, put on trial, sent for trial. Tried and found wanting. Could be months, he's saying, six months, maybe more.

Carmel

The magistrates' court might have simply been a matter of procedure, but for us it felt like a plunge deeper into the abyss. *This is actually happening*, I kept thinking.

I'd been in court before, supporting clients, but now

we were on the receiving end – the defendant and family. It made me feel grubby and resentful.

Naomi went to lie down when we got home; her energy levels were very depleted and I was worried about her emotionally. She seemed to be increasingly withdrawn, as though the only way she could function was to make herself as small, as absent as possible.

When she was a little girl, she loved to hide in small spaces, fold herself into a ball under the low table in the lounge, in the old ottoman where we kept soft toys, and whenever we got anything in a sizeable cardboard box she'd beg to keep it and clamber inside. Never a hint of claustrophobia. Hide and seek was one of her staple favourites for years. But those games had culminated in giggles and shrieks as she jumped out or was discovered.

Now I pictured her like a wounded animal, retreating from the world, growing quieter and smaller, the flesh shrinking on her bones until she became silent and desiccated.

I couldn't get her to eat much. She was spending a lot of time alone and in bed and I suspected depression. I tried to get her to see the family doctor, but she wouldn't even consider it.

'I don't want to; why should I?'

'You're struggling, Naomi, I think you're depressed.'

'I'm not depressed. What can the GP do anyway, stuff me with pills?'

'If they help.'

'No. I'm not going,' she said.

'Counselling, then?'

'Just forget it.'

If only she'd accept some help. Anything. And the thought came unbidden: *before she goes to prison*. The traitorous, appalling prospect growing ever larger.

I heard her crying in the night. And she seemed to find

it hard to summon interest in anything, even the fluffiest, least demanding magazine I brought home or the breeziest daytime TV shows.

I began to wonder if the trauma that had prompted Naomi's amnesia had also affected some part of the brain that influenced personality. After all, I'd seen that with my mum. The old Naomi, the slightly ditzy, funny, spontaneous girl, was now lethargic, colourless. It could be the grey fog of depression smothering her energy, but what if she never came out of it?

There had been a reporter in court and the evening paper let the world and his wife know that Naomi Baxter (25) of Northenden, Manchester, had been charged with causing death by dangerous driving in the case of Lily Vasey.

We got phone calls. People who weren't close but knew us well enough to have our phone number. Friends of friends, people who come for New Year's parties and we don't see from one year to the next or who I'd met through the massage course. They called up, to express their shock: was it really our Naomi, was there anything they could do?

I don't know what was more difficult, the twittering interest of those individuals or the shattering silence of others. The Cynthia Stillers to whom we had become pariahs to be shunned.

For a few days I fended off any queries from Naomi about seeing Suzanne, saying she had a lot on, then that Jonty was back from Aberdeen and they had plans, then that Ollie wasn't sleeping much. Not that Naomi mentioned her sister often.

It was during one of her visits to the hospital outpatient clinic, in the waiting area, that she interrupted me reading my book to say, 'I texted Suzanne, she's not replied. Is there something wrong with her phone?'

181

Oh Jesus. How to answer. There was no way to tell her without it cutting her to the quick. But I couldn't lie to her; she didn't deserve lies.

'Suzanne's upset,' I said, 'about the accident, about you driving.'

The expression on her face altered, the glower of guilt, plain as when she'd been a child caught doing something she shouldn't.

'She's finding it hard to deal with.'

'With me?' Naomi said, her voice wavering.

'Yes,' I said. 'I'm sorry.'

She bit her lip, her brow creasing. 'So she's dumped me, has she?'

I hesitated too long, framing the words, confirming her guess. When I began to try and explain, she just said, 'It doesn't matter, we were never that close anyway.'

Writing off twenty-five years of sisterhood, of shared mealtimes and holidays, of games and outings and celebrations and squabbles. Tears and kisses and secrets.

'Is that really how you feel about it?'

'Don't bother with the whole social-work bit.' She rolled her eyes.

'I'm not being a social worker, I'm your mother,' I said.

She left her chair then, ostensibly to get a cup of water but effectively ending the conversation.

I put my head in my hands, closed my eyes and tried to calm my pulse. When we got home I rang the GP. Maybe Naomi was refusing to try tablets for her troubles, but I needed something otherwise I was going to fly apart. I could feel the pressure growing inside, an explosion waiting to happen, the fuse burning, crackling, fizzing along. Saw myself, arms and legs and head shattered, flung, soaring away from each other. A crash-test dummy.

Naomi

Suzanne never forgets and she never forgives. She's got a big black book in her head and everyone's slightest misdemeanour is listed in precise detail, in permanent ink. I used to wish that once, just once, she'd mess up big time. Find out what it's really like to make a mistake, to jump the wrong way, to fail. To feel small and shabby and miserable about yourself.

I've tried so hard to impress her. Slaving for my A levels and getting good grades, sticking at the degree even though it was really tough and I often wanted to give up. But the most I ever got from her was 'Pretty good', in this *I can't quite believe it* voice, half expecting her to say that the grades were easier to get than when she sat them.

And then I couldn't get a job and we were back living at Mum's and I'd nothing to show her. Only Alex. Nothing to prove that I wasn't a slacker and a loser.

And now this.

And she's not the only one, not the most important one. How they must hate me. Lily's parents, her brothers, all the rest of her family. Hate me without even knowing me, without any idea of what I look like, or what my personality is like or what I feel about what I have done.

I can't even apologize to them, say how sorry I am, because if I did that then it would be like admitting I'm guilty, and everyone agrees that I have to plead not guilty.

Sometimes I feel like giving up and owning up, saying, 'Yes! I did it, I suddenly remember! It's all come flooding back. I was careless and I was drunk and I just never saw her, didn't realize we were so close when the bumper or the wheel or whatever hit her.' But I can't even do that because I'd be perjuring myself, you see. Because I *can't* fucking remember, so how the hell can I stand up in court and say 'x and y and z happened and I'm terribly, terribly sorry, punish me now'?

I don't think the guilt will ever go away. Even if they convict me and send me to prison. The awful leaden feeling inside, like an iron fist, cold and hard and unforgiving. Nothing can bring Lily back. There's no magic formula that can bleach away the stain of what I've done. It's only right that someone pays. If it was Ollie that had been hurt I'd want someone to pay for it. I wish there was something I could do to show them how sorry I am, how truly, truly sorry.

Becky and Steve come round. They talk about her wedding dress, then fall quiet and she looks a bit funny. She says, 'You might want to take your Facebook page down.'

Steve goes bright red, like a tomato. 'People mucking about.'

I grow cold. 'What've they done?'

'It's just juvenile,' Becky sighs, 'prats.'

'What is it?'

'There's a wreath, your name on it.'

'And comments about your driving.'

'Right.' I get my laptop then and there and go to the page. I don't want to read any of it but some of the words jump off the screen: *slapper, crazy bitch, killer.* These must be people who know me, people who are my Facebook friends.

'We could report them,' Becky says.

I shake my head. 'Not worth it.' And anyway, most people would probably agree with them.

I deactivate my account. I'm gone. Don't exist any more.

When they've left, I look on Alex's page. It says: *Status: single*. I feel like I'm trespassing. I close it down quickly. It's like I can't be part of that world any more.

Carmel

Evie came round for the evening. Naomi was up in her room, which gave me a chance to tell her about the rift between Suzanne and her sister.

Phil had been relatively sanguine about it. 'Give her time, you know Suzanne. High horse, higher principles.'

'She'll be feeling things more intensely after the baby,' Evie pointed out. 'Perhaps when things have settled down . . .'

'When have you ever known Suzanne to change her position?'

'Here.' Evie filled our glasses. 'Suppose Naomi's found not guilty? There is a chance of that?'

'According to Don, yes,' I said.

'How would Suzanne see it all then?' Evie said.

'Well, she's pedantic, so in theory she'd accept the legal arguments, but she'd probably say that morally Naomi was still guilty. She's so . . . righteous.'

'There's nothing you can do really. Just keep the channels of communication open, keep seeing her and Ollie and Jonty,' Evie said. 'What about Naomi, have any of her friends been around, been here for her?'

'Yes, Becky and Steve, they've been brilliant.' Naomi hadn't kept in close contact with many friends from schooldays, but Becky was one of them. She had gone to work in the family business after school, where she met Steve, who'd just started as their online sales manager.

'And when's she next in court?' Evie took a drink.

'Next month, for the committal hearing,' I said.

Naomi

Waking up, and the dream starts to dissolve. I try and snatch it back, catch it, cling to it. I was happy. We were in a hotel, Alex and me, a plush room and a trolley with food on it, white curtains billowing. An outside terrace, ours, with steps to the beach. Alex had been surfing, he came running up the beach and I ran to meet him and he kissed me and his lips were warm and salty. Not cold like someone fresh from the sea. And in the dream I wasn't frightened, there was no fear, no sick apprehension, no cold ball of shame in my belly. It was like Adam and Eve before the fall or something. How we used to be.

But now the dream is just an aftertaste, sweet in my mouth, making it fill with saliva, an urge to retch coming. In the toilet, I heave but nothing comes up. It happens a lot. I mentioned this at the hospital, at one of my outpatients visits, but they didn't have any theories about it. Certainly didn't think it was anything significant in comparison to all the other physical stuff I've got going on.

I know what it is.

I can't stomach myself. I make myself sick.

CHAPTER EIGHTEEN

Naomi

I go to the cemetery. It's huge. There are old graves from hundreds of years ago, and tombs too, smothered in green, some of the stones cracked and tilting.

There are roads and pathways. I don't know where to start. There is the chapel. I remember vaguely coming here when Nana Baxter died.

I follow a woman who is carrying flowers into the office building with the clock tower. I'm holding a bouquet too, brightly coloured, red and yellow and purple and white. I didn't write anything on the card. I don't want to upset anyone. I shouldn't think Lily's family would want me here. I'm sure if they saw my name on the flowers they'd tear the heads off and shred them into little bits.

In the office I give Lily's name. The woman checks on the computer and tells me it's in the section on the other side of Nell Lane, and gives me a plot number.

It's quite a walk and I'm sweating and my ankle is very sore. The trees on the way are vast and old and the air is full of flies and butterflies, and where the sun cuts through the trees, dust swirls round and round in long spirals.

There are no trees in the new bit, lots of new graves. The main road runs close by, the traffic loud and constant. My mouth is dry. I didn't think to bring any water with me.

Lily's grave has a marker but no headstone yet. I suppose they have to get it carved. There are lots of toys and flowers, cards and helium balloons that have sunk to the ground now.

There are three vases with flowers in. It's hard to find space to lay my flowers down without disturbing anything, so I put them off to one side.

There is a lovely photograph of her in the centre in a white frame. She's looking at the camera full on and laughing and she has a straw sun hat on. Perhaps it's from a holiday.

'I'm sorry,' I whisper, 'I'm so sorry. I am sorry.'

The blare of a horn from the motorway startles me and my heart jumps in my chest.

I walk back to the bus stop and go home.

'It's good you've been out,' Mum greets me when I get in.

I'm parched. I get a drink of water and gulp it down. 'I went to the grave,' I say.

She pauses. I can see she's wondering what to say; she wasn't expecting this. In the end she says, 'All right then,' and gives a nod.

They say she died instantly. That she didn't suffer. But the people left behind, the people who loved her, they must be in agony.

I keep thinking of prison, being locked up, and the sort of people who'll be in there, and the bullying. It frightens me. But everything feels scary these days. Most of all the inside of my head. I have these horrible thoughts, like a commentary scrolling on a loop, like the way on the news they have a running stream of headlines at the bottom of the screen. And it never stops and it continually distracts you from what the newsreader is saying.

My commentary goes on and on. It's even worse when I'm with other people and I'm trying to act normally but I'm worried that they can tell what I'm really thinking. And see what an awful person I am.

Like Becky and Steve come over and Becky talks about stuff at work or a band they saw or the latest on the wedding, and I look like I'm interested but in my head I'm like, *And why do you think I care? You with your happy face and your dull, pretty boyfriend and your safe little lives. Why are you here? What are you for, exactly?* Awful, nasty thoughts.

I hate myself for being like this. I am such a fake. I am full of poison. Pathetic. You think they'd have noticed by now.

My last regular visit to the surgical consultant. The person who deals with me I've never met before. They ask the usual questions and I don't have to undress or anything. I'm still losing weight but I tell them it's because I'm eating more healthy food. It's what they want to hear and it doesn't really matter. I'm still a size ten, hardly fading away. I like the thought of fading away. Nothing drastic or sudden but a slow decline. So I'd go from like I am now to slightly see-through like a ghost and then eventually drift into thin air.

The doctor says, 'And how are you in yourself?'

'Not so bad,' I lie.

In myself I am a total fuck-up.

Mum brings me tea and toast if I'm not up in the morning. She tries to talk to me, invites me to go shopping or offers to treat me to a haircut. She goes on and on, like a fish on a hook, flapping this way and that until I want to push her out of the room. Push her down the stairs. And then I feel so horrible for even thinking like that.

The only escape is sleep, but I can't sleep enough, not as much as I want to. I wake too early, still tired, when the house is cold, and I lie there trying to force myself back under, but my mind won't be quiet. Or I go to bed and lie awake for hours, the tension setting in my arms and back like concrete, my skin itching, the sheets mashed up as I toss and turn. I did try listening to music on my iPod, but so much of it makes me cry.

I miss Alex. It was the right thing to do: why should he be saddled with me after all that has happened? Besides, it could have tainted his reputation at work, too, couldn't it? Like when we first got together and I wanted to put him on my Facebook page. He was okay with that but he said if there was anything dodgy there like drunken pictures or stuff about drugs it'd be better to take it down because he has to be squeaky clean if he wants to be a solicitor. It's like those teachers who put totally inappropriate stuff up there and then their kids at school find it and they end up being disciplined or sacked or whatever. Alex needn't have worried – I'd nothing scandalous on there. But if we'd stayed together? *Status: it's complicated – partner in prison :-(*

Carmel

Naomi's behaviour was getting worse and I was more and more worried. I tried to broach it with her again. 'Evie's given me a number, someone you can talk to.'

'Mum . . .' she began to object.

'Try it, please, one session. If it's crap, you don't have to go back.'

'No,' she said. There were tears standing in her eyes, and her hand shook as she picked up her phone.

'What are you frightened of?' I asked her.

190

'I don't want to talk about it,' she shouted and walked out. I don't know if she meant she didn't want to explain her refusal to me – or that she didn't want to talk to a therapist about her feelings.

On the Saturday night, the shop alarm went off. There were sporadic outbursts of attempted break-ins; sometimes Phil'd be called out three times in a week, then things would calm down.

I always hated it when the call came. Worrying about him, what might happen if the burglars were still there. If he might be ambushed and forced to let them into the shop.

I lay awake, my mind circulating round our troubles, rolling them over in my mind like a millstone, a great lump of granite, dense, unyielding. Then I heard the sound of the car and him coming into the house. In our room, he shucked his clothes off in the dark.

'Hi,' I said quietly. 'What was it?'

I heard him expel air, then a hesitation that made my senses prick up. 'Phil?' I saw the security grilles, the windows smashed, the walls bare, stripped of guitars and saxophones and clarinets.

He grunted. 'They'd kicked the shutters enough to trigger the alarm, bent one corner.'

'They didn't get in?'

'No. Graffiti, red aerosol.'

'Great. I suppose you could paint the lot red. Would it still roll up?'

He didn't answer. The air in the room felt heavy, as if a storm was coming and the pressure had surged. I switched on my bedside light. He winced in the glare, stretched his neck as though trying to ease the exhaustion. He said in a tired voice, 'They'd written: *Guilty – rot in hell.*'

I was half a beat, half a breath behind. Naomi, a

message about Naomi; someone had made the connection between Naomi Baxter, charged with causing the death of Lily Vasey, and Baxter's the shop.

'Oh, Phil.'

He held out his hands. 'What can we do?' Climbed into bed.

The fallout was pervading everything, corrupting everything. Even the shop, a place I still thought of as a haven, a little nursery of creativity, now sullied and made dirty by association.

Phil and I made regular visits to Suzanne and Ollie, even though her moralizing stance was so hard to take. She was nearing the end of her maternity leave but faced her return to work with equanimity. They'd been viewing nurseries and interviewing nannies and I was shocked when she told us how much they'd have to pay for either. Wouldn't a childminder be cheaper and just as good?

'No,' Suzanne set me straight, 'the nurseries are better, more structure. Though if we went for a nanny we could expect her to do a little light housework too.'

'A little light housework?' Phil's lips twitched.

'Like your dad does?' I said.

A moment's levity. After a lurch of guilt, I realized it was okay, it was healthy. Whatever happened to Naomi, we had to function, to stick together and not crumble. And perhaps a little bit of normal banter was a salve for our wounds.

Naomi

It's hard to keep warm. I've moved my bed up to the radiator, and when it's on, I can lie there with my back

192

and bum pressed up against it and my skin gets hot, but it never reaches the cold, shivery core deep inside.

'Just go up to the shops,' she says, 'or round the park. Exercise will help, or I'll drive you to the gym, if you like.'

I can't face the gym.

'You need to get out.' She is really pushy.

'I'm fine.'

'You're not. Are you frightened of going out?'

She thinks I'm becoming agoraphobic. 'No,' I tell her quickly, so then I sort of have to prove it. 'I'll go to the park,' I say. 'Satisfied?'

She gives me a cross look. I can tell she'd like to shout at me for being awkward, but she holds back. 'I can come with you if you like,' she says.

I shake my head.

It's horrible outside. The sky's a shitty grey and there's a wind blowing and it's spitting rain and there's dog shit on the pavement. At least I don't see anyone I know, and the old man I pass ignores me. At the park the ducks are all noisy, swiping at each other with their beaks and squawking. The pond has scum on top and by the railings some crows are pecking at a piece of meat. Who feeds meat to ducks? Then as I get closer the crows fly up, flapping their wings, making me start, and I see it's a cat, torn apart, its guts like revolting sausages and its teeth bared so it looks like it's yowling. Sickening.

I go straight home, but I wait in the garden for a while so Mum will assume I've been out longer.

I can't stop thinking about the cat. It's like I was meant to find it. A message for me.

Carmel

My mother sits off to one side in the lounge, away from the row of high-backed chairs, as she no longer watches television and her interaction with the other residents and staff is minimal.

In the early days we used to visit in her bedroom and have some privacy, but as her mobility deteriorated along with her personality, I gave up on that. The nurses use medication to buffer her agitation and the accompanying aggression. It makes her sleepy. Now and again there'll be flashes of lucidity of a sort, when she'll wake and speak; nothing illuminating, though, more like the static of a dicky fluorescent strip light than a ray of sunshine, usually accompanied by a nasty retort.

I pulled a chair up to sit beside her and spoke in a low voice. There was nothing wrong with her hearing. 'Hello, it's Carmel, your daughter, Carmel.' I reached out and put my hand on hers. At eighty-one, her hands were lined but not deeply wrinkled, not shrivelled like those of the oldest residents.

She was dozing, her head down. I talked a little bit but she kept her eyes closed. I told her again about Ollie and her being a great-grandma. Knowing she retained no new information and had lost most of the old too.

A string of drool spooled from her chin to her arm. I took a tissue from the tray table in front of her and dabbed at her chin.

She woke, her eyes unfocused. Her hair was still done every three weeks, when a hairdresser visited, and she had a short grey bob, which suited her. The clothes hung off her now; she was steadily losing weight, indifferent to food and drink, on a special diet that included supplementary drinks expressly designed to help with that. There was one of the little bottles on the table. She could really have done with someone there to feed her more often, though I knew the staff did their best. I lifted the drink to her lips and tipped it, careful not to give her too much and risk her choking. She had two mouthfuls then stopped swallowing, letting the drink flow back down her jaw and on to her bib.

I'd brought a photograph of Ollie to give her, in a frame. Once I'd cleaned her up, I got it out and held it up for her. 'This is Ollie, Mum, your great-grandson. Suzanne's baby.' I could have been showing her a tax return form for all the interest she showed. She only spoke once while I was there. 'Hopeless,' she said bitterly. One word. I'd no idea what was hopeless: me, her, the situation, the future?

I was thankful she hadn't been nasty to me. 'Go away, vulture,' she used to say. 'You make me sick. I hate you, pathetic, disgusting.' She would pinch me, when she still had control of her movements, or stick her nails in my arm or my face, stabbing them like a fork. She was stronger then. Nowadays the drugs helped. A liquid cosh. I missed my mum. This was not her. This drooling harridan who looked at me with loathing when she looked at all. There was someone else under her skin, in her bones, in her gaze. And I wanted her dead.

I left the picture of Ollie in her room on my way out. Next to the photograph of Suzanne as a baby in my arms. Looking at that plunged me straight back there. Suzanne was born in St Mary's Hospital one blustery March night. I still find it hard to describe those early days. The elation, the worry, the exhaustion, the piercing moments of joy and fear. My breasts hard as rocks and leaking milk, the awful backache the labour left me with, as though my pelvis had been dislocated. The tiny being we'd made, with her huge wise eyes, face crumpling in hunger, the fuzz on her head pale thistledown. Raging thirst and ravenous hunger and weeping at the beauty of the way the sun sliced through the trees. Times when I wanted it all to stop for a bit, so I could rest, retreat, worn down by the incessant calls on my energy. My fingers clumsy on the tiny buttons, eyes itchy with fatigue, resentment in my own throat as her cries grew louder. The overwhelming weight of the love I had.

Later, in my working life, at the times when I had to take the weighty decision to remove a child from a family, I knew that they had experienced all that. And I understood in my bones and my blood that there is no worse thing in the world than taking a child from its mother. Except leaving it to suffer in her care.

Taken a child, that was what Naomi had done. Not with legal documents and papers outlining risk assessments and medical reports. And not to give the child a better life, a safer world, a chance to heal. There was no greater good in Naomi's story. No redemption. She had snatched the child, stolen her life, all the hope and love and promise, and condemned her parents to the hell of a future without her. To the purgatory of what might have been.

CHAPTER NINETEEN

Naomi

'You need a shower or a bath,' Mum says.

I stink. It doesn't bother me, but she's not having it.

She gets one of her tablets from the cupboard, something to help with anxiety. She makes a point of taking it in front me. I think I'm meant to learn by example, ask to see the doctor.

'I'll run it for you, if you want a bath,' she says. 'There's some smelly stuff left over from Christmas.'

'Okay, thanks.'

In my mirror I can see the scars from the operations. A line red and knotted across my belly. I'm still supposed to do physio; the instruction sheets are in one of my drawers, I think. The place on my cheekbone where it was grazed has shiny thin skin; they don't know if it will grow back properly. I may need a graft in future. I am marked. That seems fair, really. You hear about people walking away from a car crash without a scratch. But I'm well and truly scratched. Inside and out. I have no spleen. Before all this I'd no idea what a spleen did, where it was. Now I know it helps with cleaning the blood and is a major part of the immune system. They stuck me full of inoculations afterwards to stop me getting pneumonia or septicaemia or meningitis (I remember when Suzanne had meningitis, being scared she wouldn't get better). I've been advised to get a flu jab each winter. Every day for the rest of my life I'll take a low-dose antibiotic. We also have a stash of high-dose ones to be used at the first sign of fever.

The bathroom is full of steam and smells of mandarin oranges and pine leaves.

The water is milky and really hot. When I climb in, my skin prickles. I bend my knees and lie right back, my head resting on the lip of the tub.

The water covers my stomach and my breasts, slippery and so warm. I would like to melt away in it, to dissolve. To drain away down the plughole.

Sliding in further, I wet my hair and water fills my ears. There is shampoo on the side and conditioner. But this will do. I'll be clean enough to satisfy Mum.

I think of Alex, wonder how he is, what he's doing. Whether he's met someone else yet. I haven't touched myself, haven't wanted to, since the accident. It's like that part of me is dead. Another reason for breaking up with him. Like he'd want a frigid girlfriend.

There are drops on the tiles like tears, and mould along the edge of the bath, black spots on the sealant. My legs are hairy, something else I've neglected. My razor's on the shelf.

I see blood in the bath, a soupy red, and me floating, lips blue, and Mum screaming. I scramble out of the bath quickly, water slopping over the side. My heart is bumping painfully in my chest, my head giddy. Frightened at the possibility. Frightened at the temptation. It would be so easy.

She calls up to me on her way out as I'm towelling dry: 'See you later.'

She's changed my sheets, opened the window. The air is quite cold in my room. There's a vase of mini sunflowers on the desk. I start to cry. The yellow hurts my eyes. It will always feel like this, always.

I can't bear it.

Carmel

There was knocking on the door, persistent, impatient.

When I answered it a lad was there, a teenager. He was casually dressed and wasn't carrying a folder or a bag with goods for sale, or wearing any ID.

'Is Naomi here?' he said, and there was something in the quake of his voice and the brightness of his eyes that put me on alert.

'No, she's out,' I lied.

'Well, you tell her she's a fucking bitch,' he said, his face creasing and reddening, eyes blazing. 'You fucking tell her. Right? You tell her!'

I stood my ground in spite of the rush of adrenalin that prickled my skin.

'And who are you?' I said as levelly as I could.

'Robin Vasey.'

Lily's brother. 'Robin,' I said. 'I'm so sorry—'

'Don't fucking bother.' He jabbed his finger my way. 'It's too late, it's too late. That fucking bitch—'

'Mum?' Naomi called from the hall.

'Go in, go upstairs!'

Naomi

He's shouting and Mum's telling me to go upstairs but my feet are glued to the floor, fused to the ground. My legs won't move.

Hot shame floods through me and the pressure is back, the heavy weight, something lodged over my heart, squeezing and pressing. A cloying taste as saliva bathes my mouth.

His face is all screwed up and bits of spit fly out when

he yells, and I wonder if he'll hit me, if he'll push past Mum and thump me.

I think that would be right.

He keeps jabbing his hand at me, pointing, accusing, looking past Mum. All the dirty names, raining like stones: *bitch, cow, slag.*

He's boiling over with rage, like he'll explode.

Mum is trying to talk and calm him down, but he just keeps shouting.

I feel dizzy, like I'm going to fall over, then he turns and walks away a few steps and runs back again. 'You're dead,' he shouts at me. 'You're fucking dead.' And he picks up one of the big white cobbles at the edge of the drive and hurls it at the house and runs. I can't see it hit from where I am, but there's a clang as it strikes the lounge window, no smashing sound, and then I see it roll on to the path.

I wish he'd broken the glass.

Carmel

My legs were weak. I shut the door and said, 'Ignore him, he's upset.'

'He's right, isn't he? That's what people think.' Naomi went upstairs, despite my calling her back. I sat down, waiting for my heart to stop racing.

Lily's brother. The poor kid. He'd have looked us up in the phone book probably, trudged around the houses where Baxters were listed until he found the right one. Full of rage and hot grief and missing his little sister. Screwed his courage to knock each time. To ask his question. Deliver his message. Was it him who daubed the shop?

Phil wanted to tell the police, but I talked him out of

it. 'It's hardly a crime. He loses his little sister, the family's torn apart, and what can he do? Nothing but this.'

'Turn vigilante.'

'Come on, he called Naomi a bitch; it's not exactly a cat nailed to the door, is it?' I had a moment's vertigo, the missteps that came every so often when I would think, *How did we get to this? How surreal is this conversation?*

Phil winced and bent forward.

'You okay?'

'Indigestion,' he muttered.

'You never get indigestion. Do you want a Rennie?'

'No.' He straightened. 'It's going off.'

'Perhaps you should see the doctor?'

'Don't fuss, Carmel.'

Bloody cheek. 'I'm not fussing, but it might be a good idea.'

'Well, I've my next lot of blood results next week, so I'll be there then, won't I?'

What if it was serious? I thought of my dad, a squirt of panic in my chest. 'It's great that they can pick these things up nowadays,' I said, trying to reassure myself as much as Phil.

'Don't tell Naomi,' he said.

'Tell me what?' Naomi came in. She was so very pale. I had to get her outside more. She'd get rickets at this rate. Neither of us said anything.

'Well?' she said.

'Your dad's got high blood pressure, he's having it monitored.'

'He'll be all right, though?' she said.

'Course,' Phil said.

Naomi was four months old when my father died. Dropped dead, literally. A heart attack that felled him like a tree. Left him prone on the petrol station forecourt. He'd gone to refuel and use the automated car wash. A foggy October afternoon. He was only fifty-nine. Looking forward to retirement in the next few years. I suppose nowadays he'd have been on aspirin or statins already, his high risk identified in the annual check-up. Given advice on diet and exercise. Perhaps they'd have inserted a stent to widen the artery.

I'm glad he never lived to see Mum get ill. And I'm glad I don't have to tell either of them what Naomi has done and see the expression in their eyes.

Naomi

I keep thinking about Lily's brother. I wonder how he felt about his sister. He's much older, and a boy. Would he have played with her, given her piggybacks or taught her how to use the Xbox, or was he too busy with his own mates? Maybe she got on his nerves, always wanting him to watch her dress up and sing like Lady Gaga or whatever. Perhaps she was a spoiled, whiny little kid who told lies and got him into trouble. Or a tomboy who kicked a football about and did martial arts. Did he boss her about?

Suzanne always had to be in charge. Whatever we did, it had to be her idea or she'd refuse to play. And if I carried on anyway she'd stop playing. Once there was a gang of us on holiday; we were camping by the coast on Anglesey, and Suzanne and I met a bunch of other kids and made a den for ourselves in the dunes. And we had this game where we all had to go and hide and when Suzanne blew her whistle we had to race back to the den like we were under attack, like we were in a war or something.

Then I said we should take turns with the whistle. That's all.

And she just went back to the tent. We tried playing without her but the other kids said it wasn't as good. They liked her bossing them about.

And if I ever stood up to her and said, 'We always do your ideas, why can't we do mine?' she'd just say hers were best and mine were stupid. And I'd hit her and she'd be glad because then she could go and tell on me.

The things I see when I am awake are almost as bad as the things in my dreams.

But it's not just in my head; it's real, it's out there. You've only got to look at the TV, people being blown up and tortured, streets with rubble and lost shoes and dead bodies, bloody. Starving kids, and women being raped, and everyone just acts like that's normal. The way of the world. Which is going straight down the toilet with global warming and animals losing their habitat and the ice melting and people without enough water to drink.

The headlines in the paper are the same: no work, economies collapsing, murders, terrorist attacks. You have to walk round like you're in a shell, sealed off from it, or you'd go barmy. It gets to me. It scalds like hot oil on bare skin. I try and avoid it now. But I can't escape my own thoughts. This witch in my head, gloating, obscene. Cackling at me and forcing me to see all the dirty, sick things in life. And she's got her nails in my brain, skittering against the inside of my skull.

I've stopped trying to remember. I don't think it'll ever come back.

The dreams I remember too clearly. They coat me like dust or tar. Last night there was me and this dead body, a woman, naked, and her skin all waxy and purple. I've killed her. I'm begging Suzanne to help me hide her before I'm found out, and Suzanne's shouting at me, 'How could you?' And I know there isn't much time and I'm digging with my hands, tearing grass out in cold lumps, breaking my nails and gouging the ground. Dread coiling through me like a snake. I roll her into the grave and I'm shovelling soil over her with my arms and she starts climbing out. I'm pushing her down, my hands on her face and her shoulder. She's very thin and very strong. She has mottled white eyes like hard-boiled eggs and blood in her mouth.

All day today I've had her in my mind. This dead woman. I should be thinking about Lily Vasey, about her being dead, not some zombie I've invented.

Mum calls me downstairs. I go down because if I ignore her she comes up to fetch me. Ollie's there. Suzanne's gone to have her hair done. I don't know if she realizes that whenever she leaves him here, Mum encourages me to play with him. Probably not.

He's a bit different every time he comes. He'll be holding his hands or trying to grasp things, or making sounds he's just discovered. He likes it if I get on the floor and let him lie on my stomach. He reaches for my hair.

But I look at him today, lying there and chewing on this plastic dinosaur he has, and I don't feel safe with him. The witch is whispering in my ear. I'm not to be trusted. He's so small and vulnerable. A moment's madness and his skull could break, crushed like an eggshell.

'Pick him up,' Mum says.

What if I just snap, lose control? The possibility jolts through me. I shake my head. 'I don't feel so good.'

'What's wrong?'

'Headache,' I say. My hands itch. 'I might go and lie down.'

She sighs. 'Can't you just make an effort?'

It *is* an effort, this is an effort, everything's a fucking effort. Standing and blinking, breathing and keeping my thoughts hidden.

Ollie bashes himself in the eye with a fist and starts to whimper. Mum scoops him up. 'Take some para-cetamol,' she says to me, then she shushes him.

I do as she says, swallowing the tablets with water as I look out of the kitchen window.

There's a sudden movement in the corner of the garden, shaking a bush there, and my skin tightens. All the hairs on the back of my neck stand up and my bowels turn to water. It's the corpse coming to find me, climbing out of the grave. The shock hurts my chest. I squeeze my eyes shut tight and look again. A squirrel darts across to the back gate.

I hold on to the sink, trembling.

Mum's getting Ollie's lunch out. 'You want to feed him?' she asks.

'No. I'm going to bed.'

I don't look at her, I don't need to. I can imagine she's exasperated with me again. Her lips'll be pressed tight together. She might even roll her eyes. But I can't explain it to her. If I said it out loud – *I might hurt him, Mum, there's these awful pictures in my head, the things I could do* – it would just make it all more real. I just want it to stop. I just want some peace.

CHAPTER TWENTY

.

Carmel

Almost three months after the accident and five weeks after Naomi had first appeared in the magistrates' court, we returned there for the committal hearing. She was withdrawn for much of the time, barely responding to the scene around her, or even to us when we asked her something. Her nails were bitten down to the quick.

At one point she stood up suddenly and said she was going outside. She looked panicky and her face was ashen. I got up too and she grabbed my arms.

'We need to stay inside the building,' Don said apologetically, 'in case they call us.'

Naomi was making a sort of rocking motion, like someone preparing to bolt.

'I feel dizzy,' she said.

'It's warm in here.' I tried to downplay her reaction. 'Let's go to the ladies'.' I was thinking she could wash her face, put cold water on the back of her neck and cool off.

She continued to rock, looking to left and right.

Phil stood up. 'Come on.' He put his arm around her. 'Stretch your legs.' He edged her along and they walked off down the corridor.

Don shot me a sympathetic look and said, 'It's a stressful situation.'

'Yes,' I agreed. 'I'll get her some water.'

By the time Phil had walked her round the building,

she was calmer again. Back to being quiet and distanced. She drank some water.

When she was finally called in, she gripped the sides of the dock so hard her knuckles were white. She confirmed her name and address and date of birth and the magistrate asked Don if he consented to the case being heard at Crown Court. That was about it.

Afterwards Don had a quick meeting with us. He had a file which he patted as he spoke. 'Now that we've got the full case papers, my job will be to see how we challenge their case. That means questioning everything. Can they prove Naomi was driving? Can they demonstrate beyond any reasonable doubt that her driving was dangerous? Can they present evidence that shows that her driving was the sole cause of the cyclist's death? And on all those points we look for gaps, for absence of evidence, for weak areas. We introduce uncertainty, we query everything. Given what you've told me about the state of the vehicle, there will be very limited forensic evidence.' He put his hand on the papers. 'And there is no CCTV coverage included in here. The road traffic investigation unit estimate the car was doing forty-six miles an hour.' *In a thirty-mile-an-hour zone.* 'We will get our own experts in to consider that. Speeding of itself is neither dangerous nor careless. No evidence has been recovered indicating any mechanical fault.'

Now that he had the complete case file, his investigators would be visiting the scene of the crash, measuring distance and angle, studying the road traffic unit's report and assessing every little bit of factual evidence before making their own interpretations. They'd comb through the witness statements for errors or gaps and set out to find anything additional that might contradict or undermine what was in the file.

I had felt helpless for weeks, swept along by the

current of events and failing in my attempts to revive Naomi's memory, but now that Don had talked in concrete terms about what defending her would mean, I saw some small chance for me to contribute. Why didn't anyone stop her driving? I thought.

'I can talk to people,' I said.

'You don't need to bother,' Don said.

'No, I will – I already have, anyway. Hoping to help with her amnesia. Anyone who says anything remotely helpful, anything that's not in there,' I pointed to the file, 'I'll pass on to you. I can't just sit here and . . .' I shut up: too emotional. Don's cheeks grew rosy at my little outburst.

Phil was bothered by my keenness to get involved. 'Shouldn't we leave it to Don?'

'Look, I've no objection,' Don said. 'I know you're a reliable person, you're used to dealing with people, but I will say now that I *can* cover this – it's part of my role.'

'I have to do something,' I said again. 'What about Alex – are we allowed to talk to him?'

'If he's willing. The law says there is no property in a witness; neither side owns them, and their evidence can be considered, even used, by both.'

Naomi watched us debating, then said, 'You don't have to do it, Mum.'

'I want to – maybe I need to.'

'What do you expect to find?'

'Some things don't add up: why did you drive in that state? Why didn't anyone stop you?'

The next person from the barbecue that I rang up heard me out then said, 'Sorry, no.'

'If it's a question of time . . .'

'It's not that. I, erm, I don't want to get involved.'

'But you wouldn't be, not real—'

'I think what she did was appalling. I don't want anything to do with it.' And he hung up.

Somehow Suzanne got to hear about my efforts, and when I called round she took me to task. 'Why are you still hassling everyone, Mum? What does it matter? The facts are staring us all in the face. What are you wasting everybody's time for? Is it some sort of distraction?'

'I'm trying to make sense of it,' I said.

'It doesn't make sense,' she said sharply. 'That is the whole point. Naomi has a solicitor; it's up to him to go and talk to people or whatever, isn't it?'

'And he's doing that,' I said.

'Well leave it to him,' she said. 'It's embarrassing.'

'What?' She'd really got my goat. 'Embarrassing? A child's dead,' I stood up, 'your sister is at risk of going to prison and you're worried about being embarrassed?'

'Don't shout,' she said. 'There's no point to what you're doing. You're like some neurotic crusader, except there's no crusade, is there?'

'The truth,' I said.

'We all know what the truth is, and it's ugly and horrible and you won't accept it. Because you can't bear to see Naomi in that position. But she is.'

I picked up my car keys and made to leave. Her outburst had shaken me. I was angry and smarting but I did not want to fall out with her and I knew if I stayed I'd say something I'd regret. 'I'll give you a ring later in the week,' I said as evenly as I could.

She gave a nod. Neither of us moved to embrace.

Doggedly I carried on. Some people I rang didn't respond when I left messages. Perhaps Suzanne had warned them off: *my mum – she's coming apart at the seams, ignore her.*

209

Naomi

It's hard to concentrate. I feel sick and shaky and my head hurts. My brain is a numb grey rock. Thoughts sneak round it unbidden, quick as lizards. And behind the boulder there's a thunderstorm cracking and raging, a hurricane howling.

The items are there on the chest of drawers.

The vodka from the kitchen: the bottle is dusty, who knows how long it has been there? Mum and Dad never drink it. Perhaps it's left over from a party. Perhaps Alex and I bought it front-loading before a night out. We had some great nights. The best ever, the one when I knew I really loved him and he loved me back, was up in Newcastle. The bands were awesome, just out there, and everyone dancing, and we were pretty mashed up but in a nice way. No toilet-hugging. We went to chill out for a bit, thirsty and breathless. We got some water and some crisps. And he was staring at me with this soppy grin on his face.

'What?' I said. 'What you looking at?'

'Move in with me,' he said.

And my stomach flipped over. I felt so happy that I was nearly in tears. 'You sure?' I said.

Then he came even closer, whispered in my ear: 'I love you. I want us to be together.'

I kissed him and then I dragged him back to dance because I needed to jump about. We went for breakfast at a place near the river. Shared a fry-up because we'd not got much money left.

Now I shake my head; no point in thinking of that. I take another drink of the vodka. Oily and sharp at the same time.

Then there are the pills; three different sorts. From the bathroom and the kitchen. Hard to know if I've got

210

enough, but I think so. I'm very tired, my eyes feel dry and sore, but I can lie down in a minute.

I take a load of pills, about half of them, washed down with vodka. I don't take all of them yet, because the other thing on the chest is the note. Which I haven't written yet. But I think I should.

I don't want them to feel bad, you see, and if there's no note then they might think all sorts and blame each other or themselves. And they mustn't think I don't love them. I do love them, that's why I'm doing this. So they understand that this is the best thing for everybody. Mum and Dad and Suzanne and Alex can get their lives back and I won't be there dragging them down. Lily's family – they'll have their 'life for a life', won't they?

I know I'm a coward because I can't face another day. Each minute with the storm in my head and the claws gouging inside me. I want it to be over.

I'm sweating now, like when you have a fever, shivering too. So I don't think I can write a lot.

I put their names at the top. I smudge Dad a bit but you can still read it. *To Mum, Dad, Suzanne and Alex.*

The letters wriggle on the page and I have to close one eye. I'm very thirsty so I have another drink.

I thought I might be scared, but the only thing I'm scared of is it not working. That would be awful. I just want the peace; it will be peaceful. Not to feel at all, not to feel anything, not to wake up and have that awful sense of desolation, of hopelessness.

I am sorry. I write that next. *I am so sorry.*

The dizzy feeling is getting stronger. I take more pills. All of the ones that are left.

I read my note. *I love you all so much*, I write, and the words slope to the left, like they're dizzy too. *Please forgive me and remember I love you and I never wanted to hurt you.*

211

My fingers ache and I sign my name as quickly as I can manage because everything is moving around.

I leave the note next to me on the bed.

I try to think if there is anything else. The waterfall is in my head. The ink fills my eyes. I am falling, falling and flying.

CHAPTER TWENTY-ONE

Carmel

S ometimes I checked on her. But not always. Sometimes I had to restrain myself. Bite down on my
urges, sacrifice my own need for reassurance for her right
to be independent, to be treated like an adult.

I almost didn't. It was getting late. Nearly midnight.
I'd just got back from Evie and Lucy's. We'd had a meal
and a good chat. There were even moments when I
forgot about our troubles, so I was more relaxed when I
got home than I had been earlier.

I hesitated outside her door and then carried on to the
bathroom to brush my teeth. Leave it, I told myself. But
the familiar anxiety was rising slowly, and as soon as I
acknowledged it was there, I knew I'd not get any sleep
until I'd dealt with it. It was almost like OCD: the
voodoo that if I checked there'd be nothing to worry
about and if I didn't something terrible would happen to
her. A stupid ritual to placate the gods.

So I crept back along the hall and turned her door
handle as quietly as possible, though there was always a
tiny squeak in the mechanism.

The smell of vomit hit me immediately, acidic and
repulsive, making my mouth water, and I gagged in a
reflex response.

I snapped the light on and a wave of dread slammed
into me. She was on the bed, something terribly wrong
in the colour of her face and the sick on the pillow.

My heart hammering, my spine tingling with fear, I

touched her neck, calling her name over and over again: 'Naomi, Naomi, Naomi.' A chant to summon her.

I couldn't feel a pulse, couldn't tell if she was breathing. The panic was bright in me like a fire and I screamed for Phil and stuck my fingers in her mouth. ABC. ABC. The mnemonic from first-aid training in my head. There was nothing in her mouth. I breathed into her, ignoring the sickly smell, and began CPR.

Phil was there, he didn't need telling; he called an ambulance. They seemed to take forever but later we learnt it was just eight minutes. He was talking as I kept pumping away, telling them the names of the pills she'd taken, answering questions about her status, about her health. He had her note in his hand and this desperate, harrowed look on his face.

I was cursing her, this child of mine, cursing her and praying. I could not bear to lose her. Could not bear it. I would have torn open her chest and squeezed her heart with my bare hands if I'd had the means. There was a tide ebbing and flowing in me, rolling from fear to fury and back, currents swirling as I tried to make her breathe.

I don't remember much about the ambulance arriving. The paramedics had a preternatural calm about them, as though they were running at a slower pace than the rest of us. I wanted to hurry them, my words spilling like coins from a jackpot, brash and fast and noisy.

They put a mask on her, I remember that, and they used a defibrillator. They injected her with something. I knew, because they did those things, that she had died.

For the second time she had died.

And then we were at the hospital and she was stable, they said, though they didn't know yet how long she had been without oxygen. Or what the consequences might be.

She was so lucky. There was no brain damage. But she refused to talk to us at first. Shrank from our touch and screwed up her eyes. The mental health service got involved and recommended discharge to one of their rehabilitation units. She was deemed to be at risk of serious self-harm.

To be honest, I was relieved she was not coming home. Not yet. I didn't trust her, and the strain of watching over her would have been intolerable.

Phil and I went back and talked and wept, him making big barking noises like some seal, which tore at my heart. It was impossible to resist the impulse towards self-recrimination: *I should have seen it coming, should have dragged her to the doctor, should have known!* Yes, I'd realized she was getting depressed but I'd no idea that she'd been suicidal. *I should have known.*

'I was thinking of Petey again,' Phil said, his eyes watery. 'Oh God, if you'd not gone in . . .'

'But I did.' I held his face in my hands and kissed his forehead.

We tried to put one foot in front of the other. There's no avoiding the particularly cruel guilt that suicide or attempted suicide bestows on those who love the person involved. Like with Petey's death, relatives and friends struggle not only with grief but a profound burden of culpability. It's a false burden – we are not responsible for the person's choice to end their life, we do not have the power – but on an emotional level it is very hard not to feel that we have failed in our care, in our love. That if we'd only been better, stronger, wiser, more worthy of love they wouldn't have killed themselves.

Phil and I have must have spent most of that ensuing week talking about Naomi, and what she'd tried to do. It haunted us, even more than the accident had done, if that were possible, because this was deliberate, planned, intentional. Our daughter had not wanted to live any more.

I felt as though something had been ripped away inside. I've never felt so vulnerable, so hurt. Betrayed, even.

I berated myself for not having spotted the signs; with all my professional training, I should have seen, should have known. Her behaviour in the last few weeks, the way she acted at the committal hearing. Phil listened to me pick away at it. He was wounded too. He rang the Samaritans. He said it helped, it was good to talk to someone completely objective, who didn't know any of us, whose responses weren't coloured by shock or surprise. Who could talk very practically about the position he was in and what he realistically could and couldn't do.

We weren't allowed to visit for the first couple of weeks, while Naomi was assessed and plans were put in place.

It was a respite.

I was critical of myself, but I found it even harder when Suzanne came round. 'How could she?' she asked, looking sad rather than cross. Tears glistened in her eyes. I wondered if she regretted her break with Naomi and had some sympathy for her sister, or if she was actually just sad for us, for what we were going through.

Then she talked about the baby and how Jonty was busy with the editing, and I felt myself growing more and more tense, my comments curt and parsimonious. She didn't notice. Until I let fly. 'We needed you, Suzanne; *I* needed you, not just Naomi, and you let us down.'

She flinched. 'Just because—'

'No.' I raised my hand to quieten her. 'I'll say my

piece. You decided to wash your hands of us, of your sister.'

'Well, she'd been drinking.' She stuck her neck out. Raised her chin, still determined to stand her ground.

'That's not the issue. Whether she was drink-driving or not, a terrible thing happened: to the little girl and her family, and to your sister, who was in the car and nearly died and is facing a prison sentence. And you have been spiteful and uncaring and judgemental.'

'Mum . . .' Her lip trembled.

'I needed you on my side. You called her selfish, remember? You're the most selfish person I know.'

Her eyes filled with tears; the spots of colour on her cheeks faded. 'Look,' she started, 'if I'd known she was going to—'

'Consequences,' I laughed, 'that's the point, isn't it? We *don't* always know what's coming. But family, Suzanne. We will live the rest of our lives under this shadow. Not only what happened to Lily Vasey, but Naomi's suicide attempt. How bleak do you think things got for her? Can you imagine?'

'You're blaming me?' she said, quivering.

'No, I'm not blaming you for that. But I am angry with you for letting us down. Naomi spent half her life looking for your approval, desperate to please her big sister. You've no idea how much your rejection hurt her.'

'She tell you that?'

'I could see it,' I said through clenched teeth.

There was a pause, and I felt weary, tired to the marrow.

Suzanne cleared her throat, touched her earring. 'What do you want me to do?' she said in a small voice.

'I don't know. That's up to you. Think about it. An apology might be a start.'

'Right,' she said. And left.

And I swallowed the tears that threatened and tried to stop shaking.

Naomi

Most of the people on the unit are friendly. There's one who doesn't ever talk, who doesn't even seem to see or hear anything that's going on. Which must be nice; she just looks through everything. She's about Mum's age, dresses quite smart. She has bandages on her wrists.

There are two other women, look a bit like mother and daughter but they're not related, and they talk all the time. Like something bad might happen if they pause for breath. Nosy, too, but they don't give you a chance to answer, just talk about their own mental health or what the unit's like, what treatments they're on.

Then there's a really shaky guy. He just looks like he'll shatter. Everything startles him and he trembles constantly. I don't know if the shaking is a side effect from the drugs or if he's got some physical problem or what.

The staff are sound, generally. There's one bloke, though, and he's always picking on people, he has this really sneery, patronizing way of talking, but he's the only one really.

We're here to be assessed and treated and then hopefully returned 'to the community'. There's a secure unit across the way, but that's for people who might be a danger to others, rather than just to themselves, or those dead set on suicide who have to have someone with them every single second.

You get assessed when you first come in and they decide what treatment to start, then you keep on seeing either a doctor or the psychiatrist maybe every second or third day except weekends. But in between, all the staff in the unit are assessing you all the time, not just whether you take your medication but how you relate to people and if you join in with things and if you eat the food, which is revolting. Some people here have eating disorders and it really can't help: if you haven't got one when you come in here, you'll probably have one by the time you leave. The staff, they're always asking how you're feeling and encouraging you to think about the future. Getting stronger and going home.

There isn't any set pattern to the sessions with the psychiatrist. Though she usually asks me if I've had any suicidal thoughts or impulses. Today I say no. Then she asks me how my night was.

'Okay,' I say. 'I slept a bit better.'

'What would you like to talk about?'

'I don't know.'

There's a pause, and we let it stretch out a bit, then I say, 'I had a dream about the accident.'

'Tell me about it.'

'There was Alex and me, we were in a boat, not a car, and we were trying to steer it but it kept going the wrong way. Then it was just me, I was all alone, and there was a bump and the boat changed into a car. I got out and looked underneath and there was a body there.' I feel a bit sick as I say it. 'And I drove off. That was it.'

'Did the dream wake you up?'

'Yes.'

'And how did you feel?'

'Dirty, rotten.' It's something I've said before. The sense that there is something spoiled in me.

'Anything else?'

'Frightened. I was running, even though I was in the car.'

'And Alex wasn't in the car with you?'

'No.'

219

'You said there was just you, on your own. And we talked about isolation the other day. Do you feel isolated?'

'Pretty much.' This makes me tearful. 'Apart from Mum and Dad and Becky, I suppose. And I miss Alex.' Sometimes I think maybe I'll get back in touch with him again.

'But not Suzanne?'

I shake my head; my stomach cramps at the thought of her. At her dislike of me, her disapproval.

'You said before that you are angry at how Suzanne makes you feel?'

'Yes. She only has to say some little thing and it makes me feel lousy.'

'That's an old pattern?'

'Yes.'

'And in the past, how would you respond if she said something that hurt you?'

'I'd answer back or brush it off but inside I'd be really upset.'

'Answer back?' she echoes.

I smile. 'Like she's a teacher or something.'

She nods. 'What would you like to change?'

These are the hardest questions. Whenever I'm supposed to look ahead or think of the future, my throat closes and my eyes burn. 'I want to feel all right again and I don't want to go to prison. I want everything to change.' I shake my head. 'I want to rewrite history.'

She gives a half-smile, even though I'm getting upset. It's reassuring in a funny way. People here aren't scared of shows of emotion and that helps make them less scary.

'There's an exercise I'd like you to do.' She reaches for a piece of paper from the side table and hands it to me. 'Take this with you and draw a picture of your family, stick figures, whatever works, but I want you to do it

220

without thinking too much about it, in just five minutes. And don't alter anything. Bring it next time. Okay?'

We have an activity room where we do art therapy and music and that. I often go there to avoid the telly, which is on all the time in the lounge; sometimes I get the urge to punch it out, then I would be Miss Popularity. I never could draw, but they have other stuff here too, like modelling clay. I do that. I remember Suzanne and me as kids spent hours with Play-Doh, making little meals, cakes and pizzas and spaghetti shapes, with the machine thing that we had; like a giant garlic press. It smelt of salty marzipan. I used to lick my palms afterwards to get the taste. When I think of that, I feel like crying.

Soon I'll be allowed visitors, and after that the plan is to discharge me. I'm not ready to go home yet, even though it can be stressful living like this with a bunch of strangers. And it's hard to sleep. One of the girls, bit younger than me, she has these episodes, screaming in the night, seeing things crawling on her. She wakes everyone up. She's a bit like Grandma, having delusions. At least it's good Grandma's in a home and not a hospital. Good for us more than for her; she'd probably not notice the difference. Sometimes I think this is good practice for going to prison. But I guess prison will be much worse. Heavier, darker. I don't have to share a room here, I suppose that's one big difference. We're in a new building; most of us have a single room with en suite. The main thing here is the boredom.

It's like being marooned or something. Like I'm on a raft, floating far away from my previous life. I can't imagine seeing anyone in here from out there. And in here people don't know who I was. Only who I am now. The one who ran into the little girl, the one who made a serious attempt to end her own life. A mentalist.

We're all in the same boat, so no one's judging me.

Some of the people make me laugh; we all try and cheer each other up and look out for each other. Some of them seem quite tough, but you know they can't be really or they wouldn't be here. There's a sort of tenderness; does that sound naff? But there really is. We're all fragile and we're kind to each other.

Lots of time we spend outside, in this little garden area, all enclosed. Most people smoke, the staff as well, and although there are notices everywhere about it being a non-smoking environment and no smoking on hospital trust property, they let us do it outside.

I am now very good at Scrabble.

I'm not looking forward to seeing Mum and Dad really. I just feel so shitty. They're gonna be so hurt by what I did, and I can't ever put that right.

CHAPTER TWENTY-TWO

Carmel

I was on shift the next weekend and it was busy, dealing with a man who was mentally ill and threatening to knife himself at his sister's house. I attended with the police and got him sectioned. I couldn't help thinking of Naomi, of course, though she was a voluntary admission, choosing to go in after her overdose.

Sunday we had a call out to a family where the police were arresting the mother for supplying drugs. She had three kids under five needing emergency foster-care provision as Dad was in prison and she was estranged from her family.

The woman was understandably distraught, screaming, 'You can't take my kids, you can't take my babies!' while I tried to calm her down and explain that it was only a temporary measure until she was bailed and able to look after them. In the longer term, though, she'd be facing time in prison if convicted, and then she would be separated from them, possibly for years.

There were three police officers there. The arresting officer made a great show of disgust and impatience at her behaviour, raising his eyes to heaven and sneering. In general we have good relationships with the police – they understand our role and vice versa – but this bloke was an exception. He'd written her off without another thought: drug-pusher equals scum. He'd have seen her transported, the kids given up for adoption, quick as you like. But every case needs judging on its own merits.

Some drug-users would let their kids starve (literally) rather than spend drug money on food, but others manage to care for their kids quite adequately, as do some alcoholics. Where the family unit is supportive and nurturing, the only thing achieved by removing the children is catastrophic long-term emotional damage to all those involved and consequent social and criminal problems. My initial impression of the kids was that they were clean and well fed. The place was messy but not dirty.

I managed to get her to stop shouting and sobbing and explained what would happen next. One of the officers came with me while I sorted out some toys and clothes for the children. We took them downstairs. The mother was already in the police car by then, the other two officers standing beside it smoking.

I caught the tail end of the arresting officer's remark: '. . . by dangerous driving. Horrendous.' He practically jumped when he saw me, then jutted his chin out and said more loudly than necessary, 'All sorted?' I could feel his disapproval and imagined the way he'd talk later: *She swans in acting like the Big I Am and her own kid was pissed out of her skull and ran over a nine-year-old.*

I nodded, unsmiling, and got the children in my car. When I meet new people and tell them I'm a social worker, this is the situation that springs to their mind. But the greater part of my job is checking that children are safe, cared for and fed. Children are removed if offences have been committed against them, but we'll find family to help whenever possible. I'm on the fire-fighting end of it. Emergencies. Long-term decisions about permanent removal are never made on a wing and a prayer; there are reams of forms to be filled in, assessments to be made, reports from other professionals to factor in. And sometimes we get it wrong. We are only human.

Though you'd never think that to read about us in the papers or see us vilified on TV. The public, the opinion-makers, the politicians want it every which way. We must be immediate, decisive, fearless in acting to remove children or disabled people or the elderly from harm, yet we are expected to do so with inadequate staff and resources, and when we fail to protect a child, no matter how manipulative the parents or carers have been, we are savaged. Regarded as do-gooders, as bleeding hearts, we are sneered at as agents of the nanny state, the faceless bureaucrats who snoop around and tell tales and break up families. We are the Cinderella profession. The overriding stereotype of a social worker is the person tearing a child from a weeping mother's arms. A bogeyman in office clothing.

The next time I saw Suzanne was to babysit while she and Jonty had a night out for their anniversary. It had been in our diaries a while and I rang the night before to check their plans hadn't changed. Neither of us mentioned our argument over the phone.

Jonty was still getting ready when she let me in. She looked lovely, in a red silk dress and heels, her hair up in a French twist.

She showed me where Ollie's bottle was in the fridge and how to use the bottle-warmer, which looked like some piece of space travel kit. She was talking a little too quickly and I knew she was on edge. She told me at some length about the restaurant they were going to, and then said, 'How's Naomi?' I knew this was what she really wanted to talk about.

'Okay, I think. Better than she was.'

'Good. I am sorry, Mum,' she said. 'About, well . . . everything. Letting you down. I just overreacted, I suppose. Didn't think it through.'

I nodded, wondered if she'd say more, but that was it. She went to fetch her shawl and chivvy Jonty along. I brooded over it all evening. Would she apologize to Phil, too? Had she any intention of saying sorry to Naomi for abandoning her? Naomi wanted to steer clear of her sister as far as I could see. Maybe that was for the best. She was an adult, after all.

By the time Suzanne and Jonty came home, raving about the menu and the wine list, I had decided to let things slide. The ripples from the accident had affected all of our relationships, not just our individual dealings with Naomi herself. They had weakened my relationship with Suzanne. She would still be a big part of my life, but I could see who she was with a clearer, keener eye, and a more critical one. I thought that Ollie would be the filter for our love. That we'd stay close through sharing affection for him.

Naomi

When I come home from the mental health unit, Mum makes us sit down, the three of us, and talk about it. Dad isn't sure: 'Carmel, do you really think—' but she interrupts him. 'We need to face this, be completely open about what's happened. Not tiptoe about, or shove it under the rug. That doesn't help anyone. Now . . .' She looks at me, all in practical mode, but her hands are shaking. 'We love you very, very much . . .' There's a lump in my throat. '. . . And I understand that things must have felt . . .' she struggles to find the word, '. . . unbearable, but we will do everything we can to help you get better.'

Dad just nods.

'It's important to keep some structure in your day,' she

says. 'So, no lying in bed till lunchtime. And we'd like you to cook once a week and help with the supermarket shop. And do one of the chores.'

I used to do the hoovering and Suzanne used to do the dishwasher. Then when Alex and I moved back we didn't really do anything. Well, we did our own washing and cooking.

'The dishwasher,' I say.

They don't want to leave me alone in the house at first. Sometimes I go with Dad to the shop, and he finds little jobs for me to do, like sorting out the guitar strings or rewriting the price lists or cleaning. Sometimes I forget what I'm supposed to be doing. It's a side effect of the tablets. Like being smothered in a duvet, everything's muffled and numbed. My mind slips away all the time, like one of those random carrier bags blowing down the road, snagging on things but not for long. Aimless, empty.

I'm glad that I don't feel so much any more. It's the only way I can manage. I have sessions at the outpatient mental health clinic. The woman there, I like her, she never pushes me and if I start to get stressed she lets me talk about something else.

Each session she has to ask me the same things. 'How have you been this week?'

'Okay,' I say today.

'Any voices or visions?'

'No.'

'Suicidal thoughts?'

'No.' They're further away, they don't dominate like before, but they're still there. Like a stream burbling in the background. Sometimes they get bigger, bloom large as if a quick zoom has magnified them. Like if there's a knife left out on the kitchen counter or when I'm putting a scarf on, when I get a new bottle of tablets. Let me count the ways . . .

'Do you feel that you're making progress?'

'Yes. I haven't watched the news or anything, and I've been out every day, just walking.'

'How's that?'

'All right, yes.' These are things we've identified to help me get stronger, to avoid any extra pressure.

We have a pact, the psychiatrist and me and Mum and Dad. That if I'm going to hurt myself, I'll ring one of the numbers on the card or tell someone here.

Mum's cut back on her shifts so she's around more. She helps me with some of the Jobcentre stuff when I need it, otherwise they'll cut my benefit.

The plea and case management hearing at the Crown Court is set for a week on Monday. When I think of that, my heart burns, even with all the tranquillizers. Next week I meet the barrister. Don says he's very good. I'm not going to give evidence at the trial, but I'll be there in the dock.

Mum keeps on about it, pretending it'll be okay. The girl's family will be there, of course; I expect they'll all come, including Robin, the one who came to our house and yelled at me. *You're dead.* Well, I tried.

Carmel

I found it hard to go past her bedroom door if she was in and it was shut. Especially at bedtime. I decided to be frank with her about it. 'Naomi, I need to be able to check on you, if I feel worried.'

She looked at me, a whisper of alarm in her expression.

'If I knock on your door and you answer, that'll be fine.'

'Okay.'

'And if you're asleep and don't hear me, I'll look in on you – if I need to. Just for now.'

She nodded once and her eyes filled with tears and she said, 'I am sorry, Mum.'

Hugging her, warm and precious, I said, 'I love you. I love you no matter what you've done, no matter what happens. You know that.'

The vigilance, the state of being on alert to any dip in her mood, continued. It was very hard to relax, though my own medication helped me to keep functioning.

The days went on. Our lives went on. One morning I found Naomi in the kitchen, checking the cupboards. 'I'm going to the shops,' she said. 'Are you here for tea?'

'Yes.'

'Have we got rice?' She peered in the bottom cupboard. 'Oh, yes. I think I'll do chilli.'

'Great.'

'Becky rang. I'm going to go with her to look at this hotel.'

'For the wedding?' I said.

'Yes. We're doing a few and shortlisting them for Steve.'

I glanced at her. 'Wedding planner now, are you? Steve lost interest?'

'Think he's lost the will to live,' she joked.

There was this ghastly moment as we both heard what she'd said.

'Oh God,' she groaned, and shook her head.

And we both smiled and the danger evaporated. It felt like something had shifted. I think the counselling and the medication made a big difference. She was getting stronger, was more active and engaged. But it still felt poignant, precarious, like the last day of a holiday that has to end, or the last visit with an aged relative. Because there was still the trial to come, and a very uncertain future.

My quest had changed from recovering memories for Naomi to trying to establish if anyone had seen them leave the barbecue. And find out why they'd not intervened. Or if Naomi really had fooled everyone, Alex included, by appearing perfectly capable.

Alice, an old friend of Jonty's from childhood, was Ollie's godmother or the lay equivalent. She had come down to Manchester for the barbecue. She had a horsy, outdoorsy style to her. When I'd first chatted to her at Suzanne's wedding, I hadn't been surprised to learn she lived on a farm. She raised rare-breed sheep.

Alice was very sympathetic, full of condolences, almost gushing when I rang her. Before I even had a chance to ask her anything, she went on, 'It was such a shock when Jonty told us. I thought Alex was driving them back. She was pretty far gone.'

'Yes, I think a few people assumed he'd drive.'

'Even Naomi.'

'Sorry?'

'Naomi said Alex would drive,' Alice said.

The hairs on the back of my neck stood up. No one else had mentioned this. 'Are you sure?' Could Naomi have been confused about the arrangement? Then, when she realized she was too pissed to make a sensible decision, just pretended she could handle it?

'Yes, I asked her if they were staying over. Or if they wanted to share a taxi; we were in a hotel in town. She obviously didn't want me to think she would be driving.'

My mouth was dry, my hands clammy on the phone. 'You couldn't have misunderstood?'

'No,' she said. 'And he was on fruit juice.'

'What?'

'Well, for some of the time at least. Naomi and I went in to get more wine from the ice bucket and I offered it round, but he had a glass of juice.'

I was quiet for a moment, disturbed by what she said. I remembered Martin talking about the vodka and orange. *Rocket fuel.* Alex had been drinking but had made it look like he wasn't. And at the hospital, when he'd first told us the awful details, asking him if Naomi was drunk. His response: *No, I'd never have let her. She'd offered to drive, I was celebrating. She was fine with it.* Denying she was drunk. Was *he* too drunk to tell?

'If only they'd stuck to the plan,' Alice said.

Don was very interested in what I'd heard from Alice. 'It raises questions,' he said, 'and that's good for us. Why did Naomi say that and Alex say something different? It also helps us with a very first plank of the case – was Naomi driving the car? Was she expecting Alex to? Was he complicit? Did he ask her to? Did she just offer?'

'Why would she do that?'

'You know alcohol loosens inhibitions. People imagine that their abilities are not impaired. Serial drink-drivers will boast that they drive even better after a couple of drinks. It's bullshit. But it's not impossible to imagine Alex and Naomi reaching the car and her offering, downplaying the number of drinks she's had. A journey she's made dozens of times, a fine evening.'

'Except she's never driven like that before.' I was still sceptical. 'If only someone had seen them getting in the car.'

'At present, with this little gem, the prosecution will find it hard to prove she was driving,' Don said.

'But if she wasn't, that implies that Alex might have . . . but Alex saved her life.'

231

He held up a hand. 'We don't imply *anything*,' he emphasized the word, 'other than doubt. That's the bottom line. Uncertainty, lack of surety. Niggling doubt. Was Naomi behind the wheel? No one saw her. Was the car being driven dangerously or carelessly; was it even an acceptable standard? A young woman, unblemished history, no previous offences whatsoever, not even a speeding ticket. The prosecution will find it very hard to get a jury to convict, to say there is no shred of doubt that she committed the offence.'

There was hope. But I couldn't help thinking of Lily Vasey and where that left her family. I asked Don. He replied with the words I used so often in trying to comfort my daughter: an accident. Tragic, unforeseen, random, an accident.

CHAPTER TWENTY-THREE

Carmel

I pictured Alex and Naomi leaving. They'd parked opposite, outside the second of the detached houses on the cul-de-sac, not the one that had been sold. Julia had said something about Fraser helping the neighbours, the dog people, to move some stuff. Had he noticed Naomi leaving? I rang to ask him. He hadn't – he'd gone home by then, the bulk of the job done. The couple, the Langhams, had given up their kennels and moved to the coast, Blackpool. Setting up a bespoke holiday company for people wanting something special from a weekend in the resort beyond a trip to the Pleasure Beach and a stick of rock. It seemed like a bizarre switch of field. Julia didn't have their number, but she gave me the business name and I found them online.

As soon as Mrs Langham realized I was not a potential customer, she became impatient. I imagined they were under considerable pressure, the first few weeks into running a new business, especially as the recession showed no sign of abating. And the leisure industry relied on people with disposable income, which was in ever shorter supply for most of us.

No, she said, she hadn't noticed the car, or anyone driving off in it. She exhibited absolutely no interest or curiosity about my call.

I asked to speak to her husband. 'Neville's out,' she said. 'I can ring back.'

She gave a gusty sigh and told me to try after eight. I

233

did, and finally got to speak to him. He wasn't as brusque as his wife, but he was sorry he couldn't remember anything particular. He'd been ferrying their furniture to the new house much of the time. Disappointment rolled over me like a bank of cloud. I was thanking him prior to hanging up when he said, 'Did you already talk to Larry?'

'Larry? No.'

'My brother-in-law. He was giving us a hand.'

Larry lived in Birmingham. He sounded suspicious at first: as soon as I introduced myself, he launched into a spiel about not wanting cold callers. Then he cottoned on to what I was asking: had he seen a couple drive away in a Honda Civic, the day of the removals, about eight in the evening?

'Yes,' he said, 'bloody idiot nearly pranged my rear end. Had to brake sharp, like. It was a hire van, so the last thing I needed was shelling out the excess on the insurance. I'm a loss-adjuster myself, but these van hire firms, there's no leeway if you cause any damage.'

Oh, Naomi. If only she *had* bumped his van. The ensuing kerfuffle would have delayed them leaving, Larry or Alex would have seen she was unfit, and Lily Vasey would still be playing out and giggling with her schoolmates and watching telly or having bedtime stories with her family.

'You saw them get in the car?' I said.

'Yes.'

'Could you tell she was drunk?'

'She was, by the looks of it. But the way he shot backwards, he wasn't exactly sober himself. Or maybe he'd not passed his test.'

My heart stood still and there was a roaring in my ears. 'He was driving?' I said, dozens of objections crowding in the back of my head.

'Yes. Why?'

I began to cry, and poor Larry didn't know what to do.

'I'm sorry,' I squeaked. 'I'll have to go, but I'll be in touch. Please, remember what you've just told me.'

Phil was in the living room, the day's paper, crossword almost completed, on the floor beside his chair. Eyes closed. 'Phil?'

He heard me and stirred, came to. 'Yeah,' sleep thick in his voice. He must have seen how I was shaking; his manner abruptly changed. He shot to his feet. 'What?' Came towards me. 'Carmel what is it?'

The words were like a clot in my throat, painful, filthy.

Phil's face was riddled with incomprehension.

I began to explain, tripping over phrases and fighting against the chattering of my teeth.

He made me sit down and poured me a glass of water. 'Have a drink.'

Tears were streaming down my face.

'Naomi's still out?' I checked, anxiously.

He nodded. 'Back soon.' Becky and Steve had taken her to see *The Artist*, an award-winning homage to silent film. Something safe; so many things were treacherous nowadays. You never notice how much death is in our stories and films and dramas until you try avoiding the topic.

After. When the world turned sour and the scales fell from our eyes.

Naomi

'Alex was driving!'

'What?'

235

Mum's face is livid with intensity and her eyes are blazing. 'Alex was driving – one of the people moving out across the road, they saw him. He got in the driving seat.'

What the fuck? My guts cramp and I feel sick in the back of my throat. Suddenly I wobble, nearly fall. She grabs me, pulls out a chair and sits me down. Blood thunders in my ears. *Alex was driving? So . . . I wasn't? I wasn't driving? It wasn't me who . . .* Something collapses inside me, falls away.

I stare at her, the words all bitty and choppy in my mouth. 'But Alex said—'

'He lied,' she says, crouching down, her hands on my knees. 'He lied, Naomi, he blamed you.' She starts to cry, then tries to stop, half laughing and wiping at her face with the heel of her hand. 'And Monica lied too.'

I feel giddy, darkness filling my eyes, confusion like choking smoke. *He loves me. No, Mum's got it wrong, she's raving, she's desperate.* 'He wouldn't do that. How can you say that?'

'It's true!' And she talks fast, all about how things fit together. 'It makes sense, darling, don't you see. You told Alice he was driving and you kept on drinking, you didn't care because *you weren't going to drive.* And Alex – he made it look like he was abstaining . . . like he was on fruit juice, but he'd got vodka in it . . .'

She gets up now, talking even faster, and I'm finding it hard to take it all in. 'He was drinking secretly because he must have promised he'd drive back.'

A little glow of heat grows in me, small and uncertain as a birthday candle, barely alive, but there's also a gale blowing, a gale of horror and bewilderment. *He lied? My Alex. My lovely Alex. He blamed me and he told them all, all the world.*

Dad looks at me, disbelief bright in his eyes, as if I can

236

give him the nod and say, *Yes, that's right, I was the passenger*. But how can I? I can't frigging remember.

Then Mum's calling Don and he promises to come round. There's this tension in the air and Dad just keeps shaking his head. And I really do feel sick. I just get to the toilet in time. Puke my guts up, till my throat is sore and there's a bitter taste that doesn't go even when I've brushed my teeth.

Everything's so unsteady. Like I'm standing on dry land after months at sea and the ground is roiling beneath my feet. Balance shot. That fleeting look of relief I saw when I broke up with him – was that because of this, because it would be easier to keep up the act without me by his side?

No. She must be wrong. There must be a mistake. Alex – he just would not do that. He's a good person. Perhaps we stopped on the way and changed seats? The person who saw us might have got the wrong end of the stick – like if Alex opened the car door for me and the guy assumed he was going to get in but Alex gave me the keys. That would make sense. And so Monica did see—

'Naomi!' Mum says it sharply, like I've been ignoring her. 'Get the door!' She's on the phone to Evie.

Don listens, and he's typing on his iPad like mad and he gets all the details from Mum and rings this Larry bloke there and then even though it's late. He says who he is and why he's calling and he tells the guy he's a key witness and is there any chance he can come up to Manchester to make a statement.

Larry must stress about it, I think, because then Don offers to come to Birmingham if that's easier. I make tea while this is going on. I think about that image I have of the glossy food and grope about in my head in case there's anything after that about us leaving, about this new version of how it went, me getting in the passenger seat, Alex at the wheel, him dragging me out of the passenger side, not the driver's side. Blank. A big fat blank.

'Naomi, it's stirred enough.' Mum takes two of the cups for Dad and Don. I bring ours.

'He'll be here just before lunch tomorrow,' Don says. He's almost breathless. 'With his account I can go to the barrister – it will almost certainly mean approaching the CPS and getting them to consider whether to proceed.'

'But wouldn't it just be this Larry's word, and Alice's, against Alex and Monica?' I say.

'Larry is an independent witness; that adds extra significance to his account. An independent witness has no stake, no vested interest. That goes for Alice too.'

I don't know what I feel. Puzzled, mainly. Shellshocked. Lost.

'And your collarbone,' Don says, looking across at me, 'the left-hand side: the mark of Zorro.' *Has he lost the plot?* He draws a zigzag on his body. 'Where the seat belt cuts into you – different depending on where you sit.'

'And the bruising, there,' Mum says quickly.

'Why the hell didn't the police consider that?' Dad frowns. 'Or you, Don?'

Don shrugs. 'If it looks like a fish and it swims like a fish . . . They'd no reason to doubt Alex's account, and nor had I. There are huge variation in injuries in these situations; for every case that proves a point, there are others that contradict it. And we'd no forensics to speak of from the car.'

'We believed him,' Mum says.

'But we can add this medical evidence to the new witness evidence – even more for the CPS to consider,' Don says.

'I thought he loved me,' I say. 'He was . . .' I blow my nose. 'And the job and everything. Why would he do that?'

'To save his own skin,' Dad says.

'And that little girl, everybody thought . . .' I hit at my head; it feels like it'll burst. 'Why can't I remember?'

'Shush, shush.' Mum pulls my hands down.

'What if you had?' Dad says. 'There's something weird here. Because you might have come round and it might all have been clear as day and he'd have been exposed immediately.'

'The amnesia was a gift for him,' Mum says, spitting mad. 'And we told Monica, remember?' She whips round to look at Dad. 'That first time we went to visit, he wasn't there but Monica was. We told her Naomi couldn't remember anything.'

'Everyone believed him,' I say. '*I* believed him.'

We sit up very, very late after Don has gone; nobody wants to go to bed. We talk about safe stuff, old stuff from when I was little or Dad's punk rock days. Every now and then one of them leapfrogs forward to now and the bombshell, thinking of another angle on what's happened. Another clue we should have spotted. I don't have any of these eureka moments. I'm stunned on top of being doped up. And I really can't believe it. Any of it.

I can't believe I drove the car too fast and swerved and hit the girl.

I can't believe he did.

Or that she died.

I can't believe he said it was my fault.

I can't believe his mother lied too.

I can't believe he let me think I killed her.

It's all unravelling, but it's like I'm watching from the sidelines, an observer, seeing myself, studying my own reactions, or lack of them.

I thought he loved me.

Carmel

My first feelings were shock and sadness. Alex had lied: from the moment of impact he'd told everyone that Naomi was driving, he'd blamed everything on her. It seemed so callous, so selfish, and I found it hard to equate with what I knew of him.

I pictured his face that day at the hospital. The effort of telling the story. A story that was a sham, smoke and mirrors. On the heels of my sorrow came a roaring tide of anger. Not content with the devastation of the accident, with the cost of a nine-year-old's life, he had then allowed Naomi to be pilloried, causing the rift with Suzanne, her own guilt and shame, her depression and unhappiness, her attempted suicide. And his bloody mother had held his hand every step of the way. Prepared to sacrifice my daughter to save her son.

It was like turning a picture the right way up. Or seeing writing reflected in a mirror, impossible to decipher until you face the other way and see the words plain and clear. The moment when a puzzle gives up its secret: the little twist that releases the metal ring, the answer that completes a crossword, the rotation that solves the pattern on the cube.

Naomi drinking without any caution, believing Alex was driving them home. Alex apparently declining alcohol with a glass full of vodka and orange. People assuming he'd drive. And he had.

We did finally go upstairs. Phil was practically foaming at the mouth. 'That little shit,' he said as he got into bed.

'I guess once he'd said it, there was no going back. He was trapped.'

'Is that an excuse?'

'No, just an observation,' I said. 'And he must have

240

told Monica the truth pretty early on. She told us about passing them in the car and tooting the horn before we'd even seen him, remember? Setting herself up as a witness. Backing up his story.'

'How did he ever think he'd get away with it?'

'He did for long enough. Oh Phil, what a mess. Poor Naomi.'

I shifted over to his side and we kissed. I wrestled myself into a comfortable position, my hand on his chest, taking comfort from the beating of his heart.

CHAPTER TWENTY-FOUR

Naomi

W e've been waiting all afternoon for Don to call, and when he's still not been in touch by half past five, I ring him. It goes to voicemail. 'What if the man didn't come?' I say to Mum. 'Or he's messed up his statement?'

'I think Don would have told us,' she says, but she doesn't sound very definite.

We're sitting down to eat when the door goes and Dad brings Don in.

'I wanted to come in person,' he says.

My heart flip-flops. It's bad news. It must be.

'It's been a pretty frantic day,' he says.

I bite my cheek hard and hold my breath.

'I presented the eyewitness account to the barrister early this afternoon. I also put to him the statement from Alice about Alex agreeing to be the driver and the medical evidence that points to Naomi being the passenger. He felt it amounted to an overwhelming challenge to the prosecution case.'

My eyes prickle. Mum glances at me, blinking rapidly. Dad swallows.

'The CPS case officer saw us just before the end of the day. She agreed. There are some formalities to be gone through, but all the charges against you will be dropped without prejudice.'

I gasp, a cough and a cry all mixed up.

'Dropped?' says Dad.

'Yes, the charges will be withdrawn; Naomi will be in the clear.'

'And Alex?' says Mum.

'Up to the CPS. But there will be further investigation and I'd say there's a good chance of him standing trial himself. Same charges, plus attempting to pervert the course of justice. Which his mother may also face.'

It's all I can do to nod that I understand.

'The bastard!' Dad thumps the table and we all jump. 'He'd have watched you go to prison in his place. The little shit! And that fucking woman!'

Mum shakes her head, her hand pressed to her mouth.

'Everything you've been through,' Dad says, and he pulls me to him and hugs me.

'Oh thank God,' Mum says. 'Oh Don, thank you so much.'

'And you,' Dad says, waving his hand at Mum, 'like a bloody terrier.'

Mum pinches the top of her nose and says, 'Don't, you'll make me cry.'

It's weird, this atmosphere of relief, of celebration. But it's not that simple. How will they feel? The Vaseys? One minute they've got their villain and a day in court, a chance for justice to be done, and the next it's ripped away.

Once Don has left, we finally eat and then Dad puts Bob Marley's *Catch a Fire* on and strums along to it. It's been played forever in this house. Mum rings Evie and Suzanne and texts some other people.

'Why don't you call Becky?' she says.

But I'm not ready for it yet. 'Maybe tomorrow,' I say.

I think of how right they are together, Mum and Dad – how I can't ever imagine them splitting up. And how Suzanne has Jonty, who adores her. And Alex? *Oh Alex.* I thought he was the one. The love of my life. How wrong can you be?

The smell of coffee fills the kitchen, coffee and oranges and toast. My stomach turns over.

'How are you feeling?' Mum's up already. Dad's gone to work.

'I'm going to see Alex.'

Her eyes flare with alarm. 'Do you think that's wise?'

'I don't care.'

'I can come if—'

'No.'

'Maybe you should wait,' she doesn't give up, 'until we know what's happening with the new investigation.'

'No!'

She gives a little sigh and starts clearing the table.

I make a cup of tea and take it upstairs to drink.

The photos that used to be up on the wall are in the bottom drawer of my desk. There are tons more on my laptop, but I've not looked at any of them in months. This handful were my favourites.

One of Alex, close up; he'd just turned to the camera and I snapped him. He's laughing, his eyes bright, and he's beautiful. I trace his face with my finger.

There's one of us on the flume at Alton Towers, screaming our heads off, drenched. And one in a group, on our birthday, his and mine, at a club in Newcastle. He bought me the turquoise dress – I dragged him round all afternoon trying things on – and I got him a watch.

And the picture of him at the beach. His hair was longer then, and it was a grey day, windy. He's not smiling; he looks thoughtful, his eyes wrinkled a bit because of the wind and his mouth open just a little and the sands and pine trees behind him.

Finally the blurry shot of us kissing, one that Becky took at a party.

Are they all lies, too?

It's cold outside, and bright. The glare burns my eyes. I should have worn my shades. I can feel the bite in the air with each breath. Maybe I'm more sensitive to it since my lung collapsed.

Under the blanket of the medicine my nerves are shredded. There's a hum at the back of my skull like a fly's trapped in there, a bluebottle, and the dizziness forces me to walk close to the walls and hedges and take extra care stepping off the kerbs.

There's a walk to the bus stop and then a walk at the other end.

It should be summer, but the wind is from Siberia or somewhere.

My mouth goes dry as I turn down his street. There are loads of flowers in pots and baskets outside the house, just like before. I used to think his mum was a really good gardener, but Alex said she got everything already planted up from the supermarket or the garden centre and just chucked the lot when they faded.

The car's not there, the Honda; he must be out. Then I kick myself. The car was totalled. Idiot!

I ring the bell and fight the urge to run away. I have to see him. I need to know.

He opens the door and my chest hurts. He startles like I've slapped him or something and his face goes white, really white, like he's seen a ghost. I am the ghost. The girlfriend that was.

'Hey,' he says. He is so tense I can feel it coming off him like a smell.

'Can I come in?' I say, like a vampire asking permission.

'Er . . . yes.' He lets me in and we go in the living room, all open-plan. No sign of his mum. His plaster casts have gone; he looks fine. Pale but fine.

'You want a drink?' he says, his voice sounding creaky, uneven.

'No thanks.' My nails are hurting my hands. I open my fingers, look at the new-moon marks.

'You okay?' he asks.

'You were driving,' I say, sounding more uncertain than I meant to.

He looks at me, gives a little fake laugh like I've said something not very funny. Then his eyes start to change, darken. 'No,' he smiles, putting me straight, 'I don't know what you're—'

'Someone saw you.'

'I wasn't driving, you were driving. What the fuck are you—'

'You were driving and you said it was me.'

'You're off your head.' He glares at me.

'Why did you lie, Alex? About me?' Stupid tears stop me going on.

'I wasn't driving!' Outraged, like I am ridiculous.

'They saw you!' I yell.

A spasm tightens his face. 'No!' he says. 'No,' he repeats vehemently, shaking his head. 'No fucking way!'

'They saw you get in the car. You ran her over.'

He doesn't speak. His breath is noisy and harsh. I gulp and swallow and try to work out what to say.

'I loved you.' I stand up. 'I loved you so much and you, you bastard, you fucking bastard . . .' I'm shaking so much it breaks the words up like a machine gun. Rat-a-tat-tat.

'You've got it all wrong.' He says it in a pleading way, as if he's begging me to believe him. But I don't. Oh God, I don't.

He's on his feet too, his hands on his head, clutching at his temples.

'You knocked her down,' I shout. 'You did it. How

could you lie?' I can't breathe, all the snot in my nose, and I'm blubbing and snorting.

'Naomi,' he says, and he's twisting and turning his body like I'm wringing it out of him. Except that's all he says, just my name.

'I could have been locked up for that.'

He's frowning hard, his mouth shut tight. He flinches, rubs his nose with his hand, starts to talk, but I carry on. 'I thought I had done it. I believed you, you and Monica. I tried to kill myself.'

His head jerks up and back, withdrawing. His expression changes, mouth open, derisive. He thinks I'm making it up.

'Overdose,' I say. 'My mum found me. Been in a psychiatric unit too, after that. You prick.' It comes out as a squeak between my teeth. My chin itches from the tears.

'I thought you were dead!' he explodes. 'I thought you were dead. You weren't breathing, you . . . I hadn't any idea that . . . I never meant to . . .'

I wait for him to go on. The air electric, my wrists tingling, my spine on fire.

'If you were dead, there didn't seem any sense . . . My job!' he cries.

I don't know how long I stare at him. My mind numbly processing what he has just said.

'You talk her into it?' I finally say.

His mouth works, he blinks, then half a shrug. I get it. 'The other way around. Because she'd do anything for you. For your fucking career. You selfish, shitting bastard! And that little girl . . .'

I haven't heard the car, but suddenly Monica's in the room, eyes blazing. 'Get out!' she says.

'Mum . . .' Alex says.

'You don't say a word.' She points at him, then looks back to me. 'Get out or I'll ring the police.'

'And say what?' I'm trembling. 'That you lied for him so I'd pay the price. That I didn't count?'

'Get out!'

'We know,' I say. 'There's a witness, so your little plan isn't going to work. You're not going to get away with it.'

The tiniest flicker of her eyelids, a moment's doubt.

'You bitch,' I say, amazing myself. I can barely breathe.

She moves as though she'd strike me, and he calls to her again. 'Mum!'

'Intimidating a witness,' she shouts, 'that's what you're doing. Once the police—'

'He's not a witness, he's a liar – and so are you. I thought I'd killed her . . .'

I can't go on. I run out. And out of the front door. I'm halfway to the gate, and all the disgust and the guilt that has been smothering me seems to catch light, making me burn with anger, a tide that overwhelms me, pouring over my shoulders, through my belly, filling me with a strength I didn't know I still had.

I grab the smallest pot with its pansies and ivy and God knows what, ignoring the stabbing pain as I lift it, and hurl it at the house. It shatters one of the sheets of glass in the bay window.

That's good.

I don't bother with the bus. I walk all the way home, sometimes crying. A little old lady asks me if I need help. Bless her. I thank her and tell her I'm fine.

I'm not fine. I don't know if I'll ever be fine.

But I'm alive.

Suzanne comes crawling out of the woodwork. I haven't seen her for weeks. Not since I was charged. After I came out of the mental health unit, I told Mum I didn't want to see her if she did come round. Suzanne isn't healthy for me – like the news on television or lack of sleep. So I don't exactly greet her with open arms.

'Hi.' A big bright smile. She's let herself in, so I'm trapped in the living room with her. She's dropped her Disgusted of Didsbury act and is talking all bright and quick. 'Mum told me. It's unbelievable! Alex lying like that – and Monica!'

I'm tensing up as she goes on about it, a knot in my stomach. I wonder if she feels awkward for disowning me. She never once says anything about that. I watch her mouth; she's got bright red lipstick on and her teeth look white and even. She keeps talking but I see she's avoiding my eyes. She glances in my general direction now and again, but never long enough to communicate. She doesn't see my resentment building.

I interrupt her, hot and angry and unnerved. 'You didn't give a toss,' I say. 'You sacked me, wrote me off as a lost cause, and now I'm supposed to pretend it's all okay? That it never happened?'

'There's no need to be childish.'

'I'm not being childish. I'm sick of being criticized and slagged off and looked down on by you. I know I make mistakes. I'm not perfect. But you think you are. Well – newsflash, you're not. Sometimes you're just a right cow. You can be really toxic, you know. You're only nice to people if they do things your way, if they agree with you.'

She gives a little snort and shakes her head, prancing a bit like a horse. 'You might not have been driving, but you still got in that car. You were there.'

'You think I don't know that? I might not remember, but I go to sleep thinking about that, I wake up thinking about that. I dream about it. I can't make it right, but I don't need you or anyone else telling me how bad I should feel. Go on, fuck off home to your perfect house

249

and your perfect man and your perfect Barbie and Ken fucking life. Just don't pretend you give a shit,' I say.

Her eyes flash and she swallows, and I wait for her to come back at me, my breath tight in my chest.

'Obviously I was wrong,' she says.

'And if Mum hadn't kept asking questions, hadn't found Larry? Would you have written to me in prison? Or carried on acting like I didn't exist?' I'm shuddering and my voice is all over the place.

'You're upset,' she says. As though this is an aberration. The cheek of it! I laugh aloud.

'For fuck's sake—'

'Naomi, I'm sorry. Really, I am sorry.' At last she looks in my eyes, but hers are guarded.

I don't say anything else. It feels like too little, too late.

I get up and go upstairs, and soon afterwards I hear the door go as she leaves.

Carmel

Although there was a huge relief once the charges against Naomi were dropped, like someone cutting ropes that had bound us, allowing us to breathe again, there was still a massive question mark hanging over Alex. The police were continuing their investigation; both Naomi and I were interviewed, and Naomi was told she would likely be called as a witness if it went to court. Her amnesia persisted but she could still tell them about the conversation where Alex had all but admitted to the deception. All we could do was try and carry on while we waited for news.

Don rang Naomi one lunchtime as she was filling in a job application form.

I heard the anxiety in her voice as she answered the

call, then she listened, looking at me now and again. The scar on her cheek was still vivid but a little less puckered. She was suffering from an ear infection and taking high-dose antibiotics to prevent any further infection.

'Oh no!' she said, then, 'When?' She listened. 'Monica, really? What with? Right. Thanks for letting me know. Yes. Bye.' She put her phone down. 'Alex has been charged,' she said. 'He pleaded not guilty at the magistrates' court. And they've charged Monica with attempting to pervert the course of justice.' She raised her face to the ceiling, shook her head. 'I just want it to be over.'

If they'd pleaded guilty, it would have been. 'It'll be Monica,' I said. 'Bet you anything she'll keep fighting till the bitter end.'

'How can she keep lying like that?' Naomi asked.

'Probably convinced herself it's true. Don said she did go to the gym, they've records that prove she was there – all she had to do was invent passing you, seeing you at the wheel. If she says it often enough, fervently enough, she'll come to believe it.'

'And him,' Naomi said, her face furrowed with distress. 'After all that happened, I thought he might have the guts . . .' She broke off, shaking her fists by her head in frustration.

CHAPTER TWENTY-FIVE

Naomi

I try not to think about Alex too much – it still takes my breath away, it hurts so deep. I talk about it with the therapist, going over and over it. I weep buckets for the little girl and for myself. For Alex even, and losing him. And sometimes the rage comes, clean and cold and sharp as ice. But I am not going to prison. I'm a little stronger every day.

It is another four months before we get to trial. Late January, eight months after the accident. I'm not allowed in court until I've given my evidence. I wait in a special room for witnesses with Alice and Larry from Birmingham. The solicitor for the prosecution says it'll be towards the end of the prosecution case before I'm called. I will be talking about two things – the fact that we always decided who would drive and stuck to it, and what Alex said the last time I saw him at their house.

Mum and Dad and Suzanne will be there in the court, but they are not supposed to tell me anything about the case. A couple of weeks after her 'apology', Suzanne came round with Ollie on her way back from work. She was restless and went on about her trainee like he was a right dork, and she didn't want any pasta, probably because it was dried not freshly made, for fuck's sake, and might poison her.

Ollie was cranky and I didn't know why she hadn't gone straight home. I was the only one there.

She went to the loo and Ollie cried. Real tears, and his bottom lip was trembling like the world was ending, so I picked him up and sang to him, 'Daisy, Daisy', and he was quiet enough, then he grabbed my earring, which was agony, and I swore just as Suzanne came back in.

'Naomi.'

'Yes?' I prepared for a lecture about bad language and setting examples. And she said, 'How are you?'

Was it a trick question? 'Not bad.'

Ollie gurgled and patted my nose. 'Ow,' I said, but it didn't hurt.

She nodded. 'Your hair's nice,' she said.

Good God, I thought, we'll be talking about the weather next. 'I'm going out soon,' I said, dropping a big hint. I blew a raspberry on Ollie's cheek and he chortled and patted me again. Suzanne hadn't moved. 'I need to go and get ready,' I added.

'Jonty's left me,' she said, quick and quiet, her chin wobbling.

'What?' *She did not just say that!*

'He's been sleeping with his production assistant. All the way through the pregnancy and since. Shrewsbury, Belfast, Aberdeen.' Suzanne was shivering.

Fuck me! 'Oh, Suzanne.'

'I don't know what we'll do. Probably have to sell the house, and we'll lose money on that. Won't be able to afford the nursery.'

'Oh God.' I jiggled Ollie on to the other hip, and got Suzanne to sit down while I made her a cup of tea.

'How did you find out?' I sat down opposite her.

'He told me – yesterday. Said he had something important to talk about. I thought it was going to be a new commission at work, maybe going abroad . . .' She couldn't continue. Her nose went red. She gave a big sigh.

Ollie had fallen asleep on my lap. He was amazingly heavy. I stroked his head. I didn't know what to say.

'If I can't find child care, then my job . . .' She shook her head.

'People manage,' I told her. 'Childminders are cheaper, aren't they, must be cheaper than where you've got him?' He was at a really swanky nursery.

Ollie gave a little start in my arms and relaxed. Then it came to me. 'I could look after him. Unless you're worried I'll be a bad influence.' I couldn't resist the dig.

She looked at me; hard to tell if she was intrigued or appalled.

'I'm not having much luck with interviews,' I said, 'and I need to work. You'd have to pay me the going rate.'

She nodded her head. 'I think it could work,' she said slowly. 'We'd have to agree some standards, and you'd have to pay your own National Insurance, have a contract and everything.'

Only Suzanne. 'Of course. I'm so sorry, Jonty must be off his head, everything he's throwing away. The bastard.'

I didn't intend to build bridges with Suzanne; a stepping stone or two was more than enough. But I didn't want to miss out on being an auntie, and minding Ollie would be a way of seeing him, and earning some money, without having to spend much time with her. Keeping a reasonable distance is the only way I know to protect myself from the unhealthy pattern of our relationship.

And I wanted to keep getting better. That week the therapist had asked me if I'd been thinking about the future at all. And I had. For the first time without total dread or fear, wondering what I might do next. Little things like arrange a break away or look for some new clothes.

And I've been minding Ollie ever since.

Now, waiting with the other witnesses, I can feel the pressure building up inside and the echoes of the worst times when I was falling apart. I try to breathe slowly and deeply, and distract myself. I try to connect, chat to Alice and Larry; again we mustn't discuss the trial, so we end up talking about who we like on *X Factor* or *The Voice* and Alice talks about the sheep she has on the farm.

We're all nervous, it's not just me. Alice keeps messing with her hair and she laughs a lot even at things that aren't the least bit funny, and Larry goes out for a cigarette every five minutes.

I've been warned that I could get some pretty rough treatment under cross-questioning, but I think it's the first sight of people that's going to be the hardest. Lily's parents and her brothers, and Alex and Monica. Alex in the dock.

Where he would have put me.

Carmel

We were all sitting together, Phil and Suzanne and I immediately behind the Vaseys, who arrived just after us. Everyone in their best, sombre clothes. I caught Tina Vasey's eye as the family made their way along the row of seats and tried to express my sympathy without words, and she gave a tiny nod of understanding. She wore a grey suit jacket and skirt, on the jacket a brooch, enamelled white and green. A lily.

The two boys, Robin and his brother, look so alike,

I'm not even sure which is the one who came to the house.

The solicitor hadn't been able to tell us how long it would be until Naomi was called. Might even be the next day. Before her there would be evidence from Alice and Larry and then from the police who were first on the scene and the paramedics. After them the hospital doctor and the police officer who interviewed Alex and later Naomi. Sometimes they play the 999 call in court. I was dreading that. Imagining Alex's voice, torn and frantic, stumbling to explain, high with panic: *We hit a little girl. Oh God, I think she's dead, and my girlfriend's not breathing.* My stomach hurt. My mouth was dry. I had some mints; I took one and offered the packet to Phil and Suzanne.

Suzanne was still reeling. I'd hoped that Jonty would see sense, crawl back with his tail between his legs, but apparently not. Though whether Suzanne would have given him a second chance was highly debatable. She'd thrown herself back into work, even done a couple of trips abroad, Milan and Paris, for the fashion shows, and Ollie'd stayed with us. Suzanne had put the house on the market. She was looking at renting somewhere until the divorce was sorted out and the financial situation was clear.

She and Jonty were trying to work out what contact he'd have with Ollie. It was hard for Suzanne, especially as it would mean that Ollie was going to spend time with the production assistant, who Jonty was living with. We did offer Suzanne a room with us, though I'm glad she said no. It wouldn't really have helped Naomi: too much bad blood, too big a sense of betrayal. I don't think Naomi and Suzanne will ever be really close. Oh, they cleared the air, as much as was possible. And Suzanne came to court for her sister, but I think she blew it really and Naomi's drawn a line; she's not going to put herself in the position of being hurt by Suzanne again.

There was a hushed anticipation in the room as the court officers went about their work and more people arrived. The barristers with their wigs and gowns chatted to each other. The clerk instructed us all to turn off our mobile phones and reminded people that taking photographs was not allowed. Then we were asked to stand and the judge came in, a tall woman in her robe and wig, wearing very large glasses. Once she was seated, we all sat down again.

We had speculated endlessly about what Alex's defence would be, and could only assume that he'd continue to insist that Naomi was driving and try to undermine Alice's and more importantly Larry's testimony. Even though Larry had identified Alex to the satisfaction of the police, the defence would probably try and compromise his account – question his eyesight and memory and so on.

The clerk stood up and nodded to the barristers, then he said, 'Call Alex Cottingley.'

Alex came up the steps and into the dock, every inch a promising young professional in a dark navy pinstripe suit, shirt and tie. He was accompanied by a court officer, who stood at the far side of the dock area. Alex glanced back, up to our left, towards a middle-aged man with a tan and a grey-haired woman, who I thought might be his father and grandmother. He looked ashen, terrified really. He was visibly trembling.

The clerk called for Monica next, and she came up the stairs followed by another court officer and stood beside Alex. She wore a black skirt suit and a white blouse. I felt a burn of resentment, hot in my chest, looking at them both.

The clerk spoke, asking Alex to confirm his name and

address and date of birth, the day he shared with Naomi, only a year older. Then he did the same with Monica.

I looked away. I was finding it hard to watch. In front of me, Lily's father's shoulders moved up and down, like he was taking a long, slow breath.

The jury filed in. I wondered if they were apprehensive too – or looking forward to their role. Once they were seated, the judge began to explain to them what the charges were.

Alex suddenly made a noise, a sort of sob, and I saw him jerk, bending over as though someone had hurt him. 'I can't!' he cried out.

'Alex?' Monica said, concern clear in her voice.

He straightened up. 'Oh God,' he said, and everyone stirred. 'Naomi!' he cried out, and my skin prickled at the sound of her name.

'Alex!' Monica said, steel in her tone. 'Stop it! Stop it now!'

The judge started to admonish them but had got no further than 'Mr Cottingley . . .' when Alex said, his voice cracking, 'I can't do it, Mum, I can't.'

'Alex!' Her voice cracked like a whip.

He was shaking his head, his breathing loud and uneven, in terrible distress. 'I'm guilty,' he blurted out. 'Guilty.'

The word rolled around the room and the place exploded.

Monica yelled at him, 'No! Alex, no!' and his father and grandmother were calling out. One of Lily's brothers shouted, 'Yes! Yes!' and the Vaseys fell on each other and Mrs Vasey started crying.

Alex was muttering, 'I'm sorry,' over and over again. His barrister had gone white in the face. He hadn't been expecting this.

Suzanne stared at me, her eyes wide. Phil said, 'Oh my God.' He grabbed my hand. 'Oh God.'

The clerk called for silence and the room settled, but the air was thick with tension. Monica's head was bowed and she no longer tried to communicate with Alex.

The judge asked the jury to leave while a legal point was discussed. Once they'd gone, she instructed Alex's barrister to meet with Alex.

Alex was taken down. As he passed Monica, she grabbed at him, close to hysterical, gasping, 'Alex, Alex, please, Alex.' He twisted away. Then she howled, a guttural noise that made my flesh crawl. 'Please,' she called to her barrister, 'I need to talk to you. God, please!'

Another wave of reaction washed around the public gallery and the press benches. There was some discussion between her barrister and the judge, and Monica too was taken down the steps from the dock. Then we all rose as the judge disappeared too.

Over the next twenty minutes the room buzzed with speculation and hummed with tension. I felt nauseous, despite chain-sucking mints. I thought it must be intolerable for the Vaseys, restless in the front row, talking to each other in sporadic bursts.

Finally we were instructed to stand again. The judge re-emerged from the door at the back of the court, and once we'd settled, the clerk called Alex and Monica. The jury didn't come back in and I guessed then that the guilty pleas were going to be entered.

Alex's barrister stood up. 'Your Honour, would you please put the charge again?'

The judge nodded, and the clerk rose and said, 'Alex Cottingley, you are charged that on the twentieth of May last you drove a motor vehicle on a road, namely Mottram Lane, Sale, Greater Manchester, causing death by dangerous driving, contrary to section 1 of the Road Traffic Act 1988. Are you guilty or not guilty?'

'Guilty,' he said brokenly. Tina and Simon Vasey were huddled close together, his arm around her, and she gasped aloud as Alex spoke. I felt a bloom of relief inside. I longed to tell Naomi.

'Alex Cottingley, you are further charged with conspiring to pervert the course of justice in relation to the first charge. Are you guilty or not guilty?'

'Guilty,' he said again.

Phil looked at me, nodding his head, close to tears.

'You plead guilty,' said the judge. 'You will be removed from court and remanded on bail. You will return here for sentencing once a probation report has been completed. Take him down.'

Alex turned, shaking uncontrollably, weeping, his face blurred with emotion. He made to touch his mother as he passed her, but she reared away. I felt my eyes sting.

Then it was Monica's turn.

'Monica Cottingley, you are charged with conspiring to pervert the course of justice in the weeks after the twentieth of May last year. Are you guilty or not guilty?'

'Guilty,' she said, a stammer at the start of the word betraying her nerves.

'You will be removed from court and return here for sentencing. Take her down.'

And like that, it was done.

EPILOGUE

Naomi

Alex got seven years, five for causing death by dangerous driving and two for perverting the course of justice. Monica got eighteen months for perverting the course of justice.

It helps that he finally told the truth. He must have just decided that day, that minute. Up till then he'd pleaded not guilty at every stage. But it was the right thing to do. He finally did the right thing.

I've agreed with the GP to reduce the antidepressants. I don't want to depend on them for ever. I'm still seeing a therapist.

One of the hardest things is the anxiety, worrying that I'll relapse, that I'll go mad again, not be able to cope with my feelings. But I am getting better at living with that fear, trying to ignore it, accept it even, and then get on with things. Posts I've read online from other people in the same situation make me hopeful.

I've signed up to do a counselling course. Ironic maybe. But Evie says most therapists become therapists because they had their own demons to deal with.

Sometimes I wonder about writing to Alex, or even visiting him, though I'm not sure yet what my motives are. Forgiveness or vengeance? Or is there some sad part of me that wants to make up with him?

Anyway, I'm not acting on it any time soon. One thing I have learned from all this and the sessions is that I need to look after myself before anyone else. That is selfish, but in a good way. Be kind to myself, that's what I'm trying to do. Be kind, be true, be gentle. That and acceptance.

The nightmare happened.
  Lily died.
  Alex lied.
  I am damaged.
  I accept these truths and I carry them with me.
  That's the way it is.

Carmel

She's still wounded; I don't know how far she'll come back to us, whether that irreverence, that spark, is still kindled inside. Or whether that's gone for good. She's better than she was. Looking after Ollie has given her enough money to live on while she stays with us. And for the first time she's begun talking about the future, about what she might do.

I should have trusted my instincts. That undertow of denial that I'd felt all along. I couldn't believe Naomi had been drink-driving and I was right. But when the chorus of voices, from Suzanne, from Alex, from Monica, sang in unison, the proof seemed overwhelming. I lost faith in my child. But deep down I was still resistant to what they said, and I dug my heels in. All that struggling to collect memories for Naomi, interviewing party guests, wanting to work out why no one stopped her driving off – subconsciously I was seeking vindication for my gut feelings, I'm sure.

And Alex? I'd trusted him, seen the best in him, not fully understood the depth of his ambition, his instinct for self-preservation. His hunger. Fuelled in great part by Monica, I am sure. Piecing together what Naomi said and the way they took it right up to the wire, I think Monica was equally to blame for the cover-up. Alex had lied at the scene of the crash and then confided in his mother. He probably wanted to confess once he knew Naomi was not dead (after all, she might wake up like Sleeping Beauty and spill the beans). But Monica had heard from us that Naomi's memory had failed and so she pushed Alex to maintain the fiction. The power behind the throne. Her ambition exceeding his. Naomi dispensable.

And Lily Vasey's family? Presumably Monica had no compunction in lying to the people who mattered most in all this. The people whose lives had been shattered beyond repair.

They say girls are attracted to people like their father, so I'm not sure what went wrong for ours. Because neither Alex nor Jonty behaved like Phil would. Phil is fine, by the way, having regular blood tests and advised to exercise more. It's his birthday soon. He doesn't know yet, but I'm taking him to New Orleans. Not exactly our world tour, but it's a start.

Perhaps if Alex hadn't continued to lie, Naomi would have stuck with him. We all make mistakes and some can be fatal. He's young; he might have deserved some compassion if he'd come clean once he knew she'd survived. Instead he's behind bars, all his dreams ruined.

A moment's madness, a child dead, and all those lives changed for ever.

Before.
Seems like a mirage shimmering in the heat. Elusive. Distorted.
And I would go back there in a heartbeat.